away on the tide of Santo's isses.

While it lasted, Aphra was almost convinced that his hunger was genuine—that this great handsome creature had been waiting for an excuse to take her in his arms and make her forget what she had lost, what had never been hers. Santo Datini was a mature male who knew well how to make a woman like her, fighting her confused emotions, confront the desires which in these last few days had been twisting her heart into knots. After this knew that any more talk about being ken-hearted would—to her shame—be n as a sham.

to's kisses softened, and the pressure of arms allowed her to move within their ace. 'You see?' he whispered. 'That n heart of yours is bruised, that's all. our pride. There's nothing here that ot be mended.'

Juliet Landon has a keen interest in art and history—both of which she used to teach. She particularly enjoys researching the early medieval, Tudor and Regency periods, and the problems encountered by women in a man's world. Born in North Yorkshire, she now lives in a Hampshire village close to her family. Her first books, which were on embroidery and design, were published under her own name of Jan Messent.

Books by Juliet Landon

Mills & Boon Historical Romance

The Widow's Bargain
The Bought Bride
His Duty, Her Destiny
The Warlord's Mistress
A Scandalous Mistress
Dishonour and Desire
The Rake's Unconventional Mistress
Marrying the Mistress
Slave Princess
Mistress Masquerade
Captive of the Viking

At the Tudor Court

Betrayed, Betrothed and Bedded
Taming the Tempestuous Tudor
The Mistress and the Merchant

Collaboration with the National Trust

Scandalous Innocent

Visit the Author Profile page
at millsandboon.co.uk for more titles.

THE MISTRESS AND THE MERCHANT

Juliet Landon

Published in Great Britain 2017
by Mills & Boon, an imprint of HarperCollins*Publishers*
1 London Bridge Street, London, SE1 9GF

© 2017 Juliet Landon

ISBN: 978-0-263-93260-7

Our policy is to use papers that are natural, renewable and
recyclable products and made from wood grown in sustainable
forests. The logging and manufacturing processes conform to the
legal environmental regulations of the country of origin.

Printed and bound in Spain
by CPI, Barcelona

THE MISTRESS AND
THE MERCHANT

Chapter One

Sandrock Priory, Wiltshire—1560

Almost hidden by a creamy-white canopy of apple blossom, Aphra turned to take another look at the solid stone walls of Sandrock Priory as if to remind herself, yet again, that it belonged to her. Against a cloudless sky, she saw how the ivy clambered up towards the red roof tiles where patches of yellow lichen and pale fern fronds made a vivid palette of new spring colour after so many weeks of greyness, the same greyness that had surrounded her heart with tragedy. Now, at last, she was beginning to see ahead to a new and peaceful life at the converted priory in which, until two months ago, Dr Ben Spenney, her beloved uncle, had lived and worked as one of Europe's leading apothecaries. That he had left the priory to her in his will was still a source of amazement and some concern, too, for the place was enormous and, had he not also left her his considerable fortune to go with it, she would never have been able to afford its upkeep.

Her sandalled feet shifted in the long damp grass, turning her towards the orchard where honeybees droned busily into the blossom before heading back to the hives. Everywhere she looked, new growth was unfurling through the warm soil, washing the neat garden plots with a richness that seemed to echo Aphra's new status as a property-owning woman, the new mistress of Sandrock. Only thirty years ago, the priory would have responded to the sound of bells and Augustinian canons at prayer, its gardens given over to the growing of vegetables and fruit for the refectory tables. Since its enforced closure in 1536, the buildings had been stripped of all association with religion and converted into rooms for domestic use by Aphra's grandfather, Sir Walter D'Arvall, whose illegitimate son, Dr Ben Spenney, had inherited it. Aphra had never called him 'uncle'. Their friendship had always been closer than the usual uncle-to-niece—more like dear allies whose degree of kinship had allowed a certain familiarity. Although never discussed, their special bond was enjoyed by both of them and understood by their families.

During his years of ownership, Dr Ben had housed young medical students specialising in the use of herbs, a branch of medicine that in the last decade had become more highly respectable and reliable than ever. He had shared with them his wide knowledge of plants and their properties, and had helped them to complete their degrees. The University of Padua in Italy had sent him one of their best students to study here, though he could not have anticipated that young Master Leon of Padua would fall deeply in love with his beautiful niece, Mistress Aphra Betterton of nearby Reedacre Manor. Now, in just over a year, fate had stepped in to deprive Aphra of both Master Leon, whom she had loved, and Dr Ben, whom she had also loved, but differently.

Yet while fate had taken away with one hand, it had given something back with the other, demanding at the same time that she should move on into another phase of her life that would set her mind and body to work instead of wallowing in grief. It was a huge task for her to take on single-handed, albeit with a number of workers living on the estate and who knew more than she did about how Dr Ben had managed things. She would have little time left over at the end of each day to indulge in memories, even if they were too recent to have healed completely.

Swishing her old grey-blue skirts through the dew-laden grass, she looked across to where one end of the physic garden joined the orchard, where already men were tying, hoeing, digging and weeding, their brown backs bent to the earth. A splash of bright colour amongst the greenery made her frown and look harder, then smile as she recognised the distant figure of her father wearing his favourite suit of deep red velvet. As an assistant at the Royal Wardrobe in London, Sir George Betterton had access to all the latest fashions in colour and style, always dressing up for an occasion, even for visiting his daughter on a May morning. Behind him, however, stopping to look at the patches of new growth every now and then, was another man Aphra didn't know. Nor, if she were quite truthful, did she want to, having come here to be alone without the need to make polite conversation to anyone except her family. This was an intrusion and her father ought to have known better.

Trying to suppress her irritation, she glanced down at the hem of her skirt, soaked with dew, grass stalks stuck between her toes, and her old white apron pocket bulging with warm eggs laid away by an independent hen. Aphra's thick pale blonde hair lay loose upon her shoulders, shining like silk in the sunlight, sliding back down on to her face whenever she brushed it away. Her lips showed a dusting of white flour from the bread roll the baker had given her as she'd passed the kitchen. It was not the image she would have chosen to present to a stranger.

She had time to study him before she emerged from the low-hanging blossom, wondering why her father had needed to bring him here without warning. He was tall and powerfully built with long well-muscled legs encased in a dull gold hose that matched his paned breeches of a deeper tone, like his short doublet. Judging from his tanned skin, she thought he might be a man who travelled, his dark hair lying thickly upon his frilled collar at the back, kept in place by a brown-velvet cap. As he and her father drew nearer, she had an uneasy feeling that he knew of this place, for he looked around him as he walked, at the small arched windows, the massive walls, the regulated order of the estate, the wattle fences, the eel traps in the stream running alongside the building. She thought she saw him nodding, as if to confirm what he expected to see.

'Good morning to you, my love,' her father called. 'Were you hiding?'

'Not from you, Father. Good day to you.' She lingered in his embrace, smiling into his velvet doublet, wishing with all her heart that he'd come alone, or with her mother.

He took her hands, suddenly serious, apologetic, but unable to say so. 'We have a guest,' he said, rather unnecessarily, 'and I ask that you receive him, love.'

Darting a glance over her father's shoulder, she noted two very dark brown eyes regarding her with open admiration and again she felt that he was confirming what he already knew. 'Father,' she said, squeezing his hand, 'this is not the time.'

'I know, love. I know. But I think in this case, it might be best.'

She sighed, unable to hide her resentment, but unwilling to be more discourteous than that. 'Then introduce your friend, if you must.'

Sir George's concern was plain to see as he let go of one of Aphra's hands. 'This is Signor Datini,' he said, 'from Padua. Elder brother of… of Master Leon, my dear.'

The sharp pull away from his hand and her step backwards hardly surprised him, the wound to her heart being still so raw. 'Father,' she whispered, holding a hand flat to her chest, 'how *could* you bring him here? *Here*, of all places, where I...' Glaring at their guest, her beautiful grey dark-rimmed eyes sparking with anger, she could not trust herself to finish the sentence without discourtesy.

Showing a remarkable degree of understanding, Signor Datini stayed at a respectful distance, speaking to her in a deep voice quite unlike his brother's light musical tenor. 'Mistress Betterton,' he said, 'I hope that in time you will forgive my intrusion, even in the company of your father, but there are reasons why I had to see you in person.' He doffed his cap, revealing a head of thick wavy hair.

'Who sent you?' Aphra asked sharply. 'Did *he*?'

'You refer to my brother. No indeed, mistress. My father sent me.'

Sir George had rarely heard this harsh tone from his daughter except when scolding a servant. 'Aphra,' he said, 'there are things to be discussed.'

'I'm sure you think so, Father, but I am well past caring. The time for explanations passed some time ago. Signor Datini's journey has been wasted if all he wanted was to discuss his brother's treachery. I am well rid of him. You may tell him so, from me.'

'Please,' said the elder brother, 'please try to

understand. We do not condone my brother's deception. Our family is concerned for you.'

'Very touching,' Aphra retorted, 'but I do not need their concern. Your brother and I were not betrothed, *signor*, so I have absolutely no claim to make and, even if I had, I would not. Your brother's sudden change of mind is insulting enough without haggling over who said what to whom. So if you have come here to find out whether I intend to sue, you can assure your family that I am well rid of a man as fickle as that.'

A lesser man than Signor Santo Datini would have reeled from that salvo, but he was a hard-dealing merchant and the fury behind Mistress Betterton's eyes was something worth seeing even though it was directed partly at him. He had, for one thing, come here to find out more about her and the effect his brother's stupidity had had upon her future intentions, but it would not do to tell her so. Licking her wounds, the lady was clearly in no mood for platitudes. 'I can understand how you feel,' he said, committing that very same error, deserving her quick retort.

'I doubt that very much,' she said. 'No one can.' Tears glistened in the corners of her eyes, brushed angrily away with the back of one hand. 'There is no more to be said on this subject, Father.'

'Not out here in the orchard, perhaps,' Sir George agreed, 'but I think we might offer Signor Datini some refreshment before we return. Shall we?' Extending a hand, he indicated where their courtesies lay.

Assenting in silence, she led the way to the prior's house that had been converted into a more comfortable collection of parlours, bedrooms, kitchens and service rooms where, in the last few weeks, Aphra had begun to place her personal stamp on the previously masculine interiors. Through cool stone-flagged passages she led the two men into a sunny parlour overlooking a beautifully manicured square plot that had once been the cloister garden. A servant poured wine for them, discreetly leaving them as soon as they were seated on cushioned benches. The white plastered walls reflected light from the greyish-green glass in the windows and on the windowsill stood a pewter jug filled with bluebells. A woman's touch in a place built for men.

Aphra sat next to her father opposite Signor Datini, uncaring that her face was streaked with tears or her hair was sticking to her cheeks. For months, ever since Leon's distressing letter, she had told herself that it would have been easier for her to bear if he'd been dead; the memory of his sweet deceitful words, his arms, his kisses flooded over her like a terrible ache and it seemed that, as the hostess, she would be obliged to speak of him to his brother whether she wished it or not.

'He spoke of his family,' she said. 'You are Santo, I take it?'

'I am indeed Santo, mistress. Leon told us about you, too.'

'Really? Then why the sudden change of mind, I wonder? Did he get cold feet at the thought of marrying an English woman? If that was on his mind, *signor*, you may return to Padua with the good news that there is no betrothal nor any claim for the Datini family to concern itself with.'

'Aphra! *Stop!* This will not do, my dear,' her father said. 'You cannot hold Signor Datini responsible for any of this. He was sent by his father.'

'To check up on me? On our family? Well, tell your parents I can manage well enough without their help. As you see, I am well set up with my family nearby. What more could I want?'

Bitterness and anger from his daughter were too new for Sir George to be used to them, she being usually so quietly in control of herself and every situation. 'Little mother hen' he and Aphra's mother called her, knowing how she would take to motherhood with enthusiasm one day, though not like this. The idea of having a family one day, they thought sadly, might have been one of the reasons she had been too hasty in accepting the first offer of marriage that had come her way, falling in love too easily with a young student who had not finished his training. Master Leon had not wanted a betrothal ceremony before he returned home last September to tell his parents, which ought to have rung warning bells in their minds, and did not, because he'd had Dr Ben's approval.

'Mistress Betterton,' Santo said. 'I am happy to see that you want for nothing, but I came to offer you our family's protection, should you need it. I had no idea what to expect, though I knew about Sir George's royal employment, of course. As for yourself, I am both surprised and relieved to see you living where my brother received tuition with Dr Spenney. Leon told me about Sandrock Priory. He was happy here but, as a student, he had no right to offer you something he didn't have. That was wrong of him.'

His gentle tone did nothing to ease Aphra's distress. 'Yes,' she said, 'we spoke of marriage, but we made no vows, formal or otherwise. That exonerates the Datini family from all obligations, doesn't it? Or is it me who is to blame? Is that what you think? That I seduced him?'

'Aphra! Enough of this!' her father said, sternly. 'You are letting your tongue run away with you. Say nothing you might regret later.'

'Father, I regret everything. *Everything.* Every word. Every deed. Every wasted emotion. And I regret that you have brought Signor Datini here to remind me of what I would rather forget. Why on earth did you think it could help?' Pushing herself away from the table, she walked over to the huge stone fireplace where the surround was covered with the arms of previous priors, a mass of symbols understood even by any illegitimate incumbents. Dr Ben himself had been illegitimate and his brother Paul, too, with whom Ben had been staying when he died. Both sons had been generously included in their father's will.

'My family, mistress, wanted you to know of our support and sympathy,' said Santo. 'And Sir George and Lady Betterton, too. Leon is deeply ashamed of himself.' His voice was rich with the lyrical tones of his own language.

'Ashamed with another woman, you mean?' she said, whirling round to face him, deliberately thinking the worst, tormenting herself. 'Is that what you meant by offering me something he didn't have? The freedom to marry?'

His slow blink turned his eyes away from her towards the light and she could not tell whether he was refusing to rise to her bait, or whether he wished to spare her more pain. She chose the more painful option, simply because she had become used, after Leon's short letter, to thinking the worst of him. He had given her no reasons, nothing positive to cling to, only an abject apology in a rambling tortuous English that suggested he had not found it easy to write.

She held her face with a hand on each side as if to prevent it crumpling. Her father took her into his arms and held her, her long loose hair falling down his doublet like a veil. His eyes met those of their guest over the top of her head, accepting that Santo's slight nod of the head meant that Aphra had guessed correctly and that it was time for them to leave.

Sir George's country home, Reedacre Manor, was barely an hour's horse ride away in the same county, and indeed it was fortunate that he and his wife were still there instead of at their London home near the Royal Wardrobe. Had not Signor Datini arrived there unexpectedly last evening, they would by now have been packing up for their move, for Aphra was settling into Sandrock now and physically in much better shape than a month ago. Peace of mind was what she required and Signor Datini's arrival would not help matters.

The Italian rode easily on the big hunter from Sir George's stable and both husband and wife had remarked on his graceful bearing and his exceeding good looks that made his brother seem more like a young lad than a fully matured man. He was, they decided, altogether more robust, and probably more reliable, too, after the way things had turned out. His deep voice and Italian inflections seemed to lend a certain gravity to his speech that differed completely from his younger brother's slick boyish charm.

'Your daughter is a very beautiful woman, Sir George,' he said as they turned a bend of the leafy track. 'I can see why my brother fell in love with her.'

'She is, *signor*. She's very lovable, too. You have not seen her at her best today. She's usually the gentlest and sweetest creature. I'm afraid you saw the virago. I hope you'll forgive her the incivility.'

'There's nothing to forgive, sir. She's been through a lot recently. I did not know until you told me last night that your daughter was the new owner of Sandrock. How will she manage it on her own?'

'It's early days, *signor*, and we're waiting to see. She's good at managing things, but she's young and we're concerned that she has not yet acquired the authority that her uncle had at Sandrock. He knew the place well. He was brought up there. Aphra will have a lot to learn about managing an estate as large as that.'

'Isn't it going to be an expensive place to maintain?'

'Oh, I expect so. But Dr Ben left her his fortune, too. She won't have a problem with funds.'

'Indeed? They were close, I understand?'

'How close, you mean?' Sir George was well used to hearing unspoken questions.

'Well…yes, sir. To be left all that in his will suggests…'

'Something deeper than usual? No, you're wrong, *signor*. Dr Ben was my wife's half-brother. So is Paul, in London. Paul was left a splendid house by the river when Ben was left Sandrock. There's never been any rivalry between them, but maybe Aphra was given Sandrock because he knew she'd need a place of her own one day. She and Ben were close friends with a shared interest in medicinal plants. He knew she would look after the gardens.' The soft thud of horses' hooves on the track changed to an occasional clink as the shoes hit a stone.

'You keep away from those stones, my lad,' Sir George told his gelding, watching the soft ears rotate in acknowledgement.

'Mistress Betterton has suffered,' said Santo. 'I hoped my presence might have helped.'

'Yes, it's not been an easy time for her. Normally, my lady wife and I would go to see her again tomorrow, but perhaps you should go instead.'

'You think she'd be pleased to see me, sir?'

'Now that, *signor*, is not a question even I can answer and I've known her for twenty-three years. Give it a try, eh?'

'Certainly, sir. I'd be happy to give it a try.'

Images of Mistress Aphra Betterton continued to percolate through the mind of Signor Datini as he rode in silence beside Sir George. Now he understood why his host had told him little of where and how she lived, obviously intending that he should be surprised by her new circumstances. Nor had he told him of his daughter's beauty, although Leon had. Santo had thought at the time that his brother's description was the usual exaggeration of a lover. Now he knew that it was not so and that no glowing description could have done justice to the damaged woman he'd met that morning, even wearing her oldest clothes, her hair undressed, and her lovely skin blotched with weeping.

She had not wanted him there: that was understandable. A virago, Sir George called her, yet he was as quick to excuse her as a lovable woman, adored by her family. This he could well imagine while at the same time thinking that his brother had been ten times a fool for leading her on so, a maiden, totally innocent, and too naïve to ask of him the things she ought to have known about. She was too good a creature to be treated so.

As they came within sight of Reedacre Manor, Santo looked forward to another evening with the Bettertons whose hospitality was faultless, especially towards one on whom they had little reason to look kindly. He had intended to make his way back to Italy once he had got what he came for, but she was angry and bitter, and progress would be slower than he'd anticipated. Perhaps he might be rather more welcome at Sandrock tomorrow than he had been today. Who could tell?

Aphra had not waved her father and his guest off that morning, for she had not been as reluctant as all that to see them go. Just when she was beginning to find calmer waters, those two had caused yet another storm she could well have done without. Having abandoned a perfectly good platter of bread, cheese and fruit because of her unresponsive taste-buds, she sought refuge in Ben's extensive library where, until only recently, his students had studied and compiled their dissertations. For all she knew, Leon of Padua might have sat on the very stool she now used. Would there ever be a day in which she did not think of him and wonder why…why…why? Was his brother's visit meant to find out about her family and her father's royal appointment? Was it to find out more about her, to see if she meant to make demands on the Datini family, pretending a betrothal?

And what of the elder brother? Was there an air of curiosity about his visit? She had noticed, even through her distress, how he had looked around at her new home, no doubt thinking that Dr Ben must have thought highly of her indeed to bequeath her such an amazing place. He would wonder, of course, who she grieved for most, his deceitful brother or her uncle. Since his silent assent on the subject of another woman, Aphra was now bound to admit that Leon had damaged her love for him beyond repair by leaving her without an explanation. What she felt more than the pain of love was the dark, destructive pain of rejection. She had given him her love, sure of his devotion, certain of his return, ready to wait until he qualified. Her cousin Etta had warned her about men who did that kind of thing, but she had laughed when she ought to have listened.

On the morning after Signor Datini's visit, Aphra climbed the stairs to an upper floor over the great cellarium, an immensely long room set with tables where, until recently, Dr Ben's young students had learned about the important medicinal properties of plants. The sweet aroma of dried herbs still hung in the air, although all signs of study had now been removed, the tables cleared, the benches stacked away, the tools, glasses, weighing scales and books stored neatly in the cupboards that covered one wall. The other long wall had windows that looked out on to the square cloister gardens below, where a gardener pointed in Aphra's direction to a man she knew, but would rather have avoided.

She waited for the thud of his feet on the stairs, for the cheery greeting that would be the start of an almost non-stop flow of inconsequential chatter that must, she thought, have contributed to his first wife's early death after bearing only five children. That she herself was a prime candidate for the role of wife number two had been made clear after only their first meeting two weeks ago when he had introduced himself as 'Sandrock's most influential landowner'. She had not contradicted him by pointing out that the title ought by rights belong to her, though she was sure a man would have done.

'Ah, Mistress Betterton,' he cried from the top step. 'Hiding away, eh?'

'Good morn, Master Pearce,' she said. 'No, I have no need to hide on my own property.' It was with a fleeting sense of disappointment that she greeted him, for he was nowhere near as good-looking as Leon's elder brother, who had also rattled her usual good nature. 'Do come in,' she added, wondering if he would hear the sarcasm.

Master Richard Pearce was, however, a talking man, not a listening one, and he smiled at the pseudo-welcome. 'Thankee, my dear lady,' he said, striding forward ready to claim a kiss, this time, it being the custom for ladies to offer lips instead of cheeks.

But Aphra had not allowed it before, custom or not, nor would she allow it this time, so took a step backwards round a corner of the table. She didn't like being called his dear lady, either, already resenting the hour to be squandered in this man's presence while sharing with him the revered space that had been Ben's.

'Thought I'd look in on you,' he said, looking

around him as he lifted his cap, assessing the potential of a room this size while removing a roll of parchment from beneath his arm, 'and get you to sign this, if you'd be so kind.' Laying the roll upon the table, he pulled it out, looking for something to weight each corner. Seeing nothing suitable to hand, he walked over to the wall, removed four precious books from the shelf and slammed them down as if they were bricks instead of leather-bound herbals, written and illustrated by hand two centuries ago.

It was during this insolent performance that Aphra saw, from the corner of one eye, the brown-velvet cap of Signor Datini rising slowly and quietly up the staircase until the whole of him stood just inside the room, shadowed by the wall. Immediately understanding the unwelcome presence of Master Pearce and Aphra's impotent anger, he made no attempt to be seen by the self-important visitor, placing a finger to his lips to indicate his complicity. Having only a moment before wished that her neighbour had been Leon's brother, however inconvenient his appearance, Aphra could not help but feel a certain relief that he *was* here, after all. 'My signature?' she said, craning her neck to see what the document was. 'I would have to read it first.'

'Oh, no need for that,' said Master Pearce,

sweeping his hand across the map. 'Simply a formality, that's all.' Jabbing a finger at each part of the map as he spoke, he rattled off various points known to her. 'Here's you at the priory and this is the boundary of your land in Sandrock, see? All round here, from the old shire oak, to the stream where it crosses on to my land, to the east field over here, to the west...'

'One moment, Master Pearce,' Aphra said. 'There is my mill. On my side of the stream. I believe the boundary is well beyond that, not as it's shown here.'

Master Pearce straightened to his full height and smiled patronisingly at Aphra. He was well dressed in a matching doublet and hose of sober charcoal-grey brocade that flattered a figure tending towards corpulence, his narrow ruff supporting several chins and ruddy cheeks bulging beneath a thick thatch of greying hair. Thirty years ago he would have been called handsome, though now his nose was red and fleshy, his eyes hooded by deep folds of loose skin. 'This is the newest version,' he said, still smiling. 'There was a dispute last year... Dr Spenney and I agreed... it seemed sensible to make some adjustments, my dear.'

'Sensible to whom?' A deep voice spoke from the shadows.

Master Pearce was quick on his feet, swivelling round in complete surprise, his grey eyes bulging with alarm and annoyance. 'What? Who are you, sir?'

Aphra had been prepared for the intrusion. 'Allow me to make the introductions, Master Pearce. This is Signor Datini, a guest of my parents.'

Signor Datini moved forward into the room with an admirable nonchalance. Caps were lifted and brief bows exchanged, Master Pearce being quick to ask the first question. 'Your profession, *signor*?' he said, looking him up and down as he tried to guess.

'I am a merchant,' said Santo Datini. 'My home is in Italy, sir.'

Fractionally, Aphra's eyes widened, quickly hiding her astonishment before the elder visitor winkled out of the Italian more in half a minute than she had bothered to find out in an hour. 'So,' continued Master Pearce with some hope in his voice, 'you will not be conversant with English law.'

'I am indeed fully conversant with English property law,' Santo said, 'or I would not be of much use as a merchant, would I? In Italy, the English system of justice is much admired and all merchants must understand how it works or quickly run foul of it.'

'I see,' said Master Pearce, looking from one to the other with a frown. 'And you are here to assist Mistress Betterton, then?'

'I have been asked to assist Mistress Betterton in certain matters,' he said, smoothly. 'I would certainly need to take a close look at any changes to the extent of land belonging by ancient right to her and to witnessing any signatures.'

He sounded, she thought, exactly as a lawyer would sound. Rigidly formal. And if she had not already heard him speak, she would think this was how he would always be, in professional mode, utterly convincing. Was he speaking the truth? Leon had said nothing of this to her. Or had he, when she was not listening? What was more, she knew, as did Signor Datini, that Master Pearce was not speaking the truth when he appeared to be claiming that Sandrock Mill was his. The miller might have tried to short-change her over his rent, but she knew he would not have paid her at all if this man had been his landlord instead of her.

'Is that so?' said Master Pearce, already removing the books from the corners of the map. 'Well then, perhaps we should leave this for another occasion. These things can get incredibly complicated, can't they?' He let the roll spring back into his hands.

'And I shall have to unearth the priory's map, shan't I, to be sure of getting it right?' Aphra said.

'Excellent,' said Santo, smiling his satisfied merchant's smile. 'That should leave us in no doubt about who owns what. Don't you agree, Master Pearce?'

'Indeed. Now, if you will excuse me, mistress, I must attend to my duties.' He bowed, curtly, pausing on the top step to look directly at the Italian. 'Have you *really* come all the way from Italy, *signor*, to assist Mistress Betterton?'

There was only the merest fraction of a delay in Santo's answer. 'Wouldn't you?' he said.

If there had been any doubt in the elder man's mind about the Italian's expectations here at Sandrock, they were dispelled by that reply. He turned, disappearing an inch at a time.

Aphra smoothed a hand over the tooled leather bindings of the nearest book as if to comfort it. 'He's been here almost every day since I arrived. I don't like him,' she whispered. 'I wish he would stay away.'

'And would you have signed?'

She shook her head. 'Probably not. But he would have stayed and talked till kingdom come to convince me.' She smiled at Santo's shout of laughter.

'Your idiomatic English,' he said. 'I shall never get used to it.'

'But your knowledge of English law?' she said, quietly. 'Was that a bluff?'

'Bluff?' he said, twitching his eyebrows.

'Pretence,' she replied.

'Ah...bluff. Yes, a little. But I'd wager I know more about English property law than he does.'

'Or his lawyer?'

'Argh! He'll not have a lawyer. He'd have to pay him, wouldn't he?'

'So shall I, *signor*, for your professional assistance and I cannot afford you. You may as well go home.'

He tilted his head this way and that to catch her eye, without success, and he could tell that she was in no mood for a confrontation, just as she had not wanted to deal with Master Pearce's claims. He chose to ignore the command. 'May I sit?' he said, purposely distancing himself from that man's appallingly bad manners.

'Please do,' she said, seating herself on the other side of the table. 'Are you really a merchant, *signor*? Or was that a pretence, too?'

'I am indeed, mistress. Did my brother not tell you?'

'I don't know,' she said, looking at the table between them. 'I don't remember what he told me. I'm trying not to remember. I don't *want* to remember.' Her voice shook.

'No, I can understand that. But be assured that what I tell you will always be the truth.'

'Forgive me, *signor*,' she said, 'if I regard that with scepticism. My belief in men's words is at a low ebb. Your brother lied to me and so might you be doing for all I know. Since then, I've learnt to believe very little and to trust no man.'

'Then listen to me, *madonna*, if you will. As a newcomer to land ownership and to the sharp practices of others, like him, for example, you may find yourself in need of a man like me who can speak with some authority. A man who has your interests at heart and for no ulterior motive.'

'That sounds too good to be true, *signor*, but I've already said I cannot afford you.'

'I'm not looking for payment, only for your friendship, since I cannot be of any help to you unless we are friends, at least.'

'At least? What does that mean, exactly?'

Saints alive, he thought, *she's as prickly as a holly bush.*

'Trust,' he said. 'I suppose it means you must trust me. After your experience, you find that difficult. But if you could perhaps try to see things from my point of view, my offer of help is to make up, in part, for my brother's failings. It's something I want to do for you, to help you through your grief, to make these first few months less difficult. It will cost you nothing, except perhaps a meal now and then.'

By the time he had finished explaining to her, her hands were covering her face, her shoulders shaking with sobs, and soft mewing sounds were sifting through her fingers, dripping with tears. He sat in silence without moving, knowing that this would not be the last time she would weep for her losses. He wanted to take her in his arms and hold her safe against the world, to shield her from more harm, to heal the wounds caused by his brother whose foolishness he could understand but never condone. And then there was this charismatic man called Ben. Had she come up here to this room to find comfort in his workplace? How close had they been?

The weeping was brought under control soon enough, followed by a whispered apology. He was quick to put her mind at rest. 'Think nothing of it,' he said. With her knuckles she wiped the tears from her face and pushed a strand of damp hair away into the thick plait that hung down her back, revealing the fine bones, the high cheeks and delicate ears, the delicious tilt of the nose and well-defined mouth, the graceful sweep of her throat and neck. Yesterday's faded old clothes had been replaced by a plain bodice and skirt of dull rose pink over a white chemise, the lacy top of which could just be seen at the neckline. Santo thought of all the women who had wept in his presence, but could recall not one as exquisitely lovely as Aphra Betterton. 'Do you know where we might look for a map of Sandrock?' he said. 'If we both knew exactly where the priory land lies and who rents it, we shall have the advantage of Master Pearce. Do you agree?' For a moment, he thought she might insist on going it alone, that pride might get in the way of common sense, which would be a pity.

Her eyes rested on his face, then on his hands and back again to his eyes to find that essential element of honesty. 'But there will be questions,' she said. 'Village gossip. That man will already be telling all he meets about Mistress Betterton's Italian assistant.' This was a conversation she preferred not to have. Ignoring her parents' advice to wait, she had come to Sandrock alone to take advantage of the seclusion where the only decisions to be taken concerned the running of the household and gardens and the direction Ben would have wanted her to take in recording his plant collection. Relatives she had aplenty. Rela-

tionships she did not want. Especially not from
the same quarter as the previous one and its di-
sastrous consequence. And after their short and
decisive meeting yesterday, why had this man returned to offer help when she had already made
it clear what she felt about that?

Yet look how efficiently he had dealt with the
problem of Master Pearce. How comforting it
had been to have the Italian merchant there to
speak with a man's authority and without the
condescending argument that would surely have
followed if she had tackled the man on her own.
She knew about merchants. Her cousin Etta was
married to one. Hard-dealing, worldly, tough and
knowledgeable, and difficult to shake off when
they saw something they wanted. So what *did* the
man want? Her trust in men had fallen to rock-
bottom since Leon's departure and his inexplicable change of heart. Now, the appearance of
his elder brother, capable, handsome and more
mature than he, threatened to disturb the co-
coon of pain she had built around herself. With
that in place, she could keep everyone out and
fuel her reasons not to trust, not to make herself
accessible, not to welcome any man's company
for whatever reason. Now it looked as if she was
being manoeuvred into accepting him as an assistant, which she knew she needed, right here

where they would be obliged to meet on most days. What madness was that?

She sighed, thinking of the effort she would have to make.

'*Madonna,*' he said, gently.

'What?' Her head was turned away, trying to avoid seeing him.

'I understand your problem.'

'How can you possibly understand?' she replied. Pushing herself away from the table, she walked to the window to the medley of greens seen through panes of rippling glass. 'I wanted to be here on my own and now look what's happened after only a couple of weeks. Anyone would think I'd had no experience of handling estate matters when in fact I've assisted my mother for years while Father was away in London. I was sure Sandrock would be the same, that there'd be nothing here I'd not know how to deal with, and now all this nonsense of my neighbour wanting my mill, a dishonest steward and probably much more, for all I know.'

'Your steward is dishonest?'

'Oh…' She shrugged. 'He's hiding the accounts from me. I'm assuming…'

'I'd soon deal with that problem, mistress.'

'Needing help was never part of my plan. You were not part of my plan either, *signor.* You are the brother of the man whose deception has cast a blight on my life.' Aphra was not usually given to dramatics, but now she turned from the window to face him with her arms thrown out wide as if to demonstrate the enormity of her folly.

'Then try looking at it another way, mistress, if you will.'

'I don't want to look at it another way. There isn't another way.'

'There is,' he said, struggling to hide his smile. 'You simply think of me as your assistant instead of...'

'You see?' she yelped. 'That's exactly what I mean. Try to forget you are his brother. That's what you were about to say, isn't it? As if I could. As if I have not tried and *tried* to put him out of my thoughts. He was here, in this room, and Ben, too. I see them walking through the doors, in the gardens, the library, the church. They are everywhere and I thought that my being here would help me to lose them at my own pace. Slowly. It was the suddenness,' she whispered, 'that was so unfair.'

He nodded in sympathy. 'Yes,' he said, 'but, you know, in my experience it sometimes happens that what one thinks of at first as a hindrance...'

'Like you.'

'…like me, can become quite the opposite if you give it a chance. This situation was not planned by either of us. I thought you'd be living with your parents, not managing this great place on your own. You didn't know I'd be sent to England to offer some help to the woman my brother loves, but what a folly it would be to refuse that help rather than to make use of it.'

Aphra didn't move, didn't want to be persuaded by words that made complete sense. 'There is something in what you say, *signor*, except for your brother's love. That was false, wasn't it?'

'No, it was not false,' he said. 'Leon has not stopped loving you.'

'How can you know that?'

'Because he's told me so.'

She stared at him, only half-believing, then came back to sit facing him at the table. 'Let me understand this,' she said. 'Yesterday when my father was here, you implied that he was already married when he was here in England.'

'I said he was not free. He was in fact betrothed when he spoke of marriage to you, mistress, which he had no right to do. A betrothal is binding, as you know.'

'Then why could he not have said this in his letter? It was garbled. It gave me no indication…' she spread her hands, helplessly '…no facts at all.'

'Yes, I know.'

'You *know*? How do you know?'

'I helped him to write it. He was terribly upset. He asked me to help him.'

'So it was a family decision, was it? I see.'

'No, you do not see,' he said, countering her rising anger with his voice. 'But there is nothing positive to be gained by delving further into the matter. He is now married at my father's insistence. Leon's problem is loving too easily.'

'Well, thank you for that!' she said coldly, getting to her feet with a very noisy scraping of the stool on the floor. Her eyes blazed at him, the colour of gunmetal. 'He loved too easily. How inconvenient for the Datini family. And how many other gullible, love-starved women did he speak of marriage to? Was this a habit of his, this loving too easily? How many other letters did you help him to write, to avoid the unpleasant truth?' Her voice grew harsh as it rose in anger, her sarcasm wilder, hitting out in all directions.

Santo knew better than to attempt an answer to such questions, knowing that if he waited, she would hear the echo of her tirade and begin to calm down.

Simmering, she crossed her arms over her

breast. 'Loving too easily,' she muttered. 'Yes… well, that might be said about me, too. Perhaps we both mistook the signs. I certainly did, but then, what do I know about it? I thought love was like that. Straightforward. Uncomplicated. What a fool I was. Are you and your brother alike in this loving too easily, *signor*? You have a wife and family in Padua, I suppose?'

'I am neither married nor betrothed, mistress. Not yet. But when I spoke of my brother loving too easily, I did not mean to imply that he was indiscriminate. I meant that, by nature, his passion for goodness and beauty is highly developed. He feels things deeply, in here.' He laid a fist upon his chest. 'And he appeared to believe that he might be released from his obligations if he explained matters to those concerned. But my father is a man to whom honour and loyalty is everything, and he refused to allow it. Leon has been obliged to keep his promises. It's the law. Our family name carries considerable weight in Venice, you see.'

'So, a prestigious marriage, then. Arranged, was it? Or a love match? No—' she lifted a hand '—don't tell me. I don't want to know. I wish her well of him, whoever she is. What a pity he lacks that prized honour and loyalty.'

'As I said, mistress, he was distraught not to

be able to follow his heart. He blames himself for what's happened and begs you will forgive him.'

'Then when you return, *signor*, just remind him of the love he has lost, will you? And tell him how I'm being courted by a wealthy old landowner who has his eye on my very large estate, too. And since that is my only value now, I might even work my way through a succession of noble old husbands who can add to my material wealth, until I—'

'Stop!' Santo said, emphatically. 'This bitterness will not help matters.'

'Then what will?'

'I will,' he said. 'Give me leave to assist you, even if only for a few months while we sort out some issues, like the accounts and estate management, for example. If you haven't yet seen the map of Sandrock, you presumably have not examined your property yet, have you? And you've already encountered some inconsistencies? Well, I can keep nuisances like old Pearce out of the way, if that's what you want. I know from Leon that Dr Ben was more interested in his work than in being the owner of an estate like this. I would not get under your feet, mistress,' he added, gently. 'I shall keep out of your way. And although I cannot rescue the love you lost to my brother, at least I can pour oil on troubled waters, if you would allow it?'

Aphra did not reply immediately, but when she did, it was with a question about him. 'What about your own work at home?'

'I have some very capable managers and I have couriers to keep me informed. I have ships that come into Southampton and London, neither of which are too far from here, are they?'

'What about the gossip?'

'There are other male employees who live on the priory precincts, surely?'

'There are. The bailiff. The churchwarden. The priest and the steward.'

'Then perhaps I could be allocated a room, somewhere? I brought two men and a groom with me, all of them discreet and trustworthy, and English-speaking.'

'Your baggage, *signor*?'

'Is with your parents at Reedacre. Should I go and collect it, and tell them of our arrangement?'

Taking her face between her hands, she closed her eyes, whispering to herself, 'What am I doing? *What on earth am I doing?*'

With one lithe movement of his body, Santo came to her, standing close. 'It's time to move on,' he said. 'Share the burden with me. That's why I was sent.'

She nodded, eyes still closed, sighing again as questions filtered through her mind.

That is not why you were sent. Not all the way from Venice for my sake. I'll not believe the Datinis care so much. So what is it you came for?

'I'll find you some rooms,' she said, turning away, feeling the warmth of his body follow her.

Share the burden with me, he had said. It was what her father had offered, too, when she had moved into Ben's old home, but she had assured him of her ability to manage, having had years of experience helping at home while he was in London. Had she shown any signs of being unsure, she knew he would have insisted on having his own managers here each day, an imposition she was anxious to avoid when her only desire was to be alone with her wounds, healing them in her own time. Spending so much of his time at the Royal Wardrobe, Sir George had little enough to spare in keeping her safe from the intrusions of neighbours. Master Pearce would never have challenged her ownership of the mill had she not been so vulnerable. And now she knew her parents would not hesitate to approve of the arrangement to allow Signor Datini to stay. But how approving would the villagers of Sandrock be?

Chapter Two

As soon as she had given her reluctant agreement, Aphra knew that this was indeed the madness of a woman not thinking clearly. To accept the help of a man at this unsettled time, when her emotions were so confused, was something she had been determined never to do. What had she been thinking of? Had it been his warmth as he stood too close? Why had she allowed that, when no stranger ought to have come so near?

Barely half an hour after Signor Datini's departure, she sent one of the young estate workers to ride after him with a folded piece of paper taken from Ben's store on which she had written her change of mind. He must not return to Sandrock, but go back to Padua, she had told him. She would manage well enough on her own.

Convinced that that was the last she would see of this unnecessary interference, the control which had almost slipped away now returned, helping her to justify the growing theory in her mind that there was some malevolent alchemy at work between herself and men that must be prevented from worsening.

Only last year, when she and her cousin Etta had been with the royal court, an attempt had been made on her life which others present had believed was intended for the Queen. Her own family knew differently, but the foolish young man responsible had suffered a traitor's death and Aphra had been more deeply affected by this than she had disclosed to her relieved parents.

Then she had lost Leon, whose letter had made little sense to her, leaving her hurt, angry, confused, rejected and bitter. After that, her beloved uncle had died in London in what she felt were mysterious circumstances that had not yet been explained fully except to say that he had complained in the past of chest pains. Ben had said nothing of this to Aphra when he'd visited Reedacre Manor on his way to London, but by then she had had Leon's letter and their conversation had been mostly about her pain, not Ben's. He, too, had been profoundly shocked to hear of Leon's deceit and had offered her what comforting words he could, but nothing in his manner had warned her that they would never speak again.

Her parents had dealt philosophically with her tragedies, pointing out that men were no more likely to deceive than women and that death visited at will and often without invitation. The recent death of old Lady Agnes, Aphra's grandmother, had not been altogether unexpected, but none of them could have foreseen Ben's sudden demise, a man in the full flood of life and brilliant at his profession. These losses in such a short time should not, they had told her, be seen as particularly significant, but they had discounted the desperate young man last summer while Aphra had not, nor had they taken into account their daughter's vulnerable state of mind that preferred answers to the random workings of fate.

They had refused to take seriously her decision to remain unmarried for the rest of her life, but nor had they tried to persuade her otherwise. It was not her father's way to propel her into a marriage of his choosing, not even for an only daughter, for he and his wife had fallen in love at first sight and knew the workings of passionate hearts. For Aphra, however, her mind was immovable on that point, though she had not yet been successful in making her intentions understood by Master Richard Pearce.

Signor Datini's visit had made her aware, though, of some issues that ought to be addressed without delay if Master Pearce should push forward his claim to some of her property, one of which meant finding the map of Sandrock that the man said had been replaced by a newer version. In itself, that was not so surprising, for land had been redistributed since the priory had been sold to Aphra's grandfather for his own personal use. Doctor Ben had not wanted to keep all the fields under his control, so had sold some of them to the village freeholders, though Aphra did not believe this included the flour mill standing well within her boundaries.

The estate accounts were another issue she ought to have attended to by now, having been put off too many times by Master Fletcher, the steward whose job it was to discuss them with her every week. So far, she had not seen them at all and had come to the conclusion that she was not meant to, but a confrontation with the steward was not an inviting prospect when she would have to tackle it on her own.

Sleep evaded her that night, as it so often had recently. The full moon cast a silver light through her window, washing her room with a soft glow that changed all colours to monochrome, transmuting decisions into doubts and back again as the events of the day wandered through her mind. Questions remained unanswered. Why had Leon's brother come all this way to see her? Why would the Datini family care about her? To share the burden, he'd said. What burden? Did they think she might pester him, perhaps? Write to his tutors at Padua? Did they feel some responsibility for his actions or was it just to discover more about her state of mind?

Hugging her woollen shawl around her shoulders, she gave in to those thoughts that had not been allowed an entry in the daylight. Now she understood how foolish she had been in accepting Leon's plans for their future before any formal agreement was in place, yet at the time his passion had lost nothing by the irresponsibility of it. She had been cool, at first, while he had visited her ailing grandmother as she was nursing her. There had been more to concern her than the good looks and charming manner of the young man sent by Dr Ben from Sandrock and it was only when he accompanied her and her cousin Etta, now Lady Somerville, to London that she discovered how much they had in common and how easy he was to talk to.

Gradually, over several weeks, their friendship had deepened and, in an unprepared moment of closeness, they had declared a love for each other that had crept up on them almost unawares. She had trusted him completely. In her happy eagerness, she had allowed him a few innocent intimacies as a natural expression of her generosity and, it had to be said, her curiosity, too. They had talked of a future together while riding high on waves of desire, which Aphra now realised must have been Leon's way of securing both her interest and her loyalty. He would be back in the new year, he told her, to continue his work with Dr Ben, the details of how they would live being lost in a haze of sweet love-talk and affirmations of fidelity.

At the time, it had not occurred to her to press him, a student, for more than vague promises and even now she could scarcely believe how easily she had been deceived. For his elder brother to say that he still loved her was nonsense when he had made legal promises to another woman. Perhaps Signor Datini had said it hoping to soothe her wounded pride but, if so, it had no such effect. She wanted no more to do with the Datinis.

Of more pressing interest to her was to discover what she could about the manner of Ben's sudden death and the question of his prepared will. A man did not usually make a will until he knew his days were limited. Only then did he decide who would make best use of his belongings. Did this mean that Ben had anticipated his own death? And if so, then why? From what cause? And why had he told no one?

The moon had sailed on well past the window by the time Aphra found sleep at last.

Scarcely had she spooned the last of her porridge into her mouth when she was visited by the priest, Father Vickery, who had been a novice at Sandrock Priory with the late Dr Ben Spenney and whose long, lean frame signified a lifetime of austerity. His thick white eyebrows were almost hidden by a fringe of hair, the tonsure being a thing of the past. His voice, now several shades darker, was still musical.

'Father,' Aphra said, indicating a stool, 'what a pleasant surprise. Will you be seated?'

His grey woollen habit, now threadbare, could not hide bony knees poking into the fabric as he sat. 'Good morning, Mistress Betterton. I would not disturb you at this hour except for a matter of some importance,' he said, accepting with a smile the beaker of ale. 'It concerns our steward, Master Fletcher.'

'Ah,' Aphra said. 'What a coincidence. He's at the top of my list of people to see today.'

The priest was already shaking his head. 'You'll not be seeing him today nor any other day,' he said. 'I've just seen the back of him riding away on one of your horses, leading a packhorse behind him with all his possessions on it. And some of yours, too, I wouldn't be surprised.'

Aphra stood up, frowning in anger. 'How long ago was this, Father?'

'Just a few moments ago. I called to him, but he clapped his heels to the horse's belly and trotted away as fast as he could go. It was no good me running after him. Not with my knees.'

'Indeed not, but somebody should. I could go after him myself, in fact.'

'Nay, mistress. Best to let him go. We need a better man than him.'

'That's not the point,' Aphra said, peering through the window. 'If he's taken anything of mine, I want it back. And I want to know what he's done with the household accounts. They're private, Father.' She headed for the door. 'Perhaps you'd care to come with me? On horseback, of course.'

Father Vickery winced as he rose to his feet and gulped down the rest of the ale. 'Gladly,' he said, stretching the truth a little.

His willingness, however, was not put to the test for, as they walked into the cobbled court-yard together, the multiple clatter of hooves reached them from the arched gatehouse where a party of riders appeared led by Signor Datini. Behind him, flanked by two mounted men, rode Master Fletcher with hands bound behind him, followed by two packhorses led by a groom. Looking back on this incident, Aphra could never find adequate words to describe her emotions, especially when her expectations of seeing both Signor Datini and Master Fletcher ever again were nil. Not on that day or any other. Fortunately, it was Father Vickery who found suitable words of welcome, even though he and Santo had not met, until now.

'Well...well,' he said. 'Welcome back, Master Fletcher. Word gets round rather quickly in a village of this size, doesn't it? Well caught, sir,' he called to Santo. 'You see what a difference your presence can make? More difference than Ben's, I'd say,' he added under his breath. 'So this is your Italian lawyer, mistress?' he said to Aphra.

'He's not...' Aphra stopped herself. If word of an Italian lawyer had leaked out with the help of Richard Pearce, then why bother to refute it if this was what good it might do? So instead of arguing with him about being here when she'd sent him packing only yesterday, she introduced him to the priest as if everything the latter had said was true.

'You'll be staying with us for a while, *signor*?' said Father Vickery.

'Until Mistress Betterton has no more use for me, Father,' Santo said as if his invitation had never been in doubt. 'I took the liberty of changing the direction of our friend here, until we'd had a chance to check on what he's removed. He insists that everything here belongs to him, but I believe he didn't include the horses. They are yours, mistress?' His eyes twinkled mischievously as he saw how she tried to hide her embarrassment and he knew she was not finding the situation easy to accept.

'Master Fletcher knows they are. I am sorry to find he's a thief, as well as an inefficient steward, but I did not expect him to leave without any kind of explanation. Did you take my ledgers with you?' she asked him.

Stumbling down from the saddle, Fletcher stood uneasily with bound hands and the beginning of an angry bruise on his cheek, his expression loaded with guilt. 'No, mistress,' he said. 'I left them in the cottage there.' His nod indicated the neat little house built into the corner of the courtyard where the stewards of Sandrock had always combined home and office. Stewards were usually educated men with a good grasp of accounting and management skills, though Master Fletcher and his new employer had met only a few times, briefly, and now Aphra blamed herself for not attending to that side of things before it had come to this.

'He'd better be locked in the cellar until we can notify the magistrate,' Santo said, looking around him. 'Is that the door, over there?'

'No, wait!' Aphra said. 'Master Fletcher and I need to talk about this first. Untie him, take the horses back to the stable and unpack those bags.'

'One of them is mine,' Santo reminded her.

'I know that, *signor*. Have it unpacked. Bring Master Fletcher into the house, if you will. You are welcome to come, too, Father. You know the steward's duties as well as I do. And have the ledgers brought in here. We need to see what's been going on.'

'Nay, mistress…please!' Fletcher pleaded, rubbing his wrists. 'You'll not like what you see. Give me time…'

Aphra turned away to the house. 'I shall not like anything at all until I've seen them, shall I? At least I'm giving you the chance to explain yourself instead of running away from the problem. Come in here. Sit down. Have you eaten today?'

'By the smell of him,' Santo said, 'he's already helped himself to your wine. You're surely not going to feed him, mistress?' Protectively, he placed himself between her and the steward.

'When he's answered some of my questions, yes. A half-starved steward will be no good to me, will he? Is there not a Mistress Fletcher somewhere?'

Fletcher passed a hand over his eyes, pulling his features downwards in one heavy sweep. He was not an unhandsome man, though he was unkempt and showing signs of strain brought on by some deep unhappiness. 'No,' he whispered, glancing at the priest. 'Father Vickery knows… she…' His voice broke as his features screwed up in pain.

'Last year,' said the priest, quietly. 'Died in childbirth. She and the babe. Their first. Only been married two years. Buried here, in the churchyard.'

'Yes, I see,' Aphra said. 'Accept my sympathies, Master Fletcher. I take it that's when you forgot to keep the accounts, is it? Since then?'

Fascinated, Santo watched as she took control of the situation, sending for porridge, bread, cheese and milk for the man who had just tried to make off with her belongings from the cottage after cheating his way through years of work poorly supervised by her predecessor, Dr Ben. No wonder the thought of an Italian lawyer on the premises had been the last straw. He thought what a remarkable woman she was, more concerned for the man's genuine distress than for her own inconvenience. He watched the man begin to eat, his table manners perfectly acceptable, although the absence of a wife had clearly had an effect on his personal hygiene. Santo drew Aphra away to one side, leaving the priest and the steward to talk. 'What do you intend?' he said. 'To keep him on? It's a risk, you know. As your new Italian lawyer, I ought to advise you against it. He was taking your property.'

'As my new Italian lawyer,' she said with a sideways glare, 'you lack compassion, *signor*. As a merchant, you could oblige me by justifying your decision to ignore my request to go away and by going through the accounts with him and Father Vickery. He knows what ought to be included in them, so between the three of you, you should be able to come up with some results. If he has nothing to look forward to, he has no reason to co-operate, does he? If we put him back…'

'You're going to give him another chance?'

'Of course I am. It's obviously the loss of his wife and child that's caused the problem and, anyway, where am I going to get another steward who knows as much about the place as he does? They don't come two-a-penny, you know.'

The handsome face widened into a smile, making her heart flutter. 'I like that. Two for a penny. That means, not easy to find. Yes?'

'Yes. Unlike some Italian merchants who cannot take no for an answer.'

The smile stayed. 'I did not think you really meant it, mistress.'

'I *did* really mean it,' she growled, returning to the table. 'But now you're here, you may as well make yourself useful.'

So for the rest of that morning and well into the afternoon, Santo and Father Vickery sat with the steward with the ledgers spread out before them while they ate, drank good ale and tried to rectify the housekeeping mess. After seeing a similar kind of disorder in the steward's cottage, Aphra got three women from the village to scrub the place out, to wash the stale bedlinen and clothes, and to replace them with some that had been used by Dr Ben's students. The few items of furniture were polished and supplemented by others, the little cot removed, food placed in the kitchen, oil in the lamps, firewood in the hearth, and a widow found to housekeep and cook for him who needed just this kind of employment to put money into her purse. Aphra's money.

To his credit, Father Vickery offered to double-check the accounts with Fletcher before submitting them to Aphra each week, which they all understood to be both a help and a safeguard against any back-sliding. Unintentional the deceptions might have been, but Aphra could not afford to turn a blind eye to mismanagement, as Dr Ben had apparently been doing.

'I think,' said Santo, sitting down to supper in Aphra's comfortable parlour, 'your uncle was more interested in his medicinal studies than in household management.'

'And I,' said Aphra, arranging her skirts as she sat opposite him, 'failed to deal with that side of things as soon as I came to live here. Have we lost a lot?'

He liked the sound of the 'we' in her question. 'That's difficult to tell now,' he replied, 'but the purchases and sales have not all been recorded properly so it's quite likely that your uncle has been cheated over the year. That will have to stop. Perhaps it's a good thing that word is getting round about your lawyer being here to keep an eye on things.'

'That,' said Aphra, primly, eyeing the dishes being placed on the table, 'is something I must discuss with you. As you say, word is getting around, and that's what I don't want. That's why you should go back to Italy, *signor*.'

'But now you've changed your mind.'

'I have not changed my mind. I would not want you to return to Reedacre Manor in the dark, but you cannot stay more than one night. You and your men can use the rooms across there.' She pointed through the window to the stone-built dwelling across on the other side of the square garden. 'It was once the visiting abbots' house. Plenty of space on both floors. I've given a man the task of looking after your needs. And tomorrow, you must leave Sandrock and return to my parents' house. Your help today is appreciated, but now I shall manage on my own.'

'But you may recall,' Santo said, 'that Sir George and Lady Betterton have now left Reedacre Manor for London. When we said farewell this morning, they were of the opinion that my help here would be a good thing for you.'

'They would. It's a big place.'

'And you really do not need a man's help?' he said, persuasively.

'Not the help of a man like you.'

'A man like me?'

'The brother of the man who deceived me,' she said. 'Did you think I'd welcome you with open arms, *signor*? My memory is not so short as all that.'

'I believe that's what the English call "tarring everyone with the same brush", isn't it? I am not to be confused with my brother, mistress. He was guilty of a gross misjudgement. I am a merchant and I've learnt not to do that. Laws are there to be kept. If I were untrustworthy, no one would do business with me. My family's good name would suffer, which is why my father insisted on Leon keeping his word.'

'I'm glad he did so,' Aphra said, daintily picking up a rabbit's roasted foreleg and deciding which bit to nibble. 'I would not want a husband who breaks promises so easily.' She pushed a dish towards him. 'This is sage and onion stuffing,' she said. 'It goes well with rabbit. I did not mean to tar you with the same brush as your brother, Signor Datini. I am sure you are honourable in all your dealings. But I made a decision to be alone here, after what's happened, to give me time to reflect and to carry on some of the work my uncle began with his plants. I intend to supply London doctors with the raw material, as he did. They don't all grow the plants they use in medicines, you know, nor do they buy them from just anyone. Only from growers they can trust.'

'That's an excellent line to pursue, mistress. You have the gardens and the men to tend them, and your uncle's research, too. One cannot allow years to elapse before picking up where he left off. They're not all perennials, are they?'

Not looking at him, Aphra continued to nibble at the meat. 'What do you know about perennials?' she said. 'Was that a shot in the dark?'

That smile again, diverting her thoughts, fractionally. 'Another one,' he said. 'A shot in the dark. No, I know that perennials seed themselves and multiply each year, and that others are known as biennials, appearing for only two years, and that others must be re-sown every year. Annuals. My brother told me that.'

'He was Dr Ben's most talented student.'

'Was he? I didn't know that. He didn't say. But I know he was trying to establish a system for naming plants that everyone would understand. He found all the various names very confusing, to say the least.'

'It can be dangerous, too. Mistakes have been made because of wrong identification.'

'Which is why apothecaries and doctors trusted your uncle and a good reason why you should follow in his footsteps, mistress. And if you could manage to keep the apothecary's foreign imports separate from your household accounts, Fletcher would be able to give you a clearer picture of exactly what materials you're buying and for how much. You also need records of what herbs you're exporting, too.'

'What do you mean?' Aphra said, pausing in her eating. 'That the medicinal plants are mixed up with supplies of sugar loaves and spices? And barley?'

'Yes, I'm afraid so. I cannot believe that your household needs bulk supplies of alkanet and juniper berries and senna, does it? All that ought to be in a separate book kept only for the apothecary department, or the stillroom, or wherever you prepare it. Some are very expensive items. I import some of them myself.'

Wide-eyed, Aphra studied his face and knew he was not making this up. 'I didn't know that. You're right, Dr Ben was perhaps not as concerned about balancing the books as he was about obtaining the very best ingredients. We have to do something about this, immediately.'

'Would you allow me to look through Dr Ben's records to see what he's been ordering for his work? It could make a significant difference to costs.'

Aphra looked down at her pewter plate, realising that this was the first time she had wanted to eat everything on it. Yet she hesitated, knowing what this would mean. He would need to stay longer.

Santo saw her doubts. 'We have to find that map, too, you know. You have to know exactly where your estate boundaries are. Did your father not go through that with you?'

'No,' she whispered. 'Well, he might have done, I don't remember. Those first few days here were a blur. There's quite a lot to be done. Yes, I suppose we'd better take a look, but you see...' Spreading her hands, she sighed and shook her head. Her hair was dressed loosely in a thick plait with wisps floating over her neck as if she cared nothing for how she looked in his company. She had not expected him to be here. As for the next day, and the one after that, she was sure he would make out a good case why she needed him around. 'You see, I don't want people, anyone, looking through my uncle's things. It's too soon. They're too precious. Sacred, almost. Do you understand what I mean?'

'Of course I understand. But think. Dr Ben would not have wanted to make it easy for other landowners to take advantage of you, like Pearce, for instance. He left his estate to you, presumably, so that you could support yourself and not be reliant on a husband. That means you must know all about it. Nor need you do it alone. If the villagers think I'm a lawyer as well as a merchant, well then, let them. Many households have their own lawyer.'

'Does yours, *signor*? In Italy?'

'Indeed it does. A company lawyer for my father's glassworks on Murano.'

'And what about your work? Do you not have business in Padua to attend to?'

'You asked me that before and I told you. I have managers, couriers and captains. They are in constant contact with me.'

It was dark by this time and, looking out of the window before answering him, she saw only their reflections in the glass, the cluster of candles casting a brilliant glow between them. She saw how he watched her and once again knew that this was not only about assisting her on the estate, but something else that required him to stay at Sandrock until his mission was completed. She wished she knew what it was. His eyes were dark, admiring and perceptive, and she knew that he found her attractive. She had learned to detect that look in men, though it made no difference to her unreceptiveness. Never again would she allow herself to fall in love. Never again would she be so generous, or so foolish. Perhaps she would allow him to stay for another day or two—after all, her heart was still hard and cold, and not for sharing.

'Then I shall let you know tomorrow, *signor*. That will give me time to sleep on it. Now, will you try one of these desserts? Last year's plums, I believe.'

The rooms allocated to Santo, opposite Aphra's, were comfortable enough to encourage any visiting abbot to overstay his welcome, which he also had in mind to do. Reasonably sure of the lady's decision and of his own ability to make himself indispensable, he had his two men, Enrico and Dante, arrange his belongings around the room while he stood to one side of the window to watch the lights being extinguished in the rooms across the garden. His brother had known this place well. His foolish brother. Now, however, it was becoming easier for Santo to understand what had possessed him to behave so badly, to give his heart when he had already pledged it. Their father had been adamant and Leon ought to have known better than to expect any flexibility. Certainly marriage to the niece of the famous Dr Spenney would have boosted his career, but not at any price.

Her anger was understandable, he thought, watching the two men place things exactly as he liked them. He supposed he would feel the same way about having a man's company imposed upon him when all he'd wanted was to be alone. But that was not all, was it? His presence reminded her of Leon, the terrible bitterness of rejection and the foolishness she now felt after love had blinded her to common sense. No woman would be unaffected by that blow to her pride and to have him there, even as an aide, would keep those wounds open longer than need be.

The thought of finding an acceptable way to comfort her was not new to him. It had kept him awake for hours last night. But she had given him not the slightest indication that she might accept any comfort he could offer. Prickly, resentful and defensive, and certainly under no obligation to charm him, not even for the sake of courtesy. He would have to tread very carefully if he wished to stay long enough to find what he was looking for, for if he asked her outright, she would most certainly refuse to help. So would he, in the same circumstances.

It began to look as if Aphra's faith in Master Fletcher, her steward, had paid off when, early next morning, she passed his cottage on her way to the kitchen gardens and heard him whistling. He came to the door as she drew near, presenting his new morning face, shaved and bright-eyed, his hair washed and combed. 'Morning to you, mistress,' he said with a smile. 'I'm about to take a look at the gardens over there. I've got three men and two lads on my payroll, but now there seems to be eight of them. We'll be having half the lads in the village there, if we don't watch out.'

'Before you send them off, Master Fletcher, find out exactly who they're related to, then see if the head gardener actually needs the extra help. It may be that he needs them, with things starting to grow.'

'Right, mistress, I'll do as you say. Then I'll go and—'

'Ah! There you are!' Santo's deep voice reached them from across the courtyard just as the steward turned to walk away. 'Don't go, Fletcher. You're the one who'll know exactly where the estate boundaries are. Yes? Good morning to you, mistress. Would you give me leave to take Master Fletcher and the bailiff off to ride round the San-drock lands this morning? It's a matter of some urgency, you'll agree, if we're to understand ex-actly what belongs to you.'

'Well, I…'

'Your lawyer is correct, mistress,' Fletcher said, nodding in agreement. 'I know a few bits changed hands with Dr Ben and I have the newest map that shows the changes. You really do need to know about it. I can take you round, sir. Shall I go and get it?' He was half-inside the cottage before Aphra could think of an objection. So that was where the map was.

'You were supposed to be leaving,' she said, attempting some severity.

'Yes, but I've been thinking…'

'Of a reason why you should stay. Yes, I can see that. Have you broken your fast yet?'

'In the kitchen, with the men,' he said. 'You could come with us?'

She caught the sunlight shining in his eyes and on white teeth. 'No, I have other things to do. Go on, then. Get on with it, if it's so important.'

'One of us needs to know,' he said, reasonably. 'Four of us is better.'

Aphra turned away, speaking to herself so that he would hear and not be able to reply. 'And what will it be tomorrow, I wonder? Something equally urgent?' She did not see his smile, but felt his eyes on her as she walked over the uneven cobblestones, and she knew that her hips swung and that her hair shone silvery in the bright light.

She had not exaggerated when she'd made her excuses not to ride out with him and the men, for there was indeed much for her to do that she had ignored in previous weeks while revelling in being her own mistress. Without quite knowing why, she experienced a new, different kind of energy and a realisation that the tasks of managing a large estate on a day like this were well within her capabilities and enticing, too. There was a spring in her step as she walked down to the high-walled kitchen garden where, after watching the men at their tasks, she decided that there was enough work for all eight of them.

But as the sunny morning wore on, her involvement with the gardens, the stillroom, the store rooms and dairy, the bee skeps and the brewhouse did not prevent her ears straining to catch the sound of Signor Datini's return from his ride. Even while she gave instructions, spoke to Father Vickery and examined the church register for details of Dr Ben's funeral, her thoughts refused to stay on track, teasing her with his next attempt to stay another day and the way she would allow it while giving the impression of irritation. Tonight, at supper, he would present her with some necessary task that only he, a man, could perform and she would argue and pretend to refuse, already feeling the disappointment if he should accept her decision. Was that why she had given him the comfortable visiting abbots' house instead of a humble pallet in the students' dormitory which had once been the infirmary? It was perfect for rows of beds and the basic necessities, but not exactly homely. Perhaps she was sending out the wrong kind of message.

In an attempt to refocus her thoughts, she returned to Dr Ben's great library which she had earlier decided to make her own place of study, where his writings would have some influence on her. Botany was a complicated subject and, although every good housewife had some knowledge of plants and their medicinal properties, Dr Ben had taken it to new levels, specialising in particular qualities and remedies. She had not yet discovered what these remedies were for, though Leon had once mentioned that he and Ben were working on the same area and that on one occasion, Ben had given him access to his notes. A rare act of selflessness for a tutor to bestow on a pupil. Little wonder, then, that Ben had been so upset to hear from her, Aphra, that his best student would not be returning, after all. Did Leon have some of Ben's notes with him? And had this bad news, together with her own distress, somehow contributed to his death in London, only two days later?

Up in the library, she looked through his meticulously written recipe books and then found, in neatly labelled ivory boxes, the powdered pigments he and his students had used to illustrate certain plants, a skill they needed in the accurate compilation of herbals. There were fine brushes there, too, stacks of prepared paper and stiff vellum, and some of his drawings, exquisitely detailed, labelled and described. It was as if, she thought, he was showing her how to go about observing and recording the plants, some of which he had brought back from his foreign travels, pressed flat between the pages. So it was here, amongst Ben's painting materials, his boxes and pots of vermilion, green and blue byse, verdigris, yellow orpiment, lampe black and white lead, that the painful memories of betrayal and loss were replaced by the gentler ones left by a beloved uncle for exactly that purpose. Amongst the notes and sketches, she felt his presence next to her, pointing a finger to show her what to see and how to portray it.

As the light began to move away, Santo's quiet step upon the stairs did nothing to disturb her, though he saw in one glance how the art materials spread across the table had brought to her a peace which he himself had not. This was something he had not foreseen when he had agreed upon this mission, that not only did he have his brother's latent presence to deal with, but also that of her uncle, who had thought so highly of her that he had left her everything he owned.

He sat on the stool opposite her and waited to be noticed, half-amused by the lack of any greeting. Finally, her silver point lifted from the paper on which delicate lines had appeared as fine as a spider's web, filling him with admiration. 'So, you've returned,' she said, unwelcoming, unsmiling.

She was priceless, he thought, with her emotions still all over the place. He smiled at her, resting his arms on the table and hunching his great shoulders. 'Indeed I have,' he said. 'So now we can deal with Master Pearce and his claims. You see, that was a good enough reason for me to stay, don't you think? Apart from the other reason, of course.'

'Which you are about to remind me of, naturally,' she said, laying down the pencil.

'Naturally. I promised to assist you with estate matters. I owe you that, at least.'

'You don't owe me anything, *signor*,' she said, looking beyond him, arching her back against the strain of bending. Her white coif lay on the table where she had been resting her elbow on it, squashing it flat. 'Was the map useful to you?'

He brought the roll of parchment forward and waited as she found weights to hold its corners. '"The Priory of Sandrock and its Estates,"' he read, '"at its Acquisition by Sir Walter D'Arvall in the Year of Our Lord 1540, with Revisions made in 1559." That's only last year,' he added.

His hands smoothed over the fields and woodlands to show her how some boundaries had been moved. The fields and grand house of Master Pearce were given some attention, too, though Santo suspected that Aphra's attention lay elsewhere.

He was correct. 'If you leave this with me,' she said, tonelessly, 'I can memorise it by suppertime.' She looked up at him, surprising him with a shadow of guilt in her eyes, like those of a child caught with its mind wandering off the subject. Her long fair hair, freed from the linen coif, had fallen over her face as they had pored over the map, her eyes meeting his through a veil of pale gold that she seemed in no hurry to rearrange.

In the fading light, he found it difficult to be certain of the message sent from beneath drowsy lids, but her uninterest, together with her parted lips, her seductively tousled hair and her fragility

combined to knock him off course in the same
way, he supposed, his brother had been when
he'd offered her his entire world. Was this how
Leon had seen her before they'd made love, or
after? Had she looked at him like this, driving
him mad with desire? Did she know how she
looked? He would swear she did not, having con-
sistently shown him her coldest demeanour and,
anyway, she was not the kind of woman to care
overmuch about the effect she had on men. It
was one of her attractions. Her naturalness. Her
artlessness. A woman completely without guile.

'*Madonna?*' he said, gently.

She blinked, breaking the spell with a sudden
surge of activity, brushing her hair back with
an impatient gesture, embarrassed to have been
caught daydreaming. 'Yes? What?' she said. 'I
should be clearing this away.' Closing the notebooks and covering the paints, her methodical
hands gave no hint of the confusion in her mind
and the wanton thoughts that had sneaked across
the map as his hands had smoothed and stroked,
tenderly caressing the parchment to the musical
murmurs of his deep velvety voice. Some distant ache around her heart made her frown and
turn away quickly before he saw something she
did not know how to explain, not even to herself.

Chapter Three

After that fleeting moment in the library when the hypnotic sweep of Signor Datini's hands over the map had caused her body to respond with an uncontrollable ache for their comfort, Aphra was determined that he must go. She had seen his expression and knew from experience with his brother how easily a man's thoughts could be diverted into dangerous channels. Her own, too. After all that had happened, it seemed inconceivable that she could experience the stirrings of her heart again, so soon. Yet there was nothing to be gained by pretending it hadn't happened. He must go. Now, before such feelings assailed her again.

But Santo arrived at the supper table well prepared for the dismissal he knew would come and, before she could launch into all the reasons why he ought to return to Italy, his own excuses came with such conviction that she was obliged to take them seriously. He had noticed, in the ledgers, not only how the supplies needed for the kitchen were being mixed up with those for Dr Ben's apothecary's business, but that imports ordered last year had not yet been collected from the warehouses in Southampton and, if they were left any longer, would either deteriorate or disappear altogether. The situation must be remedied, urgently. He showed her the ledgers.

'These goods have been paid for, have they?' Aphra said, laying down her knife.

'According to our records, yes. Sums amounting to hundreds of pounds.'

'*Hundreds?* Are you serious? Whatever for?'

'Valuable ingredients, mistress. Precious stones and seed pearls. Sandalwood, root ginger and musk. Gum arabic and theriac from Venice. I import this kind of thing myself. It cannot be left there indefinitely. Besides which, Dr Ben's recipes will be needing them.'

'What…precious gems? Pearls? What on earth did he do with those?'

'I have no idea, mistress. But that's no reason not to collect what he ordered, is it? They've been paid for, so they should be here. You can always sell what you don't want. I could do that easily enough, through my contacts.'

'Who would I send to Southampton? Anybody?'

'Someone dependable and honest, with your authorisation in their pockets. I could send Enrico and Dante first thing tomorrow, if you wish. They know their way round the warehouses, and the customs house, too.'

Aphra picked up her knife and handed it to him. 'Would you mind cutting me a slice of the pork, please?'

Santo took it from her, trying not to betray the victory he felt. 'Certainly, mistress. You are agreed, then, that they should go without delay?'

The pork slice, transparently thin, crumpled on to her platter. The ambiguous nod of her head was taken for both agreement and thanks. She could not waste time in arguments when there was precious cargo to be identified, signed for and conveyed safely to Sandrock. He was right. Such rare and expensive commodities were too valuable to leave uncollected. So Aphra's decision to send him away was delayed once more. Instead of fuming over the change of plan, she felt it best to accept, for the time being, the unorthodox situation of having her ex-lover's brother on site to handle the complexities of an apothecary's trade, amongst other tasks that appeared, suddenly, to require immediate attention.

Before the end of their meal, however, an additional complication arrived in the form of a message just received from a breathless rider to say that Dr Ben's elder brother Paul would arrive on the morrow, bringing with him his lady wife, their daughter and Aphra's brother Edwin. Those four were the bare bones of the party, for Uncle Paul and Aunt Venetia never moved far these days without a retinue of servants, pack-horses and grooms, assorted maids for this and that, and hounds. Always the hounds. Uncle Paul, and Edwin, too, liked to hunt and Aphra had no illusions whatever that the first visitors to her new tenancy had come as much for the hunting as to offer her some comfort. As she read the message, she wondered if they realised how much she preferred to be on her own at this time, taking each day at her own pace. Already that preference had been compromised and now she would be obliged to introduce Signor Datini to them when she would rather not. 'Damn!' she muttered, laying the paper to one side.

'Bad news, mistress?'

She sighed. 'No. I like them. But…'

'But what? Who?'

'Uncle Paul is coming for a few days. He's a buyer for the Royal Wardrobe. My brother Edwin works as his assistant. Aunt Venetia is always very well dressed, as you might imagine. And Flora.'

'Their daughter?'

'She's twelve. She has a twin brother called Marius and an older brother, Walter. I'm surprised they won't be coming, too.' Her eyes swept up and down the long polished table, imagining how it would look loaded with food each day and how much notice she had been given to prepare it. The kitchen staff were competent, but food needed to be either caught or made. 'I suppose I shall have to take this kind of thing in my stride. Heaven knows I've had enough practice at it.' Glaring at him from beneath her fine brows, she allowed her resentment to show, though Santo could see that there was something she was not sure how to express without incivility. 'You wouldn't like to...er...?' Hiding her eyes with one hand, she tried to rephrase the question in her mind.

'Wouldn't like to what?' he said, leaning forward. 'To disappear while they're here? Is that what you're about to say?'

Guiltily, she nodded. 'Yes. If you could just—'

'No, *madonna*. That would not do. Nor can

you pretend to them that I'm your lawyer. They are family. They will find out who I am soon enough, but you are mistaken if you think you owe them an explanation.'

Her head came up, defiantly. 'Oh, yes, of course you're right, *signor*. I simply say that you are the brother of the man who deceived me and that for some *inexplicable* reason I have offered you my hospitality instead of showing you the door. Now, what's wrong with that as an explanation? Poor little Aphra. Desperate for a man. Any man. The first one who comes knocking. What an idiot, they'll say.' With fists clenched upon the table, she sat back and waited for him to speak, half-expecting him to find reasons, arguments, excuses, comforting words, justifications. But he said nothing and after a moment or two of silence she realised that he was about to agree with her, that the situation both of them accepted and understood would not be seen so charitably by others. Her parents had met Santo and seen how his presence might help her, but she could hardly expect the same kind of perception from relatives to whom he was a complete, and presumably unwelcome, stranger. Particularly Uncle Paul, who would get hold of the wrong end of the stick, so to speak, for although he was Dr Ben's

elder brother, he had little of Ben's deep understanding of the foibles of human nature.

'You could *pretend* to be my lawyer, as you've
done so far,' she said with a lift of her brows.

'Not to relatives I couldn't. I prefer to be honest unless there's a very good reason to stretch
the truth, as I have been doing.'

'And if that doesn't work, you lie.' Her sarcasm was delivered more like a compliment.

'No. But nor do I believe either of us owes
anyone an explanation when it is none of their
business. If that is truly too much for you to bear,
then it would be best for me to leave first thing
tomorrow to save you any embarrassment. If that
is what you wish, I shall respect your decision.
You have only to say.'

One fist unclenched to smooth a crease from
her table napkin while her mind spun and asked
questions she hardly dared to answer, so prepos-
terous were they. 'What about the seed pearls
and gems?' she whispered. 'And the theriac?'

'That depends on how much you want them.
Do you?'

'Want them? I certainly do. Hundreds of
pounds?'

'Well then, we'd better collect them.'

'But what about…you know…explanations?'

'Keep it simple. I am Santo Datini, merchant

of Venice trading in glass and exotic spices, rare products from the East Indies, Persia, Egypt and wines from Cyprus. My ships come into South-ampton every springtime.'

'Is that how you got here, *signor*?'

'It is indeed. It is also how my brother came to England and returned home. You mentioned that your aunt's name is Venetia. So she's not English?'

'Italian. Her father was a silk merchant. Pietro Cappello. That's how she met Uncle Paul, trading in silks for the Wardrobe.' She saw how Santo was nodding, a bemused expression in his eyes as he followed her words. 'You know him?'

'Every Venetian merchant knows the Cappellos. A very wealthy and powerful family. Your uncle made a good match there.'

'So is it likely that my aunt will know your family, too?'

'It's possible. Her father will, but he's an old man now.'

'I see. So you suggest we give them no more explanation than that.'

'If they want to know more, they'll ask. When they know I'm a Datini, they'll make the connection, I expect. But it's really none of their business, is it?'

'But what if they ask you what your business

is here at Sandrock? What exactly *is* your business here, *signor*?'

'I thought I'd explained that to you.'

'You tried, but I'm afraid I never found your explanation very plausible. My credibility has suffered, you see, along with other faculties.'

'Then I shall have to do more to convince you, mistress. Let's get this dreaded visit out of the way first, shall we? After that, you might find my help so useful to you that you no longer wish to send me packing. Is that how it's said in English?'

Aphra's deep breath was an attempt to maintain some seriousness, suspecting that he might be trying to sweet-talk her out of her enquiries into his business, which he had never answered to her satisfaction. Clearly, he did not intend to. For the moment, however, she would accept his help, for the idea of playing lone hostess to her relatives did not appeal to her at all. One at a time would have been more than enough.

Later, when Santo had returned to his rooms, such thoughts began to shame her. She and Edwin had always got on well together, even after he had left home to work as Uncle Paul's assistant instead of his father's. A year younger than herself, he had been a great comfort to her during those bleak winter months when everything had seemed black and despairing. They had not seen each other since then, when they had been too full of grief to speak of anything much except their loss of Dr Ben and Master Leon's betrayal. Now she had the chance to thank him for his brotherly concern, not resent this interruption to her peace but put on her best face to show how well she was recovering, how capable her management. She would feast them each day, bring out all the best tableware that had not seen the light of day since Ben left and send them back with praise on their lips instead of pity for her.

So, on the following day, she recruited women from the village to help the house servants prepare rooms for the guests, feeling a certain satisfaction that so many people could be accommodated without the slightest problem in a place as large as this. Soon the rooms were transformed from echoing spaces into cosy chambers with sweet-smelling rushes on the floor and polished panelling, colourful bed curtains and coverlets, new beeswax candles and gleaming windowpanes. Inspecting the food stores, she found the shelves bending under boxes of last year's fruits, preserves, pickles and honey.

The grain bins were full, the cold stores filling up with rabbits and pigeons, capons and eggs, wild boar, sides of bacon and racks of fish from the monks' fish pond. The dairy, cold and spotlessly clean, clanked and thudded to the sound of the butter churn, the skimming of cream, the soft clack of wooden butter pats and clogs on the white stone floor, while muslin bags of whey and curds dripped from hooks to make sage-flavoured soft cheeses. The aroma of baking bread and fruit cakes wafted through open doors, the sound of crashing pans and whistling kitchen boys telling Aphra that, by suppertime, she would set before her guests as fine a meal as any in London and probably fresher.

Recalling how Ben had had a fondness for good wine, she had a selection brought up from the cellar to add to her own brew of best March beer and was relieved to see that the stock was not as depleted as she feared. She had been drinking only Ben's home-grown fruit wines made from elderflower and cowslip, cherry and blackberry, but for her guests she found casks of malmsey from Crete, claret from Gascony, sack from Spain and white wines from the Rhineland. With the ale and beer, there would be plenty to choose from.

As she suspected, the huge oaken dresser in

the dining parlour, which she had not bothered to look into until now, revealed an astonishing collection of glass and silverware which she assumed Ben had kept for special occasions. As she received each piece from the young man whose head had almost disappeared inside the cupboard, she murmured in astonishment at the design, workmanship and probable value, for only at the court of Queen Elizabeth had she seen anything like this hoard. A few of the most astonishing vessels were mounted in silver gilt, made of materials she recognised. 'Surely,' she said to the young man, 'this one is made of rock crystal. But what's this one? It looks like half of a giant's egg.'

'Half an ostrich egg, mistress,' her helper said. 'Polished. The lid is mother-of-pearl. And this one, see, is half a polished coconut with silver mounts. And this one is a nautilus shell. See how it spirals? The other one is beryl, and here is serpentine marble. That's quite heavy.'

'How do you know all this?' Aphra queried.

'Doctor Ben told me, mistress. He trusted me to treat them with care. Rare materials are antidotes against poison, you see. In his business he had to use every method known to guard against mistakes. He knew how accidents can happen, even when you know what you're doing.

So he collected precious things from all over the world.'

'Yes, so I see.' The impact of his explanation did not reveal its full meaning to her as she peered into the darkness of the cupboard. 'Are those drinking glasses?' she said. 'If so, we should be using them.'

The young man brought them out, one by one, catching the glint of light on the patterned surfaces, engraved, gold-tinted, intricate, astounding. Not even at the royal court had she seen glasses like these. But the unmistakable clamour of arrivals in the courtyard, the yelping of dogs and shouts of greeting put an end to her viewing of the tableware. 'Put them on the table,' she said, briskly. 'We'll use them all.'

'On the *table*, mistress? Not on the sideboard, as they're required?'

'No, they're too precious to keep on rinsing them out at each drink. We'll have them there, one for each person. That should give them something to talk about.'

'Well...yes, mistress, if you say so. I hope they'll be safe. There's a set of eight. Best knives and spoons, too?'

'Yes. Best pewter platters. Polish them up. I must be off.' Running along the passageway, she came out into the bright light of the courtyard already heaving with horses and humans where arms opened wide to hug and swing her off her feet with smiles and the tang of cool cheeks. Aphra was suddenly overjoyed to see them all.

From his rooms on the south side of the monastic buildings, Santo heard the commotion and, for a moment or two, debated whether to appear along with the guests or wait until the greetings were over. No, he thought. The latter would look too contrived. So the courtyard was still filled with colour from rich garments, dyed plumes and plum-coloured liveries when he entered quietly through the side gate from where he was able to see Aphra's family well before being noticed himself.

Appearing to fit in well with her description of them as a lively crowd and not at all pompous, Santo easily identified the one she called Uncle Paul, a well-made smiling man whose terracotta-velvet robe swung into sumptuous folds as he released his niece from a hug. As Santo had expected from one involved with the buying of fabrics for royalty, Paul D'Arvall wore the most fashionable clothes, fur-trimmed, silk-lined, leather-edged, gold-trimmed, as did his very elegant wife, the Italian daughter of Pietro Cappello. Clearly glad to see Aphra, the lady was slender and fair and, although no longer young, still beautiful. She held her daughter by the hand, a lovely child with her mother's fair colouring and a smile for Aphra of genuine pleasure. A delicate pale grey Italian greyhound sat like a toy in the crook of Flora's arm and Santo suspected that the dapple-grey pony had been chosen to match the dog, like Flora's pale grey overskirt. Not pompous, then, but conscious of a collective image. And not one of them in the black of mourning.

The tall young man standing to one side, smiling at the noisy welcome, was the first one of the group to catch sight of Santo. This, he thought, would be Edwin, who would find it most difficult to understand what he was doing here, once he knew of his relationship to Master Leon of Padua. Unhurriedly, Santo strolled forward, looking Edwin directly in the eye as merchants did with each other, refusing to hide behind a smile. Removing his black-velvet cap, he held it to one side as he bowed, then replaced it. 'Sir,' he said, 'I am Santo Datini. Do I have the pleasure of speaking to Master Edwin Betterton, brother of Mistress Aphra?'

Edwin's bow was immaculate. 'You do, sir. Are you...?'

'Staying here? For a short duration, to be of

what service I can to Mistress Betterton, that's
all. Today, I sent my men to collect some precious merchandise from Southampton that Dr
Spenney had ordered. They were likely to have
been forgotten about, otherwise. I stayed two
nights with your parents at Reedacre Manor
before offering my services here. Sir George
was kind enough to commend me to your sister.' From the corner of his eye, Santo saw how
conversation between the others had stopped to
listen to him, how they scrutinised his clothes
and demeanour, ready to pounce with their questions. He turned to them, bowing again. He had
taken care with his dress. They would find no
fault there.

'To Reedacre Manor from…where?' said Paul
D'Arvall.

'From Venice, sir. I am a merchant of that
city. My galleys come into Southampton at this
time of the year.'

From Aunt Venetia, there was a slight ripple
of interest at the thought of galleys and merchandise. And Venice. 'Your name again, sir?'
she said.

'Santo Datini, *signora*.'

'Then you will know of my family, the Cappellos,' she said, smiling.

'Just a minute,' said Paul D'Arvall, glancing

first at Aphra, who was biting her lip, and then at Santo. 'Just a minute. Datini? Isn't that…?'

Aphra moved forward with her head held high, not knowing how, at that moment, Santo's admiration for her courage was almost too great to be contained behind his gentlemanly expression. 'Yes, Uncle,' she said. 'It is. Signor Datini is the eldest son of that family and I have accepted his offer of assistance at my father's suggestion. Already he has sorted out several of the problems that Dr Ben left.' She glanced at her uncle's frown before addressing the whole group in a tone of gentle authority. 'So if I have no problem with the situation, no one else should have any, either. Now, shall we go inside and take some refreshment? The men will help your servants with the baggage. Come, Flora… Edwin. Shall we lead the way?'

Doubts and queries brushed aside like so many cobwebs, Aphra led them into the house and the sunny parlour where only a few days ago she had torn her father's commendations into strips and where she now played the perfect hostess with enquiries into their busy lives. She was particularly pleased to welcome Edwin, threading her arm through his, convincing him within minutes that she was well on the way to recovering from her misfortunes.

Naturally, the guests wanted to know the nature of the problems that Dr Ben's sudden demise had left her with, to which the mere mention of household accounts, apothecaries' materials and acquisitive neighbours were enough to send the conversation flying off in all directions. Soon they were all in agreement that it would have been almost impossible for a young woman like her to deal with such problems alone, and although they watched carefully for the slightest sign of attraction between Aphra and her handsome guest, they were unable to detect anything more than unaffected politeness on both sides.

Once the family had been shown to their rooms, Signor Datini and Aphra had time in which to congratulate themselves and each other for dealing with the situation so cleverly. She came from the light outside into the darkening passageway, almost bumping into him. 'Oh…you!' she said, taking a step back. 'Don't go. Supper will be served very soon, now.' She would like to have said how distinguished he looked in the deep green suit of rich brocade with gold-edged slashes showing a creamy-white satin beneath. Small gold studs caught the light down the front of his doublet where gold threads created a discreet pattern of entwined leaves, his square chin supported by a creamy frill of Venice lace. The epitome of a wealthy merchant, she thought, and a far cry from his younger brother whose prospects would have been more modest without marriage into a wealthy family. Did that have something to do with his father's insistence? she wondered. Was it all about comparative wealth?

The warm aroma of roasting meats wafted along the passageway. 'I hope it won't be too much of an ordeal for you,' Santo said, softly. 'You handled things expertly, mistress. Your aunt and uncle appear to have accepted my presence here, just as we hoped they would, but your brother had little to say. Will he see me as a problem, do you think?'

'He's very protective of me,' she whispered, looking towards the doorway. 'He and my cousin Etta warned me and I didn't heed them. He was very angry about it all, so it may be that he's venting some of his feelings on you. Don't mind him if he asks some searching questions, *signor*.'

'I shall do my best to satisfy him with the truth. I have nothing to hide,' he said.

Aphra was glad to have taken such pains over their first meal together, the table covered with white linen, finest napkins, pewter polished like silver, Ben's best ivory-handled knives and the sparkling glasses Aphra had discovered, now set upon the table instead of waiting on the sideboard, as was more usual. At once, even before the cushioned benches were occupied, the exclamations of wonder could hardly be suppressed, for they all knew that this had recently belonged to Ben and passed on intact to Aphra. Now they saw, however, that Ben's taste in expensive tableware showed a side of him kept hidden until Aphra's tenancy.

The food soon covered the table in a symmetry of colour and size, entirely of Aphra's devising, and while pies were shared, fish and wood pigeons portioned, the conversation was more in muted sounds of approval than of questions that needed lengthy answers. But as glasses were filled with wine, the sounds of wonder changed to whispers of amazement at the flashing colours rippling through the intricate convolutions of the glass where, on the stem of each one, three elaborate projections like lace wings widened to touch the underside of the bowl. Each bowl and foot was covered with engraved patterns of scrolling leaves, casting the reflections downwards on to the tinted knobs and coils below.

'Hold it with both hands,' Venetia warned her daughter. To Aphra, she smiled. 'I think I know where these were made, my dear. Pure Venetian, are they not?' Like Santo's, her voice still held the hint of Italian colour, the rolling 'r' and the full vowel sounds.

'I really don't know, Aunt. This is the first time I've used them.'

'Oh, but Murano glass is unmistakable, is it not, *signor*?'

Santo agreed, turning his magnificent glass round slowly to catch the lights on the many facets. 'This is indeed from Murano,' he said. 'It's known as a winged-stem glass and the decoration on each wing is called "threading". The engraving on the bowl and foot is done with a diamond.'

'By hand?' said Aphra.

'By hand, mistress. Only the most skilled craftsmen can work to this standard.'

'You seem to know a great deal about it, sir,' Edwin said, sharply.

'I should, Master Betterton. These were made in my father's workshop.' Suffering the concerted stares of five pairs of eyes, Santo waited impassively.

Aunt Venetia saw nothing strange in this. 'That's it!' she said. 'I thought the name was familiar to me. The Datini glass workshops on Murano. So that's your family, *signor*.'

'What's Murano?' said Flora.

'It's an island just a short boat ride from Venice, *signorina*,' Santo said. 'Your mama will have been there to see the glass-blowers. The craftsmen were moved out of Venice because of the danger from the furnaces, you see. So now there are several workshops there and all the workers live there, on the island.'

'And does your papa work there, making these?'

'Not personally. He owns it and his men make other things like mirrors and lenses for spectacles.' Obligingly, the conversation veered along Flora's need to know about the glass instead of how such rare and expensive vessels came to be owned by Dr Ben. But now there was a certain constraint between himself, Aphra and Edwin whom he believed were sure to be wondering if it was Leon who brought them for his tutor. A very costly gift, they would think, for a student to give.

The guests were not late to retire to their rooms that evening, though a light touch on Santo's sleeve was taken as a request to stay behind. 'When are we to expect the men to return from Southampton?' Aphra asked him, intending her businesslike question to be heard by those guests still on the stairs.

'With the wagon, some time after noon, I suppose,' he replied.

The door behind them closed on the flickering torches and, in the dim passageway, she turned to him, angrily. 'Did you *have* to say all that about the glasses? Could you not have used some discretion, *signor*? Was it absolutely necessary to claim them as coming from your father's workshop? They *must* have guessed who brought them here?'

'Does it matter who brought them?' he said, feeling the heat of her anger from where he stood. Her cheeks were flushed, her beauty breathtaking.

'It not only matters who brought them, but why. Did you know about them?'

'You mean, that they could have been a gift from Leon? No, how could I? Perhaps you believe Dr Ben *bought* them. It's possible, I suppose, but they're worth a small fortune. Some of the finest I've ever seen. Or perhaps they were given to him by a client, as thanks. Who knows?'

Something resonated in Aphra's mind when, earlier, she had seen the other vessels of rare materials. 'Do they have special properties, these rare glasses?'

'Well, I know that the soda ash comes from Syria.'

'Not *that* kind of property,' she said, irritably. 'I mean medicinal.'

He spoke slowly as he recalled something that Leon had once told him. 'Only that any liquid drunk from a rare material can have a curative effect, that's all. But glass is not a rare material, mistress.'

'Then perhaps my uncle wished to own them because, being very expensive, they might guard against disease, or poisons, even. The more expensive, the more effective.'

'That may well be, but I'd be interested to know how your uncle acquired them. Leon couldn't possibly have—' He broke off as the dim light caught the sudden flash of anger in her eyes and the toss of her head as she began to move away from him.

'*Enough!* I've heard enough of him, *signor.* I care not!'

'Mistress, I only—'

'No! *Enough!*' she cried. 'I do not wish to hear his name again. Can you not *understand*? I'm trying to…trying *not* to…' Infuriated by words that failed to express her meaning, she swung away again only to come back to him for another try, batting his hand away as he tried to take hers, to hold it, to make her stay. 'No… no! You don't understand a thing, do you?' She panted, forcing words out under pressure. 'How I'm trying…day by day…to dismiss him from my thoughts…to start again…and now you… *you*…forcing him back into the room on the first time I have guests, when I thought only to show them how I'm forgetting…how I can manage. Oh…*go!*' she wailed. 'Just go! Go home back to Italy. You ought never to have come here. I really don't need your kind of help, *signor*.'

'Of course,' Santo said. 'You're quite right. You don't need my help, *madonna*. I shall pack my bags and go tomorrow, if you will allow me to stay overnight. You may recall that Dante and Enrico are on your errand, bringing back the supplies you need. I should meet them on the road to Southampton. I'll send the wagon back here without its escort, shall I, and take a chance on it arriving intact? Is that what you want?'

That was not what she wanted. No. She wanted him here without his deceitful brother shadowing him, reminding her of broken promises and her broken dreams. She covered her face with both hands, unable to answer, too aware of his masculine presence near her in the dark passageway where the deep sea green of his doublet glinted dimly with gold. She sensed his warmth and knew that his question was but one more reason why he should stay and that the longer she remained silent, the more he would understand her dilemma.

As a successful merchant, he was not unused to the silence of assent, though he did not usually acknowledge it by taking anyone in his arms, as he did with Aphra. Gently, so as not to startle or anger her any more, he eased her slowly towards him and held her comfortably against his body, being careful not to dislodge her jewelled black-velvet hood while taking some delight in the soft touch of her silky hair over his hand. He would like to have done more than that, but this was not the time nor, in fact, might there ever be a time when she would allow more than this. 'Men can be so clumsy,' he whispered. 'Forgive me. You have every right to be angry. Shall we try again tomorrow, *madonna*?'

Sliding her hands away from her face, Aphra nodded, placing her palms upon his chest to ease herself away. 'I bid you goodnight, *signor*. Don't break your fast in the kitchen tomorrow. Join us in here, if you will.'

'Thank you. Sleep well. And if I may offer a small crumb of advice?'

She waited.

'Don't try to solve all your problems at once.

Answers sometimes arrive without our digging too deep for them.'

In the darkness, a dull flash of gems told him that she had nodded in agreement and, as she walked away towards the staircase, the air moved around his face and the rustle of skirts faded with the soft padding of her shoes on the stone flags.

Comfortably swathed in her loose night-robe, Aphra sat on the edge of her bed to sip the warm milk and honey while her maid Tilda moved silently about the room to prepare it for sleep. Questions with too few answers passed in an endless stream in her mind, always returning to those few moments in the dark, where she had allowed Signor Datini to take the liberty of holding her. What kind of message, she asked herself, was she sending? Had his younger brother kindled in her the need for a man's comforting arms so much that she must now accept it from him, too, no matter how inappropriate? Had she wanted to pretend, for just one moment, that it was Leon instead of his brother?

There had been a time, just after Leon's departure for Italy when, full of hope, she had indulged herself to the full with memories of their times together. She had thought longingly of his company and of how their relationship had developed so quickly during those months when he had stayed with her and her married cousin Etta.

Henrietta, half-sister to Queen Elizabeth, had asked Aphra to be her companion during those months last year when their time was divided between Etta's two homes, one in London's Cheapside, the other in rural Surrey. Studying for a time at the Apothecaries' Hall in London, Leon of Padua had been invited by Etta's husband to stay with them for convenience and it had been easy for them to meet, mornings and evenings, and to foster an easy companionship where each would tell the other of the day's events, as husbands and wives do.

In medicinal plants, they had found a common interest and Leon had brought a new meaning to her life that had been missing until then, with none of the bitterness and sarcasm she had shown to his brother. It had seemed like the most natural thing in the world to give him her heart while believing in his dreams and not once had it occurred to her that she was overdoing her generosity.

She had asked her parents if they liked him and, seeing her happiness, they had agreed that he was a considerate and caring young man, accepting that there would be no betrothal until

Leon had spoken to his parents. Younger sons were obliged to tread carefully if they wanted some financial support from a father, even though Leon's potential as a first-class apothecary had been verified by the eminent Dr Ben Spenney, who had Aphra's welfare very much at heart. What could possibly go wrong?

'We wanted nothing more than your happiness,' Etta had told her, holding her dear cousin while she sobbed. 'Perhaps we ought to have been more cautious, asked more questions. But I suppose we thought that if Ben thought highly of him, that was enough. Even my lord saw no guile in him and he's as cautious as anyone could be. Even now, I can scarce believe it, dearest. We all liked him. There *must* be a good reason behind it.'

Leon's betrayal, followed by Dr Ben's sudden death, had broken Aphra's heart, leaving her with two mysteries she was in no position to solve. Then the questions had begun. Had it been everyone's approval that had made her so sure of him? Loving too easily, Signor Datini had said. She had taken it the wrong way, but it was clear that that was what she had done, too. Fallen in love without a ripple on the surface of her composure, no doubts, all sweetness, comfort and a kind of security in his arms.

He had shown her only his good side and she had not had time to see any other. She had been excited and proud of his scholarship, his future. Now, such doting was a warning never to fall in love again. Never to allow sweet words, or the comfort of his brother's embrace, not to allow her heart to skip a beat, or her eyes to admire the width of his shoulders, his hands smoothing over a map, like skin, his voice in the dark telling her not to look too hard for answers, his insistence on staying at Sandrock, his command of difficult situations, his authority. She would do better not to dwell on such things, for there could be no future in it.

Setting down her empty beaker, she went to the window to look out at the dark garden and then across to the building on the opposite side where Signor Datini had been given rooms. A dim light shone from the lower window and a shadowy figure moved across it just before the light was extinguished. Aphra moved quickly back into the room, feeling an uncomfortable twinge of guilt at her curiosity.

She had been mistaken about the real reason for Uncle Paul's visit, having believed, cynically, that it was sure to be for the hunting. After the first smiles of greeting Uncle Paul had not mentioned any desire to hunt and, at supper, Aphra had noticed how thoughtful he appeared, lacking his usual light-heartedness. Obviously, the sudden loss of his brother had affected him deeply, especially since it had happened at his house with all the resulting enquiries about how, why and exactly when. Fortunately, Paul had been able to satisfy the authorities that his younger brother was an eminent pharmacist and had been aware of his heart condition. The fact that he had left a will appeared to confirm that he had regarded this seriously, although Aphra herself had never noticed any sign of it, nor had he spoken to her about his heart, only to his brother. Hoping that there might be an opportunity to talk to Uncle Paul in private while he was here, she climbed into bed from where she could watch the slow progress of the moon on its silent voyage, its light rippling unevenly through the small thick panes of glass. How easy it was, she thought, for familiar images to appear distorted, these days.

With the first light, the view through the windows was even more distorted by rivulets of rain that came with strong westerly winds to streak the glass and send clouds lumbering across the sky. After breakfast, when only three of them remained, the gentle questions put to Aphra by her aunt and uncle about what she intended to do here at Sandrock were easy enough for her to answer. 'Oh, there's plenty for me to do here,' she said. 'Ben's herb gardens have come back to life again now and I intend to carry on, growing them to supply the London doctors. Most of them would prefer not to buy from anyone else. He was always so reliable. They send their own couriers with lists, you know. And besides that, he was compiling a record of them and teaching his students how to paint plants as an aid to recognising them. Some of the old herbals are shockingly inaccurate. That's a part of his work I can continue. I think he'd approve.'

Paul D'Arvall nodded in agreement. 'He would. And with your knowledge of herbs and remedies, you could probably treat the locals, too, my dear. You'd be as good as any town physician.'

'As long as I didn't charge a fee. But there's still some tidying up to be done. Until now, I've not felt inclined to look too deeply into his cupboards and shelves, but I shall have to make a start soon. Do you know what Ben might have wanted seed pearls and costly gems for, Uncle Paul? Apparently, he's ordered some from the Southampton merchants. It's due to arrive some time today.'

Paul frowned. 'That doesn't sound like Ben,'

he said, softly. 'He always scoffed at the quacks who use that kind of thing in their preparations. I hear that some of them grind pearls into powder so they can say what exotic and expensive stuff they've added, but I don't think Ben...well, I really don't know, love. Perhaps he wished to try them as an experiment. He liked to experiment, didn't he?'

Aphra waited, thinking that there was something her uncle might be about to add. Starting his answer so positively and then tailing off into unsureness sounded rather odd. Aunt Venetia's lengthy glance at her husband also seemed to imply that there was more, until she reminded him of something that took Aphra's expectations on to a different level. 'What about Ben's things?' she said.

'Things?' said Aphra.

'Yes...of course!' Paul slapped the table with a sudden eagerness. 'Ben left his satchel and notes with us...well...naturally, I didn't bring them sooner, Aphie, because you were too upset. But now you should have them. Shall I bring them down here to you, or...?'

'No, thank you, Uncle. If you could take them to Ben's library where I work, I'd like to look through them in my own time. Did you...?'

'No, dear,' said Venetia, 'we didn't go through

his satchel. No point, really. And his notes mean nothing to us. You may find a use for them.'

'Thank you. Was there anything else? No letter? The ring he wore? That should be yours, Uncle Paul.'

'The one on his little finger? No, my dear, we left that in place. I don't know who or what it signified, but then, you see, we had no connection as boys. I was brought up with the D'Arvalls and Ben was brought up here in the priory by his uncle, Father Spenney. Which is why he was given that name. None of us knew we were related until after my sister was married. Then the story came out and we discovered that we were full brothers. But we had very little to do with each other. It was a sad story, not knowing his mother. Well, nor did I for that matter, but at least I had a stepmother to comfort me.'

'He thought highly of you, Uncle. I'm glad he was with you…when…'

'Yes, love. We'd had a merry evening together. We loved him. All of us.'

'You said, at the funeral, that he'd complained of pains in his heart.'

'Yes,' Venetia said. 'He thought we ought to know. Just in case.'

Swiping a hand around his jaw, Paul sighed and nodded. 'Even went as far as making a will.

I protested. Said it was too soon for that. But he would have it so. He gave it to me to keep. Just as well, in the circumstances.' Leaning forward over his arms on the table, he looked intently at Aphra. 'I'm glad he left Sandrock to you, love. It was the right thing to do.'

Aphra's smile was sad, rather than happy. 'I had wondered,' she began.

'What, dear?' Venetia whispered. 'You wondered if we minded? Not at all.'

'No,' said Paul. 'Not out here in Wiltshire. London is where I work and, anyway, we can always come over for the hunting, can't we?'

'Of course you can. You're always welcome, you know that. Are the boys away at school now? Is that why you didn't bring them?'

'They're tutored at home. We have an Oxford graduate who comes in every day. Walter is almost a young man now and Marius is catching him up. Flora sometimes joins them at their lessons...' he smiled indulgently '...and she's already better than her twin at Latin, although for the life of me I don't know why she'll ever need it.'

'That's what my father used to say about me,' said Aphra, 'but without it I'd never have been able to understand some of Ben's herbals.'

'And without it, husband dear,' said Venetia with a sideways look, 'Flora would not have learned Italian as easily as she has. Would she?'

As if on cue, the luscious sounds of her language reached them through the open door, one voice distinctly high and enquiring, the other replying in the deep fruity timbre that was Signor Datini's. At twelve years old, Flora appeared to be taking the chance to practise her skills on someone other than her mother and was just then telling her companion that Marius enjoyed mathematics which, to her, was a form of punishment. 'No,' she was saying, 'we are not at all alike, but I love him even so. And Walter, but he's so very grown up these days.' She dipped a pretty curtsy to the three adults at the table, drawing in the fine cord tied to her greyhound's collar, a tiny dainty creature, silken grey with folded satin ears. 'Sit,' she whispered. Placing herself at Aphra's side, she snuggled close as her cousin's arm went round her, leaning against her knee while her parents smiled and continued their conversation, regardless of her youth.

'Can you tell me,' Aphra said, 'anything more about Ben's last night with you?'

'About his death, dear?' Venetia said. 'What is it you wish to know?'

'Was it peaceful? He was alone, I understand.'

Santo had moved silently to the stool beside

Paul from where he could see Aphra's face. Her parents had already explained to him something of the bond between her and the favourite uncle and she, too, had earlier indicated her feelings for this remarkable man. Perhaps now he might learn more about the relationship.

'Unfortunately, my dear,' said Paul, 'he *was* alone. We had all gone up for the night. We heard nothing. But I went to his room in the morning when he didn't appear at breakfast and found him on the floor, still dressed. His bed had not been slept in, so I know he'd been there all night. He had fallen. Hit his head on the corner of the clothes chest. There was a pool of blood.'

'A lot?'

'A lot. There was a beaker on the table, half-empty. It looked as if he'd drunk from it and re-placed it.'

'Half emptied of what?'

'A strange-smelling liquid. I thought it was probably a sleeping draught he'd prescribed for himself and perhaps had made it too strong. Maybe his heart had given way, after all. That's how our father died. Heart failure. Simple as that. Very sudden. No pain, Aphie love.'

Aphra's response was a mere nod of the head, for by now she held one hand across her forehead to hide the tears swimming in her lovely eyes. 'Alone,' she croaked. 'So sad…so very sad.'

Turning in her cousin's arms, Flora placed a kiss upon her cheek. 'Don't cry,' she whispered. 'I'm sure he didn't suffer, Aphie.'

'That's just reminded me of something,' Paul said, suddenly delving into the leather pouch hanging from his belt. 'You asked me if he left anything. Well, amongst other things, there was this, pinned to the inside of his gown.' Pulling out a very creased scrap of yellowed parchment, he smoothed it out on the table and passed it across to Aphra. 'I don't know what it's about. He was to have given an important lecture at the Apothecaries' Hall, you know. I wonder if it may have had to do with that.'

The three words written on it in an old-fashioned script made more sense to Aphra than to her uncle. 'Meltizar. Jasper. Baltezar,' she read. 'Are they not the names of the three magi who travelled to Bethlehem to see the new Christ? Why would he need reminding of that, I wonder? What was the lecture to have been about? Did he say?'

'About sleeplessness and pain relief,' he said. He'd been researching that for some time, as well as heart problems. There was this, too. He may have worn it to ward off evil smells. I really don't know. It was hanging round his neck, so I removed it.' Dangling from Paul's hand was a small leather pouch on a thong. 'You take it, Aphie,' he said.

She weighed it briefly in her hand, then held it close to her bodice, leaving the observant Santo Datini in little doubt that her love for Dr Ben Spenney would not easily be replaced by that of anyone else. With those two still in her heart, what chance would another man have? he wondered.

Chapter Four

Santo Datini would have been insensitive indeed not to have been a little daunted by this touching show of affection by Mistress Betterton for Dr Ben, in whose former home she now lived and saw his imprint in everything it contained. Her uncle Paul, he mused, had brought the tragedy back to her in stark reality, even down to the manner of his death, when it had been Santo's hope that time itself would relieve her of the worst of these memories. Uncle Paul's visit had done him no favours, so far. He was not a man to give up easily, but for the life of him he could not see how to get what he had come for when he had no idea where to look in a place this size, nor could he see how to make any progress in Mistress Betterton's esteem against that kind of opposition. Fortunately, he would not be asked which of the two was more important to him.

As Aphra had warned him, her brother lost no time that morning in questioning him about his presence there, which apparently Edwin found more difficult to accept than his uncle. Hoping he might discover, with Aphra, what the small pouch contained that had hung around Dr Ben's neck, Santo followed her until he was intercepted by Edwin and asked if he could spare him a moment or two. He had little choice but to agree. Returning to the now-empty parlour, they stood by the window like two wary fencers, though Santo was too old a hand at the interrogation game to be unnerved by a young man of Edwin's years.

Edwin began. 'I wonder if you could remind me who it was who sent you here and in what capacity? I am concerned for her, you see.'

'I will remind you most willingly, Master Betterton,' Santo said, gravely. 'Your concern does you justice. I was sent here by my father to make contact with your sister, to make sure she has the comfort and support she needs after my brother's unfortunate misunderstanding with—'

'*Misunderstanding?* Is that what you call it?' Edwin blustered.

'If you would allow me to finish? Thank you.

I was about to say *with my father* about the nature of his contract. He, my brother, had mistakenly thought it could be terminated, if both parties agreed.'

'*What* contract? Your brother and my sister were not—'

'I am speaking of the lady to whom my brother was betrothed, sir.'

Edwin's eyes opened wide, unblinking, his words halted by the shock.

'I see you are surprised,' Santo said. 'So was your sister. She didn't know, either.'

'Then he had no business speaking to her. Did he?'

'He was, and still is, in love with her, Master Betterton. When you have known love of that sort, you will perhaps start to understand how it affects a man's judgement. But that is not to excuse him. We are an honourable family and my father refused to allow it. At the same time, he felt that matters could not be left like that when a young woman of good family had been deceived, so he requested me to make contact with your sister and to offer our sincere apologies for the damage Leon has done. Since I arrived, I have discovered that your uncle, Dr Ben, has been taken from you, but by now the news will have reached my brother, too. Your uncle's fame has spread all over Europe. A terrible loss.'

'So you came all the way from Venice to see...'

'I came on one of my galleys, as I told you yesterday. I do business in Southampton.'

'How convenient for you that we are not so very far from there, sir.'

'It would have made not the slightest difference if Wiltshire had been at the other end of your island, Master Betterton. I would still have come.'

Edwin's attempts at aggression being less than successful, he paused before finding a more courteous tone. 'And now, sir?'

'And now, as I explained, I am doing what I can to be helpful, with your parents' full knowledge and approval. There have been several small problems where I've been able to assist her. On a place of this size, a man's authority can make things happen faster.'

'And how long do you intend to stay?'

'Until your sister decides she no longer needs my help. Not a moment longer.'

Edwin looked away, resting his behind on the stone windowsill. 'She has suffered,' he said, quietly. 'I care for her.'

'I can see that,' Santo said, answering both statements.

'It was the manner of it as much as anything else. Just a brief letter. No explanation. Did he not know what damage he was doing?'

Santo saw the young man's fists clench and knew what was going through his mind at that moment. Nevertheless, he found it interesting that Edwin believed as much damage had been done by the terrible abruptness of Leon's rejection as by the termination of Aphra's dreams. She herself had said something very similar to him. *The suddenness*, she had said. Or had he misunderstood? As an outsider, how was he to know? Perhaps, he thought, it was time to ask some questions of the lady's protective brother. 'I understand,' he said, 'that Mistress Betterton and your uncle Ben were very fond of each other and that it was this affection that led him to leave Sandrock to her.'

The question appeared to raise Edwin's hackles yet again, for his hard stare at Santo was loaded with suspicion. 'They *were fond* of each other, sir,' he said, 'but if you think—'

'I don't think anything,' Santo said, deliberately cutting the retort in half, 'except that Dr Ben was particularly fortunate in having someone to hold dear the work he was doing here. He must have known she would wish to continue with some of it and treat it with respect.'

'Well, you're probably right there,' Edwin said, grudgingly. 'But it was not only that they shared the same interest in plant medicine when the rest of us didn't. They had a very...well... special relationship. None of us spoke of it. It was not discussed. We just accepted it. It was quite innocent, but special.'

'Yes, I see. So that is why your sister is as much distressed about his death as she is about my brother's deception.'

'Perhaps more so,' Edwin said.

'You think so?'

'Well, she and Ben had known each other far longer, hadn't they? And although there seems to be a reason why she and your brother could not marry, there's no valid explanation yet for Ben's death, is there? Not yet, anyway.'

'The authorities have accepted it as a heart problem. You have doubts?'

'Every death is a heart problem, isn't it? I simply find it difficult to understand why a man of his age who appeared to be in the best of health should fall down dead, quite suddenly, just before an important lecture.'

'You were at your uncle Paul's house when Dr Ben stayed overnight?'

'I lodge with my uncle and aunt, yes. I went up to bed before them, but he looked well enough at supper. They stayed up late to talk.'

'Was he concerned about the lecture he was to deliver?'

'Concerned? Not Ben. He could lecture the hind leg off a donkey.'

'A…donkey's…hind…leg? That's another one for my list.'

At last Edwin smiled.

Santo was quick to take advantage. 'You have three young cousins, I believe. Do you get on well with them?'

'Well enough. The boys are at their lessons while I'm at work, so we don't get much time together.'

'At school? St Paul's, is it, or Westminster?'

'They have a tutor. Marius has days when he gets overtired, so they take their lessons at home.'

'Indeed? So that's how Flora learns. She's very bright.'

Edwin shrugged off the idea. Flora was a girl and too young to be of interest. He pushed himself away from the sill, making it clear that that line of questioning was concluded. 'My uncle's death came at a bad time for Aphra,' he said, 'just after your brother's letter.'

'Would there have been a good time?'

'Not for her. She adored him.'

Santo had half-prepared himself to hear such an opinion from Aphra's brother, but even so, the bald statement came as yet another discouragement to any aspirations a man might have harboured about the lovely Aphra warming to him, one day. 'My brother thought highly of him, too,' he said. 'He'll be sorely missed.'

'Did he?' said Edwin. 'So he'll be shocked to hear the news, I take it. Just think, all this might have been his if he'd played his cards right.'

Frowning at the implication, Santo thought it was time to conclude the conversation. 'I shall never get used to the English turn of phrase,' he said. 'Leon was not playing a card game when he fell in love with your sister, Master Betterton. I hope you manage your love life better than he has, but you can take my word for it that he is suffering for his mishandling of affairs. I bid you good day.' There was no reason, he thought, why he should not have the last word on the subject. Leon had certainly taken a wrong turn in the direction of his love, but there was not the slightest doubt that it was Aphra he'd wanted. Nor could he possibly have known that Dr Ben's will would be executed in Aphra's favour, or that his life would come to such an abrupt end at the height of his career.

But as Santo left the parlour that morning, he could not help wondering what Master Edwin Betterton hoped to achieve by his unmistakably hostile attitude towards him. It was one thing to be protective of his sister, but surely there was nothing to be gained by discounting the help Santo had been to her, so far, or by pointing out her affection for Dr Ben, of which he was already aware. Could it be Edwin's clumsy way of warning him off, perhaps? Or was his concern as much for Sandrock Priory and its large estate as for his sister? Was that the meaning behind his coarse remark about Leon not playing his cards right? he wondered. If so, it was clear that the young man himself had never suffered the complexities of being desperately in love with the wrong person, as poor Leon was doing.

It had rained heavily during the night and continued after breakfast with a vengeance, thundering down on the rooftops and bouncing high before running into the gutters and overflowing the rainwater barrels, flooding the ditches and pouring across the cobbled courtyard like a river, gushing into the drains built by the monks with typical thoroughness. As the downpour ended with a rainbow and a brilliant burst of sunshine, the wagon from Southampton arrived. Squelching with every step, the four men and horses waded through the water, squinting through hair and forelocks that shone like rooks' wings. Men and boys from the stables rushed out to meet them, unhitching the unhappy horses while Aphra, Uncle Paul, Edwin and Santo came to welcome the men and to organise the comforts of dry clothing and food. The contents were well protected under layers of canvas, but Aphra's concern was that some of the dry goods might have become damp on the journey. So, with Edwin and two gardeners and the two women from the stillroom, Aphra attended to the unloading of the precious wares that had travelled from every part of the known world to reach Sandrock Priory.

Checking each sack, barrel and box on her damp list, she became so totally immersed in the task that when the burly miller strode into the courtyard, she was chasing after a box of cloves which were on their way to the storeroom instead of the stillroom. One of the lads thought she'd said clover. Master Miller's red face indicated that he was very unhappy. Paul D'Arvall had met him once before. 'Morning, Master Miller,' he said. 'Plenty of water power for you today, eh?'

The scowl deepened. 'That's the trouble,' the miller said. 'There I was, thinking my wheel would have all the power it needs, but no! Nowt but a blasted trickle.'

Santo joined Paul to listen, as did Fletcher, the steward. The miller took some time to come to the point, but the gist of his complaint was that, in the night, someone had dammed up the leat that directed water from the river into his millpond without which his mill wheel had lost power instead of gaining it after all the rain. Unless the level of the millpond was kept up, the wheel would grind to a halt. 'And that's no laughing matter,' Master Miller said, though no one was laughing.

'We'd better go and take a look,' Paul D'Arvall said. 'Come on, man. Show us what they did.'

'Pearce's men, I reckon,' said the miller, leading the way out of the courtyard. As they went across the field, he told them how Master Pearce had been to see him two days ago about sharing his job with one of Pearce's own men. 'And why would I want to do that,' he asked them, 'when I've been milling since I was a lad? I'll tell you why.' Which he did, in a roundabout way, sure that this was Pearce's revenge for his polite refusal to oblige. 'He gets one of his men in my mill and then he bumps me off,' he said, waving a fist in the direction of the village.

'But he couldn't replace you without Mistress Betterton's agreement, Master Miller,' said Santo. Master Miller was sure Pearce could get what he wanted, one way or the other. And so they investigated, then went on to visit Master Richard Pearce in his grand house at the far end of the village: the miller, the steward, the mill-owner's lawyer and her uncle, who was known to her Majesty the Queen and not averse to boasting of it. This was a formidable group of men against whom not even Master Pearce could hold his own when he knew himself to be the culprit, although his excuse was that it was all a regrettable mistake on the part of his men who had been told to clear the ditches, not to build dams. Very sad, he agreed. He would remedy it immediately.

Aphra's representatives, however, were not deceived by this compliance. Pearce was a nasty piece of work who, if he couldn't get his own way in one thing, would try another. The miller returned to his mill and the other three to the priory where the sight of Aphra's stony expression warned them that an explanation was overdue. The steward suddenly had an urgent task to fulfil, but neither Uncle Paul nor Santo could escape the impending enquiry, with too little time to prepare their justification for 'taking matters into their own hands'. And had it not occurred to either of them that she would like to have been consulted before they marched off to deal with a matter which was, after all, *her* business? She had been wearing a scarf tied over her hair which, when her scolding paused for effect, slipped off to loosen a mass of pale blonde hair. Angrily, she tugged the scarf away from her neck and hurled it to one side, indicating to both men that something had seriously upset her.

'Hold on a minute,' said Paul, following his niece into the parlour. 'What did you want us to do, leave it until you'd discussed it while Miller waits to grind his flour and Pearce plans his next little trick? Be reasonable, Aphie!'

She whirled round to face the two men. 'Pearce? What does he have to do with it?'

Paul told her, in detail, what had happened to the mill leat and the water. 'These things must be dealt with straight away,' he said, 'and you were—'

'I was out *there*!' she said. 'I should have been consulted. This estate…'

'Yes,' Paul said, 'we know it's yours, Aphra. But when you have men here willing to help, you might allow them to—'

'To take any action they think fit. Is that it? Without *me*?'

'Yes,' said Santo. 'Pearce had no choice but to back down in front of—'

'*What?* You went to *see* him?'

'Of course. And he was obliged to listen. He certainly would not have listened to you. You know how men like him try to ride rough-shod over women property-holders.'

'So he listened to *you*, did he? Don't tell me he apologised, too.' Her eyelids drooped in a show of disdain as she looked away, sure she had won the point.

'He did,' said Santo, 'profusely. And if nothing else, that should warn you that he won't let it rest there. He'll find another way to get at your mill. This is the third time, remember, if you count his visit to Miller the other day. He wants your mill, mistress. Your uncle and I assumed you'd appreciate our help in this. Most women would…'

It was the wrong thing to say. 'Well, I'm not *most* women, *signor*,' Aphra replied, 'and what I would appreciate in future is to be included in any negotiations about *my* property.'

'Aphie,' said Paul, using his most soothing voice, 'you are making too much of this. We've settled the problem. Isn't that enough?'

'No, Uncle. It's *not* enough!'

'Then what…?'

'Oh!' she cried, on the verge of tears. 'Just leave me alone!' And as if to make that happen, she pushed past them to the door, reaching it just as Santo opened it.

Closing it behind her, he returned the puzzled look in Paul's eyes, watching for some understanding to dawn behind them. 'I think, sir,' he said, 'that we might have done the wrong thing.'

'We did the right thing, Santo,' Paul said, straddling the bench beside the table, catching sight of his muddy boots as he did so. 'I don't know what's got into her. I've never seen her like this before. Perhaps it's time to take our leave.'

'Is it all getting too much for her, sir? Your brother's death. My brother's deceit. Pearce making a nuisance of himself again. Us disturbing her peace? Perhaps you're right. I've obviously outstayed my welcome. I shall go and pack my bags.'

'I think I've fulfilled my duty, too. We'll not be far behind you.'

'Your duty, sir? Surely it was more than that?'

'Of course, but I'm referring to bringing the things that were Ben's. I had to return his lecture notes and personal items. I wouldn't want to keep those.'

If Santo's expression changed very slightly and then returned to normal, Paul did not notice. 'So Mistress Betterton has them now?' Santo said, casually.

'She asked me to put them in her workroom. I expect she'll derive some comfort from them. But you're right. It was too soon to invade her grief.' He swung the muddy boot back over the bench, sighing. 'Ah well! Better go and break the news. The ladies will not be best pleased.' Servants bearing armfuls of table linen entered as they left, reminding them that the midday meal was almost ready to be served.

But Paul D'Arvall's mention of Dr Ben's notes was more important to Santo than food, for while Aphra was dining with her relatives, he might at last be given the chance to find what he had come for and then leave. In this instance, conscience would have to take a back seat for, if this looked remarkably like theft, he easily consoled himself with the fact that, since she had not yet read the notes, she would hardly notice if any were missing. If the notes returned by Paul D'Arvall did indeed include those lent to Dr Ben by Leon Datini, as Santo had every reason to believe, then as Leon's elder brother, he had every right to claim them. Such was his reasoning. The only problem would be in trying to recognise which of them belonged to Leon and which to his tutor, for Santo knew next to nothing about the study of insomnia and pain relief, on which his brother had been working since he came to England.

If only Leon's notes had been taken home with him, as all the other students' work had been, there would have been no need for this inconvenient trip which, even now, was on the verge of becoming futile. But Leon had explained to him that Dr Ben had asked to borrow his latest research for the prestigious lecture at the Apothecaries' Hall, a request that had honoured Leon above anything, especially as his tutor had promised to mention him by name. As to why a tutor should wish to borrow the research notes of one of his students, Santo had not asked, assuming that it was not so very unusual.

Quite naturally, Leon also had assumed that, after his decision not to return, it would be a relatively simple matter for Santo to visit Dr Ben at Sandrock Priory and ask for his notes. And so it would, except that everything was now jealously guarded by Dr Ben's beloved niece who would be as likely to part with her right hand as a single page of them. What better way would she ever find of revenging herself on her former lover, whose name she could not bear to hear spoken?

From his room, Santo watched the procession of kitchen servants carry large dishes of food across from the kitchen to the dining parlour. When all activity ceased, he went across to the old cellarium which was now Aphra's workroom, entering it via the staircase where he had first met Richard Pearce only a few days ago. He had known then that the rogue would not give up so easily. Feeling decidedly uncomfortable at having to snoop around Aphra's private workplace, he felt almost relieved to find that the room was not empty after all, but that Aphra was there, sitting very still on a stool near the table where Dr Ben's leather satchel, various opened packets, a pile of papers tied with string and the leather pouch made an untidy heap. Whether the papers were the controversial notes or not, Santo could not tell and now it seemed unlikely that he ever would. So far, however, they were untouched and, although Aphra gave no sign that she was aware of him, he knew that she was.

Framed by the long silky hair that spilled over her shoulders, her face was pale, her lips compressed into a line suggesting anger more than anything else, he thought. 'Mistress,' he said, quietly, 'I have come to take my leave of you. I don't believe I can be of any more service to you, in your present frame of mind. My men are packing and we shall be ready to leave…'

'Goodbye,' she whispered. 'I dare say I shall manage.'

There was a finality in the words that did not match her tone. He turned to go, to see if she would say more but, at the top of the stairway, he hesitated, reluctant to leave before he'd said what was on his mind. 'Yes,' he said, 'but I dare say you'll manage even better when you've stopped feeling sorry for yourself, mistress.'

As if she had been waiting for an excuse to continue the previous argument, she leapt to her feet, facing him with her fiercely blazing eyes. '*Sorry* for myself?' she said. 'What do *you* know about how I feel? What can you *possibly* know? When did *your* life turn upside-down? When did men walk into *your* house and take control of your management? That was the very last thing I wanted, *signor.*'

Santo walked back into the room and, reaching her, saw how she struggled to hold back tears that shimmered on her eyelids. 'No one has taken control of your management,' he said, sternly. 'Everything that has been done was with your permission except today when someone had to act fast to prevent further damage. Which you chose to see as interference. And if you'd been looking and thinking straight, you'd have seen that and thanked your uncle instead of bawling at him like a common fishwife. I imagine he'll be as glad to leave you to it as I am, Mistress Betterton. Now you can get on with it. Alone.' Without waiting for the next retort, he headed down the staircase faster than his ascent, almost crashing into Aphra's brother, Edwin.

Edwin dodged aside. 'I heard shouting,' he said. 'Have you been quarrelling with my sister? Why is she not eating with us? Is it true that you—'

'Ask her!' Santo replied, continuing on his way. 'She has all the answers.' All the same, he would rather it had not ended like this. He had been assured by both Leon and Sir George, Aphra's father, that she was the mildest-mannered, sweetest-tempered woman, yet so far he had seen little of that more reasonable aspect. Obviously, he thought, she was finding it very difficult to recover from the double tragedy. Had something happened to upset her that morning, while he and her uncle Paul were dealing with the mill problem? Did she not trust anyone to discuss it with her? Could he perhaps delay his departure long enough to find out? And somehow to get what he'd come for, too?

* * *

Only moments after waving off her uncle's cavalcade, Aphra was about to return to her workroom when she caught sight of Dante and Enrico preparing to load the Datini baggage on to their packhorse. Santo was not far behind. This was the chance she needed; she must not let it pass. Summoning all her courage, she called out to him. '*Signor?* Could you spare a moment, please?'

She noticed his hesitation, his glance up at the threatening sky and the droop of his shoulders as he dropped the bags he was carrying. His reply was no more than polite. 'Certainly, mistress. Where?'

'My workroom. I shall not delay you long.'

Giving instructions to the men, Santo followed her through the courtyard gate and round the west door of the church to where her workroom took over the whole floor above the cellarium, which was being used as a dry store for the goods that had come on the wagons that morning. It also held foods for the kitchen, as well as sacks of spices, salt, tubs of verjuice and dried fruits, the massive space smelling of wheat and oats, pepper and salt bacon. Upstairs, the light from large windows flooded the room where the scent of herbs and paper, chemicals and incense wafted on the air. When Aphra walked over to the bench where her uncle's possessions were in the process of being examined, the reason for this became clearer.

Indicating the empty leather pouch, she glanced briefly at Santo as if she was aware that he would rather have been elsewhere. His last words to her had been cutting, to say the least, showing her the more ruthless side of his character which, she thought, he probably used on disagreeable merchants. 'I found these paper packages in that,' she said, 'hanging round his neck, Uncle Paul said. Do you recognise the contents, *signor*?'

Santo bent to look more closely at an opened paper that had been folded to enclose a heap of glittering yellow powder. 'Gold?' he said.

'Yes, powdered gold. And that one?'

The next paper enclosed a pile of small brownish lumps. He poked at it with one finger, then sniffed. 'Frankincense, quite good quality,' he said. 'And this one, I assume, is myrrh. It's a gum resin, you know. From Arabia. Expensive. Used in perfume. Is that what you wished to know, mistress?'

'No, *signor*, I knew that already. What I would like to know is why he would have needed to carry it in a pouch around his neck. And why would these three names have been pinned to the inside of his gown?' She slid the scrap of parchment towards him, the one given her that morning at breakfast. 'The names of the three magi. What's it all about? Do you have any suggestions?'

Santo's eyesight was good. Tilting it against the light, he peered closely at it, then lay it down again, tapping it for emphasis as he told her, 'It's written using blood for ink,' he said. 'This is dried blood.'

Aphra's gasp made him look up. 'Blood?' she whispered. 'Are you sure?'

'I've seen enough blood to be quite sure. Was Dr Ben particularly religious? I mean, fanatically so?'

'It would have been difficult for him not to be religious, *signor*. He lived here with the monks for half of his forty years. His uncle was the prior.'

'So, perhaps that explains it,' he said, unhelpfully.

'Not to me,' she said. 'Not if it's viewed in the context of all the other stuff that came on the wagon this morning.'

'Ah!' he said.

'Ah what?'

'So that's what upset you. The stuff from

Southampton. Not the fact that your uncle and I managed to deal with a problem without you.'

'Oh! For pity's sake!' Aphra said. 'Can we not put all that aside for a while and talk about *this*? This is far more important to me than what you two decided to do about the mill. If it's an apology you want, then you have it! So now can we move on, do you think, or must I do penance, as well?'

'And that's an apology, is it? Try again.'

As stand-offs went, it did not last very long, for Aphra knew that he would merely turn to go and that would be the last she would see of him. Ever. So for as long as she dared, she kept her eyes on his, watching for the smallest signal that her time was up. But even as she whispered, 'I'm sorry...forgive my outburst. I am not quite myself', he was already walking towards the stairway and the cry she had intended to keep only inside her heart now insisted on being heard. 'No...no, *signor*! Don't go! Please...please?'

He stopped and turned, waiting. 'Why?' he said.

'Because...because I need you here...to help me...please don't go. There are things here I don't understand and you appear to know about...such things...and I don't think I can manage alone. I know I said I could, but...but...' Her voice quavered on a choking sob and her hand trembled as she held it out to him, feeling the clasp of his fingers on hers, wanting to pull him towards her, to lay her head against the wide expanse of his chest, to feel the comfort of his arms. 'Will you stay a while longer?' she whispered, looking down at their hands. 'Tell your men to unpack?'

His hand squeezed hers, then let it go. 'There's nothing here we cannot sort out between us,' he said, more kindly. 'I'm sure there'll be a perfectly reasonable answer somewhere. I'll go down and tell the men to stable the horses.'

Aphra thought he might do what he had done before and hold her in his arms, but he did not. Shamed by her own uncharacteristic behaviour, she resolved not to fly off the handle as she had recently been doing, for that would drive him away faster than anything else. She wondered, nevertheless, as she waited for him to return, how it might have been if Santo had been in his brother's place and he her lover instead of Leon, and how she might, or might not, have recovered from the kind of deception she had experienced. Again, had she ever felt quite this way at Leon's nearness? And would she have pleaded with Leon to stay, after knowing him for less than a week?

Immediately, she banned the thoughts as ridiculous. She was done with that kind of thing. Men were unreliable and false, and what reason did she have to believe that the elder Datini would be any different from his brother? Besides, as she had just told him, the mystery of Ben's death was far more important to her than any problems with the mill, for since she had discovered what he had purchased in his last order from the foreign galleys in Southampton, she realised that it would be impossible to try to explain it by herself. Even in those last few moments, Santo had shown that his experience of life was infinitely greater than hers and more useful in explaining the workings of a man's mind without the emotions with which, at present, she was clouding them.

'Now,' said Santo as he reached the top of the stairway, 'shall we begin again? What is it you've found that's upset you so? I thought you knew what he'd ordered when you saw his list. Was there something else?' Lifting his velvet cap, he ran his fingers through his hair, placing the cap on the bench.

His fingers, Aphra noticed, left ridges in the thick brown mass where his cap had made an indent all round. 'I didn't actually see the list,' she said, redirecting her attention from his hair. 'It was you who told me some of the items, but

I didn't know about all the other things, which I can hardly believe would help to relieve pain and sleeplessness. If that is what in fact he and your brother were studying.'

'But surely those were not the only problems he made cures for, were they? Didn't he have cures for stomach upsets and headaches, as other apothecaries do?'

'Plant remedies, yes, but not silver nitrate and mercury and bismuth,' she said, reading from the list, 'and copper, zinc oxide and tin. Whatever would he have wanted those for?'

'We would have to consult another apothecary to find that out,' Santo said, taking the list from her. 'Saffron and rhubarb, now those are plants, are they not, but very costly. Gum tragacanth, three kinds of sandalwood, senna and musk... good heavens...that's expensive, too, and wood of aloes and ambergris. That comes from whales, you know. Difficult to get hold of.'

'Wales?'

He made a swimming movement with his hand. 'Whales. Sperm whales.'

'Oh, yes. But there's a long list of precious stones there, too...look...there.'

'Amethyst, topaz, ruby, sapphire, agate and onyx, ebony...now that's a wood. Very black and hard. Comes from the other side of the world. But what use could that be in a medicine, I wonder?'

'It seems to me,' Aphra said, 'that he's ordered things more for their rarity value than for mixing into remedies to be swallowed or smeared. No one could possibly eat precious stones, or wood. Could they?'

'Nor musk and ambergris, either. They're used in perfumes, like the myrrh and frankincense. So what is the gold for, or the tin and copper?'

'The three magi, with their gifts, is obviously of a religious importance,' said Aphra, 'but perhaps personal, too, otherwise he'd not have worn them all close to his body, would he? And written in blood, too. Surely it would not have been his own?'

'But magi, in threes or not, were supposed to possess secret information, the gift of second sight, that kind of thing. Magic, in other words. Necromancy.'

'You say *were*, *signor*, but he would still have to have believed it, wouldn't he, to wear it round his neck? But wait, something has just occurred to me.'

'Tell me?'

'Have you ever heard of the Elixir of Life?'

'Of course. Who hasn't? But you're surely not thinking that a man with your Dr Ben's reputation would chase after that kind of nonsense, are you?'

'You may call it nonsense,' she replied, 'but he told me on more than one occasion that today's apothecaries are wrong to doubt the accuracy of ancient authorities, as they do.' *My* Dr Ben? she thought. Well, let him think what he likes. 'Like Galen, and others. He believed that theory and practice should go together, not kept in separate compartments. And that's why I think he may have been exploring the old beliefs, like the Philosopher's Stone, for instance, that transmutes base metals into gold, or the Elixir of Life that hounds out devils and keeps men young. Perhaps he was simply putting them to the test. Experimenting, like Uncle Paul suggested.'

'Well, you may have something, but I believe we should keep an open mind about these theories until we've taken a good look at whatever else he has here. I know,' he said, passing the list back to her, 'that you are not inclined to disturb his things, but if you really want to know more about his unexpected death, then you must know more than you do about his life. It's not as if we'd leave things in a mess. Any search would be done with respect, methodically and tidily.'

'Yes,' she whispered. 'And you'll be here to help me?' He had been talking about 'we', but she had to make sure that he intended to stay, for she was convinced now that not only his help was needed, but also his company. Even these last few moments with him had shown how important it was for her to discuss ideas together, even if his were no nearer the mark than hers. Somehow, she felt safer with him than without him and, though she had experienced a similar feeling with his brother, this was quite different, laced with a kind of emotional excitement that she could not quite define, except to say that it was most unsettling.

'If that's what you wish, mistress. But if your memories of Dr Ben are sacred to you in some way, then I would not want to interfere with that. I understand from both you and your brother that Dr Ben held a special place in your heart.'

It was on the tip of her tongue to say that, yes, he did have a special place in her heart, but not quite the one he imagined. Like a beloved friend, but never like a lover. It had been an easy relationship, but Ben had not thudded his way into her heart the way Santo himself had, troubling her with indiscreet thoughts that conflicted guiltily with her memories of his deceitful brother and her declarations of heartbreak. If the truth be told, her thoughts of Leon were becoming more diluted every day since Santo's appearance and even then only in respect of the work he did with Dr Ben. It would not do, of course, to let Santo know this, for the picture she presented of being a wronged woman gave her valid reasons for accepting his help in trying to remedy the situation, somewhat. Nor would it do to play down the part Dr Ben had had in her life. Let him think her heart was not her own, if that's what Edwin had indicated. It suited her well enough.

It did not, however, occur to Aphra that Santo had his own thoughts, based on experience, about where exactly women's hearts lay and that Aphra's had not been quite as badly broken by his brother as she had made out. Damaged, perhaps, but not beyond repair.

'Yes, *signor*,' Aphra said, 'we were close, but I cannot believe my uncle would have left Sandrock to me if he'd believed I would make a poor curator of his works.' She laid a hand upon the pile of notebooks, still tied up. More unspoken words lay between them concerning the trust Dr Ben had had in Leon and the bitter disappointment he must have felt at what had happened. Had he intended that Sandrock Priory should be the future home of Aphra and her brilliant husband? 'I think we might go down to the stillroom,' she said, shaking out the folds of her green linen gown. 'I sent some of the supplies there this morning and now I'm beginning to wonder what he had intended to do with them. Perhaps the two stillroom maids will know.'

'You don't wish to examine the notebooks first, mistress?'

Aphra glanced at the pile, not detecting the note of hope in Santo's voice. 'I think,' she said, 'we should delay that task until we've taken a look at what else he's been using, then we might get a clue as to what he's been using them for.' Taking up the long cord that hung from the girdle at her waist, she selected a silver key from the bunch and, stooping to a cupboard beneath the bench, unlocked it and placed the pile of notes on a shelf inside. 'There,' she said, locking the door. 'They'll be safe in there until we need them.'

'Would they not be safe left on the table? Does anyone come in here except you?'

'There is no lock to this room. Even Master Pearce walked in unannounced, didn't he? Perhaps I ought to speak to the locksmith about having some locks put in. With these precious things here, I suppose it makes sense to be more careful.'

'Indeed, mistress,' Santo said. 'One cannot be too careful now.'

Chapter Five

The sun had moved over to the other side of the priory by the time they reached the large building that projected well into the herb garden and on into the leafy orchard where beehives stood like upturned baskets. This was where essences were distilled and potions made to Dr Ben's recipes, where bunches of drying herbs hung from racks, where shelves were covered by dozens of labelled jars and sealed pots, and where two middle-aged ladies continued to work as if Dr Ben were still alive to direct them. On this particular afternoon, the door was wide open to allow a cloud of scented steam to escape, its source a large glass retort gently simmering with a pale pink mush.

'First batch of rose water,' said one of the

maids, smiling at Aphra and trying to bob a curtsy as she pounded into a stone mortar with an arm-sized pestle. Her own arms were bared to the elbow and thick with muscle. 'This is last year's dried mistletoe.'

Aphra smiled back. 'And this,' she said, indicating Santo, 'is Signor Datini. I wanted to show him what came on the wagons. Has it been put away yet?'

'Not all of it, mistress,' the maid said, leaving the pounding to give her hands a wipe on her apron. 'It's over here until we can deal with it, though I cannot think what we're supposed to do with some of it. All these flasks of theriac, for instance.' She nodded towards a stack of small barrels. 'Must have cost a fair bit. Takes twelve years to make and a lot more to mature. This is the finest. From Genoa.'

'A kind of cure-all, isn't it?' said Santo.

The other maid joined in. 'You could say that, sir, but it's beyond the reach of most people's pockets. Dr Ben has it mixed with wine, or ale, or rose water, to be taken as a preventative. Took it himself, he did.'

'To prevent what?'

The two maids smiled, demurely. 'Now that, sir, he didn't share with us except to say it was good stuff. He was never one to recommend anything unless he'd first tried it on himself, you see. He always told his students that.'

'Really?' said Aphra. 'Would that not have been rather dangerous?'

'It would if you didn't know what you were doing, mistress,' said one. 'But Dr Ben did. We made this one for him just before he went off to London.' Reaching up to a shelf, she brought down a stone jar, tightly stoppered with a piece of waxed linen bound with string. 'This is arnica mixed with calendula officinalis. That's marigold to you and me. He was trying it out on himself.'

'May I take a sniff, please?' Something nudged Aphra's memory.

There was a beaker on the table, half-empty. A strange-smelling liquid. Probably a sleeping draught he'd prescribed for himself.' Uncle Paul's words at breakfast.

'Certainly, mistress. It's an odd smell, but no worse than some we prepare.'

Removing the seal, she gave the contents a little shake, then passed it to Aphra who sniffed, frowned, then passed it to Santo. 'That's certainly arnica,' she said.

'Mmm…' he said. 'I don't think I'd care to drink it, though. Did Dr Ben tell you what it was meant to prevent? Pain, for instance?'

'No, sir. He would just give us the recipe and we'd tell him how it behaved in the making-up. Whether it separated or went off too fast. That kind of thing.'

'So you wouldn't have any idea what Dr Ben was researching in particular?'

'He had quite a few students here, sir, studying different ailments for their degrees. We went along with anything they needed. We never enquired what they were for and some were good for a range of ailments. Like feverwort. That's been used for centuries for just about anything. And like the chamomile, mistress, that you drink, but you also wash your hair with it.'

Aphra had tied her hair up in her scarf, as the maids did. 'What do you do with the ambergris?' she asked, catching sight of the label on a dark glass jar.

'We make it into pills,' said the elder of the two maids. 'Mixed with wood of aloes, musk, gum tragacanth and rose water. Dr Ben usually carried those about with him, but he'd used up his supply before we could make more. Very special, they are. Too expensive for ordinary folk,' she said, replacing the jar, 'like many other things here.'

They moved on, asking about the other ingredients and finding that the two experienced maids were very well informed about the making of pills and poultices, powders, tinctures, lozenges, ointments and salves, electuaries and potions of every kind for drinking, anointing and inhaling. Many of the plant ingredients were grown at Sandrock, some of them quite rare, studied by the students, their properties recorded: roots, stems, leaves and flowers, seeds, bark and berries. But no matter how many questions they asked, none of the answers seemed to indicate that Dr Ben himself had been making a particular study of insomnia, pain relief or conditions of the heart. And although there were preparations here that dealt with the heart along with every other organ and ailment, the two maids could offer no particular evidence to suggest which way his interest lay, other than in giving his students a comprehensive grounding in herbal remedies. Which, in Aphra's mind at least, was very much at odds with the things she had found earlier in his belongings.

As they walked away Santo's attempts to rationalise their findings, if one could call them that, were not appreciated. 'It doesn't prove anything,' he said, 'except perhaps that he kept his research to himself. Perhaps those two have been preparing ingredients and concoctions that were precisely for pain relief without realising it. Why would he have told them how his recipes were to be used? It was my brother who needed to know about that, under his tutor's guidance, of course.'

'Well, I am not entirely ignorant on the subject of herbal remedies,' Aphra said, blowing a tiny spider off her hand. 'All women are taught the basics, but that doesn't explain why I saw nothing there to convince me that my uncle was exploring new ground in that particular subject and I'm sure that those two would have known if he'd had that in mind. After all, it's probably one of the commonest ailments, isn't it? Sleeplessness. Pain. His audience of apothecaries in London would certainly have been expecting to hear some new information, if there was any. So where is it?'

'In his notes, I expect. Well, some of it, anyway,' he said.

Aphra's thoughts were racing backwards and forwards, searching for an answer. 'But when I asked them what Dr Ben might have used the precious stones for, they looked at me blankly and shook their heads. They didn't know he'd ever ordered any. The elder one said it sounded to her like the kind of nonsense that Dr John Dee dabbled in and that Dr Ben had always been a bit sceptical about charms and such.'

'Did he know Dr Dee, then?'

'Oh, yes. We met him at court several times and he stayed with my cousin Etta and her husband at both their houses while I was there. He's a dear man.'

'But according to the stillroom maids, he dabbles in nonsense. Do you think he might have persuaded Dr Ben to try out some of those expensive items for his research? Even though he was wary of charms?'

'The Elixir of Life,' Aphra said, under her breath.

Santo heard. 'What? Oh, surely not! Your uncle was an apothecary, not a magician, Aphra.'

They had reached the door that led to her room where, stung by his dismissive tone, she faced him, crossly. 'Then *you* suggest an alternative,' she said. 'If Dr Dee believed in it, why not Ben, too? I've told you, he didn't close his mind entirely to other ancient theories. He was willing to give them some credit, even if he was wary.'

'But...the *Elixir of Life*?' he said, frowning. 'Hounds out devils? Keeps men young? That's a very strange area for an apothecary to venture into. It's a long way from researching the properties of plants and illustrating new herbals, isn't it?'

Aphra looked away, unwilling to see the doubts clearly written on his face. A lock of his hair, still uncovered, had slipped over his forehead before he raked it back with his fingers and, as the light began to fade, so too did their arguments. 'I don't know,' she said. 'It's time for supper. I'll meet you in the parlour. And perhaps you might ask Dante and Enrico to join us. Father Vickery and Master Fletcher will be eating with me now, on Saturday nights.'

'Thank you,' he said, turning away, wondering whether her invitation to his two deserving men was an attempt to be more hospitable or simply a measure designed to eat up the food that would have been prepared for the departed guests. On the other hand, he thought, more charitably, could this signal an acceptance of his presence at Sandrock after that heartfelt plea for him to stay and help? Not even he could have been unmoved by that, knowing how volatile her emotions were, even to the extent of allowing her guests to leave without too much regret and presumably without the kind of apology she'd offered him. And now, Leon's notes were revealed at last, albeit under lock and key. Somehow, he would have to find a way around that problem.

After the heavy rain of the previous night, the blackness beyond Aphra's workroom window was clear and still, reflecting the wavering light from two candles in the wobbly glass, like splinters reforming with each movement of her head. Sleep had evaded her after an eventful day in which her passions had run too high for comfort, a day she would rather forget, but could not, for she had done something she had been determined never to do. She had pleaded with him to stay.

If the reasons had been merely the ones she had given, needing his help, that would have been understandable. But there was more to it than that and now she could fool herself no longer about those persistent womanly thoughts that plagued her night and day, for her capricious heart had veered, refusing all her attempts to return it to the place where broken hearts suffer. She was not relieved by this recovery, having always believed that she was the kind of woman who would be constant unto death, so to feel this way about the brother of the man who had cheated her of happiness was beyond all reason.

The problem now would be how to conceal this sudden change of heart from him. For one thing, she knew herself to be relatively new to this kind of happening, unlike her tempestuous cousin Etta whose experience of men's ways was rather more sophisticated than hers. And for another, she had few doubts that the worldly and good-looking Signor Datini would have had *affaires* by the score, resulting in some serious understanding of any signs of interest, intended or not. Had he detected any from her, so far? Probably not, she thought, after her behaviour today when he had been quite prepared to leave, more exasperated than physically attracted.

Catching sight of his cap on the bench, she picked it up gingerly, as if he might be watching, running the tips of her fingers around the velvet rim, recalling the indentation on the thick waves of his hair. In a sudden urge to connect with him, she placed the cap on her head. The cap fell down over her eyes so she removed it and placed it on her lap. On the bench in front of her, Ben's leather satchel lay half-opened with something protruding from the corner. A small knife fell out with a clatter as she tipped it up, then several small balls of a greenish-brown substance rolled after it, each one no larger than a pigeon's egg. She picked up the knife to examine the woody handle, sure from her own observations that this was the unusual mistletoe wood, close-grained and pale. Then, turning her attention to the balls, she squeezed one until it crumbled, telling her immediately by its greenish grains that this also was mistletoe, pounded and mixed with something sticky, probably honey.

Wasn't that what the stillroom maid had been preparing that same afternoon? Mistletoe? The magical plant that became more potent if it grew on an oak tree? And on the edge of the orchard there were two such oaks. Had Ben been taking it? If so, for what reason? Even she knew of its dangers if the dosage was too great. Concerned and puzzled, and rather afraid of what she might find next, she took the key that she had brought with her and unlocked the cupboard containing the notes. The candle flames bent as the pile slapped the surface of the bench.

The yellowing pages of handwritten Latin were to be expected, but what she had not thought to see was that nowhere did Dr Ben's unmistakable small and precise style appear, but instead the larger and more hurried hand of Leon Datini, whose letter to her had been scrutinised countless times for extra meaning. Page after page in both books revealed that his studies were meticulous and comprehensive, set out under headings dealing with the use of herbal remedies for sedation, the preparation of bark and roots for sleep-inducing infusions, methods of distilling and blending for pleasanter-tasting medicines, the importance of knowing the moon's phases when planting, harvesting and administering, and on to the end of the book, packed with detailed information. Torn bits of parchment had been used as bookmarks, each of them marking a particular point of interest. And this, she reminded herself, was what Ben had intended to use for his lecture to the apothecaries. Leon's notes. His own most talented student. Not one word of Ben's own except indirectly through his teaching. But why? Why had he accepted their invitation to lecture on a subject for which he was *supposed* to be an authority and then borrowed Leon's material?

The answer came to her like a whisper with overtones of an apology. Because it was Leon's research that was up to date, not his own. And why was that? Perhaps because he had been more occupied, these days, with some magic, life-prolonging procedures that would not have interested his fellow apothecaries in London, but which he had felt compelled to pursue.

Still doubting that conclusion and hoping to find a more acceptable one, she lined her findings up on the bench, all the things her uncle Paul had brought from London. The parchment with the three names written in blood. Packets of expensive materials, like those carried by the magi. A mistletoe-handled knife and balls. Remedy or preventative? Which? And the notes Leon Datini had expected to reclaim on his return to

Sandrock, except that now he would not be returning. Slowly, a window opened in her mind, letting out the truth to dance before her, mocking her innocence and her stupidity. Important research. Good enough for his tutor to use. And Leon would want it back, so he sent his brother to claim it.

Anger, humiliation and deep offence held her rigid, unable to think or to feel anything other than the desire she had only recently admitted, reluctantly, to be followed by the recognition of the shamelessness of the elder brother whose pretence of help was now exposed. Why had she not seen it before? Because he had asked her to trust him. And she had. Like a fool, she had.

The candles had burned well down as thoughts whirled madly around everything he had said and done, his strategies to make himself indispensable, his pretence at leaving, then the easy acceptance of her persuasion to stay. How he must have laughed while making up the next excuse not to return home. Well then, she must beat him at his own game. Destroy the notes, perhaps? That would be sweet revenge indeed. Could she do it?

Before she could imagine the consequences, so much against her nature, her dark reverie was disturbed by the sound from below of a door latch clicking, then by the tread of feet on the stairway. Yes, it would be him. Having seen his brother's notes at last, he would be devising a way to take them, then to leave as unobtrusively as possible. Why not simply let him have them and go, and never see him again? That would be best. No revenge. No Santo Datini.

Every fibre in her body wanted to scream, *Go! Stay away from me! No! Stay!*

He stepped within the small pool of light, still wearing the suit of deep green he'd worn at supper. Evidently he had waited, dressed, for this hour. 'I saw the light,' he said. 'I wondered...'

'What?' Aphra said without looking at him directly. 'What did you wonder? Whether you could get your hands on your brother's notes and then leave? Is that what you came for in the middle of the night, *signor*?'

There was no denial, only, 'You've read them, then?'

'I've looked through them. They're good, too. No wonder my uncle wished to use them for his lecture. And no wonder you were sent to retrieve them. What a pity you could not have been honest about it.'

Promptly, he swept a stool forward and sat upon it so that his head was on her level, where now she could read his face with hardly a movement except from her narrowed eyes. 'Nothing I have said to you has been dishonest, mistress,' he said.

'Yes, it has!' she retorted, goaded by his evasions. 'It was dishonest of you to pretend that your father sent you for any compassionate reasons, when what you *ought* to have said is that your brother sent you to obtain his notes. *That was* dishonest. You cannot deny it.'

'And would you have obliged me by parting with them?'

'No. But at least I would not have been duped into thinking you or your family care a fig about me after your brother's devious behaviour. In spite of your denial, *signor*, you *are* all tarred with the same brush. All you care about is getting what your father paid for in the shape of *this*!' Angrily, she slapped a hand on the notebooks. 'So that your brother will make for himself a respectable living on what he learned here. You asked me...*persuaded* me to trust you. And like a fool, I did.'

'This is not true,' he said. 'Leon's behaviour concerned us all, mistress. My father was deeply distressed to hear what had happened while his younger son was here studying. That was not meant to happen at all, which is why he sent me to offer any help you might need to ease your distress. At the same time, Leon did not see why he should be further punished by losing the work of the past three years. That would ruin his career, as well. Is that what you want?'

'Do I...?' Incensed by this male view of the matter, Aphra leapt off her stool, tipping his cap off her knees on to the floor. 'Do I *want* that?' she cried, standing closer to him than she'd intended. 'Do I care about his damned career? Did he show due care to my reputation, when all is said and done? My first thought when I realised what this was all about, *signor*, was to destroy the notes. Does that answer your question?'

'But you will not,' Santo said. Picking up his cap, he held it between them. 'Not until you've told me what *this* is about.'

'What...? Nothing!' she said. 'I don't know. What about it?'

'It was on your lap when I came in.'

'It was in my way, that's all.'

'Really?' Carefully, he picked a long silver-blonde hair from the inside and held it up to her. 'Then how did this get there, oh, Mistress of the Broken Heart? Is your heart cheating on you, these days?' As he spoke, he slipped his other arm quickly around her waist, pulling her in close to his velvet doublet, a more purposeful embrace than that gentle hug after their angry words in the dark passageway.

But although Aphra's dreams had taunted her with disturbing images of this kind in the last few days, they had not come to her in the middle of an acrimonious argument about the exact state of her heart and the damage it had suffered, and close physical contact was at that moment an affront to her dignity. 'No!' she growled, struggling against him. 'Let go! Why in heaven's name do you think this must be…the answer… to everything? Let me go, I tell you.'

With a mighty shove she broke free of his arms, propelling herself backwards so fast that she fell over the stool she'd been sitting on. Both she and the stool fell with a crash to the floor before he could prevent it. 'Oh, let me *be*!' she cried, batting his hands away. 'I can manage!'

Taking not the slightest notice of her request, he bent to her with a hand under each armpit and lifted her to her feet as if she weighed nothing, keeping hold of her when she would have turned away, his fingers pressing through the soft velvet of her night over-gown. Lifted to him, restrained as she had never been before, she attempted to hit his face but, with the sudden rush of air and the wobble of the bench as she had fallen, the candle flames slowly guttered and died within their pools of wax just as his lips found hers. Her hand, ready to strike, was caught in black mid-air and held away while her body curved in to him, softening as his mouth beguiled her senses, drawing her cry of complaint away before it could form.

Darkness engulfed her, leaving her with nothing to cling to except his wide back and the purposeful insistence of his lips moving over hers, as if he knew that his lovemaking would be in every way superior to his brother's fledgling efforts and verifying what she had assumed earlier about his experience. Thoughts of resistance were swept away on the tide of his kisses and, while it lasted, Aphra was almost convinced that his hunger was genuine, that this great handsome creature had been waiting for an excuse to take her in his arms and make her forget what she had lost, what had never been hers. The darkness conspired to hide away all distractions, even their verbal sparring, endorsing Aphra's passive co-operation, heightening every sensation in ways she had never experienced with his brother. She had not intended to compare, but it was there, even so, for Santo Datini was a mature male who knew well how to make a woman like her, fighting confused emotions, confront the desires which, in these last few days, had been twisting her heart into knots. After this, she knew that any more talk about being broken-hearted would, to her shame, be seen as a sham.

His kisses softened, the pressure of his arms allowing her to move within their embrace. 'You see?' he whispered. 'That broken heart of yours is bruised, that's all. And your pride. There's nothing here that cannot be mended.'

Breathless, she tried to wriggle away, but was not allowed to. 'There's little wrong with *your* pride, *signor*. I know perfectly well what this is all about. Another attempt to manipulate me. It won't work!'

'No, nor is it meant to,' he whispered. 'But I believe you and I could—'

'No! How *can* you believe I want a relationship with the brother of the man who deceived me? Who comes in the guise of friendship, as you do? As a cover for stealing something you knew you'd not get by fair means?'

'This,' he said, smoothing a hand over her back, 'is not intended to manipulate you. It is simply my response to feelings we've both been aware of since my arrival. Your outbursts are no more than an attempt to hide it, so I think we should leave my brother out of this discussion. He has nothing to do with it, Aphra. He was obliged to give you up, but his feelings about that are not my direct concern.'

Angered by this apparent heartlessness, she jerked away and, with all her strength, broke free of his arms, her lips still tingling from his passionate kisses. To think clearly after that took all the will she could summon. 'I wonder that you can say that, *signor*, when it must be your brother's feelings that sent you here. He has *everything* to do with it, doesn't he? Otherwise you would not have come and I would be free to get on with things, as I was doing quite nicely before you arrived. But now we have it out in the open. You have come to reclaim the notes and I am determined that you shall not have them until I have solved the mystery of exactly what happened to cause my uncle's death. Somehow, I believe your brother must know more about that than I do.' She felt the hard edge of the bench behind her.

With his back to the window, his large silhouette loomed against the faint light of dawn that picked out the tower of the priory church nearby. The dark closeness of his body was making her heart behave strangely and she knew that what had just happened had changed things between them for ever, for if he had not seen that one hair in his cap, he would presumably not have suspected that she was warming to him. Or *would* he? He had talked of their mutual feelings since his arrival. That called for the kind of perception she did not have. Or was he lying about that, too?

But now her arguments were milling round in circles. Were they arguing about that, or the notes, or Ben, or Leon? The darkness was no help to clear thinking, the chill of the room made the hair on her arms prickle, and she drew her velvet gown closer about her, feeling very vulnerable and wrong-footed. The books of Leon's notes lay on the bench behind her and she knew that, if Santo was so minded, he could take them and go without too much opposition. She would not be able to prevent it. But in the darkness she was unable to stop him from reaching out for her, drawing her into his arms again, warming her against his body, this time with the same gentleness he had shown on that first occasion. This time, she lay her cheek against his doublet and, in the quiet of the new dawn, heard the distant thud of his heart.

'Know more than *you* do?' he said. She heard the deep boom of his voice in one ear. 'We shall not know if my brother's research can help with your uncle's death until he tells us, shall we?'

'So you'll take the notes, *signor*? I don't suppose I can prevent you, if that's what you have in mind.'

He spoke with his lips touching the top of her head so she could feel the warmth of his breath. 'No,' he said. 'You accuse me of wishing to steal them, but I am not a thief to run off with them into the night. Besides, there's something that keeps me here for a while longer.'

'What?'

'I offered you my help and you accepted it. And in spite of your claim that you were doing very nicely, you were not, were you? Apart from the estate management, you need help with your investigations, too, and I have to admit that my curiosity is whetted about your uncle's unexpected death. Leon may be able to shed some light on that, although I doubt it, but the only way we shall find out is by allowing him to tell us what he knows. Besides which, it's critically important that he has his notes back as soon as possible.'

'Why? Can't he find another subject to research?'

'And waste three years of study? No, he *must* have them, Aphra.'

She noted the urgency in his voice. It would be to do with his degree, of course. And then setting himself up as an apothecary. With a new wife and a future family to feed. 'I shall burn them,' she said, sweetly.

She felt his arms stiffen around her, then the slackening of them as his hands came up to hold her face, cupping it like a flower. 'No...no! You must not. Promise me you won't do that. *Promise* me? You cannot hate him so much, surely?'

Taking his wrists, she prised them apart. They were thick and muscular, like the branches of a tree. His kisses had been nothing like his brother's. She had never felt as helpless in Leon's arms, never as needing of his presence, never as unsure of herself and her decisions. Was she simply reacting to the circumstances? Was it the idea of being in love more than love itself? Could it be lust and desire, and having the delicious power of being able to keep a man's interest, even when it might have an ulterior motive? Could Santo Datini repeat what his brother had done and desert her? He was a merchant. One of his ships would be at Southampton to take him back at a moment's notice. She would like to have thought she was the reason he stayed, but such thoughts could only lead to more heartache. 'You will stay then? For a while?' she said, hoping to sound unconcerned, whatever his answer.

'We shall explore your uncle's possessions,' he

said, 'to find out if anything can give us a clue as to why he abandoned his studies of pain relief and left it to my brother to continue, and whether we can discover any more about why he died. So, he had a heart problem, but that doesn't seem to explain why he appeared to be turning away from herbal medicine. He was world-famed for that, not for his collection of antidotes against poison. Sounds to me as if he might have made a mistake there.'

'If you're implying that my uncle accidently—'

'Hush, *madonna*,' he said, once again pulling her into his arms. 'We should not jump to conclusions, as you have already done with that nonsensical Elixir of Life theory. And if all this takes too long, I could send the notes to Padua by special courier, but that's a huge risk. I would rather take them personally.'

'Yes, *signor*, I'm sure you would. But they're in my possession now and I shall do everything I can to make sure they stay there. The only way they'll ever reach your brother is if I were to take them to Padua myself and that is most unlikely.'

'We'll cross that bridge when we reach it,' he said. 'Meanwhile, there is something I want you to understand.'

It was almost morning light and Aphra was

desperately tired. Unpredictable things had happened that night that needed deep thought to explain them, and as soon as he had said 'meanwhile' she knew he was about to lecture her. 'Yes, *signor*, there are many things I need to understand, so allow me to mention just one.' She had laid her palms against his chest to break his hold on her, but her push had no effect on his strength and she was immediately pulled back hard, her head tipped on to his shoulder, in no position to finish her sentence, whatever it was. Once again, in the pale dimness of the new day, his wide expressive mouth covered hers to drive away all irritations and arguments from her mind, obliging her to feel the sensuous warmth of his kiss and the passion behind it.

She had missed Leon's kisses although his letter had soured those memories. But since Santo's arrival, her thoughts had strayed too often to his potent masculinity and self-assurance, to the way he walked and spoke and looked at her. Guiltily, she had tried to discipline those thoughts of how it might feel to be kissed by him, chastising herself each time.

Now, however, she knew that her imagination had been nowhere near the real thing, for whatever she suspected about his motives, it would be hard, even impossible, to refuse this kind of attention whenever he was inclined to offer it. Without enquiring too closely into her reasons for her temporary surrender, she took her fill of his lips, giving back kiss for kiss as much as she was able, tasting the moisture of his skin and caring not when her breathless protest sounded totally at odds with her response. 'No...no, *signor*. This will not do,' she breathed against his chin. 'This will cause all kinds of complications. There will be talk. It cannot go on. We have investigations to make. Nothing must hinder that.'

His arms slackened and his kiss to her forehead was, she thought, meant to appease her. 'Nothing *will* hinder that,' he said. 'We'll begin today. But now I shall escort you back to your room to catch up on some sleep. Shall you lock the notes away first?'

'You'll not take them, will you?'

'Not without first escorting you to Padua, *madonna*.'

'Tch! Foolish man. What *did* you come up here for?'

'For my cap.'

'What, fully dressed? At this time of night?'

His voice caressed her. 'How else would you have me? At this time of night.'

She felt a blush rising into her cheeks as she found the key to the cupboard.

* * *

Why did he have an answer to everything? she asked herself, closing the door of her room quietly. She glanced across to Tilda's sleeping form, almost envying the maid her untroubled dreams, so different from her own disturbed thoughts. Kicking off her leather slippers, she lay upon her bed and wrapped the thick woollen coverlet around herself, fending off the chill of the dawn walk from her workroom, but sure that Santo's instructions to catch up on her sleep had fallen on deaf ears. How could she sleep, after that? Why had she allowed it to happen when every ounce of her abundant common sense chided her for her stupidity?

For all her daydreams, for all her longings and the stirrings of her heart, she had not meant for any of them to be realised in this way, or for her needs to be made so glaringly obvious. Yes, she had known him to be more experienced than she at recognising the signs, though she had not intended for her earlier plea to be interpreted in quite that way, or so soon. But would it have been worse, or better, to let him go? Would she have been happier for his departure, just to prove to him that she was not loving too easily, which was what she had accused herself of? After suffering what she had believed to be a broken heart, why had she found it so easy to desire a man like him? What guilt would she now endure for the shallow love she had declared for his brother? What game was her heart playing to swing her from the heights to the depths and back again in the space of a few months?

Wanton. Inconstant. Indecisive. These were words that flitted through her mind alongside the warnings of future torments when Santo would reveal, as he was bound to do, that his desire for her came second to his need to reclaim his brother's research. That, of course, was what it was all about. Their desire for each other on a physical level might be genuine enough, but when he achieved his goal, there would be nothing to prevent him from doing exactly as his brother had done. One day soon, she would wake up and he would be gone with the notes and all the declarations of trust, honour and interest in Ben's death gone with him. Well, at least in that he was not able to deceive her, but whether the pain of men's deceit grew less with advance warnings she was unable to speculate.

The sensible thing to do would be to put a stop to this new development now, before it was too late. But before the echo of that advice had died away, the memory of his embrace and the thrill of his mouth on hers claimed all her thoughts, just as they had then. It was already too late. Whatever the consequences, she wanted more, not less of him.

Her eyelids drooped against the growing light as she recalled his attempt to steal another kiss before they parted in the dim passageway and the effort it had taken for her to pretend a coolness she did not feel. She had held him away with a feeble protest that had provoked only a grin from him that gleamed, even in the dark. Sleepily, she held the back of her hand to her lips to breathe in his lingering scent, for that was where his goodnight kiss had been deposited, its softness sending a weakness flooding towards her heart. Out of habit, she waited for thoughts of Leon to lull her to sleep, but they would not come, their place taken by the far more powerful ones of his brother.

'How else would you have me? At this time of night?' he had mocked, making her squirm inside the comfort of her blanket. They had both known the answer to that.

The short walk across to his rooms in the visiting abbots' house was not far enough to cool Santo's ardour. Taking Aphra as far as the staircase in her own dwelling had been a tantalising step she could hardly be expected to recognise, for her naivety was one of her most attractive features, all the more so for her attempts to seem otherwise. He could see how this same innocence was what had appealed so strongly to Leon, making him appear more worldly than he was. Why else would the simpleton have believed he could wriggle out of a betrothal in Italy that had taken their father almost two years to negotiate?

And yet, he could sympathise, for Mistress Aphra Betterton would turn any man's head and his brother would have stood no chance against the kind of desire she was able to generate without the slightest effort. He had seen it for himself. Pretence was not her forte. On the contrary, she had snapped and scolded and tried several times to send him away, even while contradicting herself, too angry and confused to think it out. He would like to have followed her upstairs to her room, where he was sure she would not sleep for some time.

He would also have liked to return to the workroom to take a look at those notes after she had indicated that they were, as he suspected, all Leon's work, the research he now needed so urgently in Padua. It began to look, he thought, as if some drastic decision must be taken if she delayed things much longer. The greatest stumbling block, however, was the spectre of Dr Ben for whom Aphra cared enough to hold on to the precious notebooks until the real reason for his untimely death was explained more satisfactorily. He had promised not to steal them, although that course might have benefitted Leon. But brotherly love could not be stretched as far as that. Nor was he willing to lose the ground he had just gained.

Quietly, he let himself into the dim hall of his lodgings, smiling as Dante's muffled snores penetrated the decorated plasterwork ceiling. He thought that if Dr Ben had been a married man with a family to make a claim on his funds, he might have found it less easy to finance his obsession, whatever it was. Those expensive rarities in his possession certainly seemed to indicate a very personal quest so private that not one of his close relatives appeared to know anything of it.

Chapter Six

'Ben…dear Ben,' she whispered, touching the new grass on the mound covering the burial. 'What was it you kept to yourself all these years? Why did you not share it with anyone?' Holding her hand still, she waited, then stood upright, lifting her skirts to skim the mossy pathway. A robin flew ahead of her to perch on another gravestone, its eyes like two bright beads, its orange-red breast contrasting with the pale greens lit by the early Sunday sun. The church bell tolled for the first service of the day and, in the distance, couples and families moved in respectable sober dress towards the great west door while one figure stood apart, waiting for her to reach him. Such an innocent gesture, she thought, but ill advised before so many inquisitive stares from villagers who had not had time to know her well.

With a nod of greeting to Santo, her smiles and good mornings were for those she met in the porch, though it was obvious even then that their sidelong glances at her handsome escort and scarce a smile for her was an indication of their assumptions. Her attempts to ask after their children and aged parents were met with a noticeable coolness and, from her position at the front of the congregation, the whispers, nodding heads and stares could be felt, so different from last Sunday's kindly regard. Aphra was left in no doubt that her virtue was already being questioned as much as her imprudence.

After the service, she took him to task. 'You must know how people gossip when they have little else to think about,' she whispered to him as they turned towards the door of the prior's house. 'In a village as small as this, everyone knows everyone else's business. One cannot move without it being common knowledge before breakfast, *signor*. I told you how it would be.'

Santo opened the door for her, allowing her to pass through, then following her down the passage into the parlour. 'So I must not attend church, mistress? Is that what you're saying?'

'I'm talking about you being here. Being seen together. You saw their faces.'

'Yes, I saw. Master Pearce kept his distance, too, I noticed. Is that usual?'

'Not at all. He looked as disapproving as the rest of them today. He usually makes some flattering remark. I'm not sure whether I prefer that or the scowl.' She could not help but smile at the dilemma as she tried to hold Santo off, who was clearly intending to take her in his arms. But the moment was interrupted by servants carrying trays of bread, cheese and bacon, boiled eggs, oatcakes, a slab of butter and jugs of ale, setting them on the table, but hesitating over the next task.

'Begging your pardon, mistress.' One of the men glanced at Santo.

Briskly, Aphra had moved away. 'Yes, set it out, if you please. We're ready to eat.' They were joined almost immediately by Father Vickery, Dante and Enrico, by Aphra's maid Tilda, the steward, the bailiff and the young churchwarden, so no more was said about the unsettling disapproval of the church congregation. Not until later, when Father Vickery lingered, requesting a private word with Aphra. The subject of his concern was no surprise to her. 'Don't beat about the bush, Father,' she said as the weary priest peered into his empty beaker. 'Here, hold it up. You'll need some more of this. Or would you prefer something stronger, perhaps?'

'Oh, no, my dear, thank you. This will do nicely. A very good meal. Your uncle laid a good table, too, but…'

'But he would not have approved of this arrangement. Is that what you'd like to say, though only a few days ago you were in favour of it?'

His white hair caught the sun like a halo, etching deep lines upon his face. He took a sip from his beaker, watching it touch the tabletop before he answered. 'I was, wasn't I? But it was inevitable and I think I must have failed to see that, in my eagerness for you to have some help here. In retrospect, I suppose a chaperon…an older lady…might have been more appropriate.'

'Inevitable, Father? What do you refer to?'

Sadly, he looked at her from beneath his bushy white eyebrows. 'That you…well…that both of you would form an attachment…an emotional attachment. And that is not something your parents gave much thought to, either, otherwise…'

'Otherwise they would not have consented to Signor Datini's presence here. Yes, I can see you're concerned about that, but when there are other men living here, like yourself, on the priory precincts, the men who came to breakfast, then how can one more be a problem? And how can you have come to the conclusion…?'

She was stopped by Father Vickery's long bony hand preventing any kind of excuse. 'Aphra,' he whispered, leaning across the table. 'Listen to me, my dear. I was up at dawn this morning. I went into the church. Then when I'd finished my business there, I wandered into the garden.' He pointed to the window. 'It was the cloister garden when I was here with my brothers. We would go there to be alone.'

'The garden,' she murmured. 'Between my workroom and here. At dawn.'

'Yes, at dawn, Aphra. I was not spying, but I could not help seeing that you appeared to be in your nightgown. With Signor Datini.'

The picture was clear in her mind as she closed her eyes with a deep sigh. 'Father, do you wish me to explain what happened last night, just to put your mind at rest?'

'My dear,' he said, stretching out his hand to take hers, 'it is not my mind that needs putting at rest. If you tell me that nothing happened, then I am bound to believe you. But others are not so charitable or trusting, and already there has been talk in the village about the good-looking Italian and what exactly his role is here.'

'But, Father, you know that…'

'Yes, I know. But others cannot be hood-winked for ever into believing he is your lawyer. Master Pearce for one does not believe it. Nor do those who saw your relatives leave so soon after rooms had been scrubbed and beds refurbished and food brought in for a week and more. Any young woman of your beauty, Aphra, must be seen to be living her life with immaculate virtue. Your reputation can be so easily compromised, my dear. To those out there,' he said, tipping his head towards the door, 'it may have looked as if your guests left in a hurry because they didn't like what they saw here.'

'Father! It's Pearce, isn't it? Spreading any scandal he can invent.'

'Not entirely. He has voiced concerns…'

'Oh, yes, I'm sure he has.'

'But so have others. Some of them just now after the morning service. Of course I told them not to spread malicious gossip and I scolded them for such tittle-tattle. But now I believe the situation must be looked at again, my dear, when it's clear that you and Signor Datini have developed feelings for each other. You have, haven't you?'

'Father,' Aphra said, laying her other hand on top of his, 'I did not intend for this to happen. Quite the opposite. I know how I feel, but I cannot speak for him. I don't know how he feels about me except what men often feel about women. All I am certain of is that he came here to retrieve his brother's research and take it back to Italy. And now I expect you will tell me to let him have it and go home.'

'And you are not willing to do this because...?'

'Because,' she said, releasing his hand, 'I seem to be making a habit of losing everything I hold dear. *Held* dear,' she corrected herself. 'I have fallen in love, Father. To part with him would...would...' Pressing her palms against the black, boned bodice, she gasped at the pain of yet another heartbreak. 'Don't judge me harshly. I believed I loved his brother, but this is quite different. He is all I desire.'

Father Vickery shook his head. 'Sometimes, my dear, all we desire comes at a heavy price, but a woman in your position cannot afford to pay with her reputation. Once lost, you would never regain it. Your parents would agree with me.'

There was nothing else she could say to that, having seen the problem from the start, her fears realised, and whether it was Master Pearce's doing or not, the gossip had begun to damage her good character and Signor Datini's honour. Going with Father Vickery to the door, she was desperately sorry that he had seen her and Santo together as they had walked back to her dwelling and just as sorry that an explanation of the situation would have sounded too incredulously simple to be believed.

Changing her Sunday shoes for her garden sandals, she headed for the open space of the large plot where herbs grew in abundance around the stillroom. Feathery fronds of fennel swayed against fluffy coriander, poppies, stocky borage and several varieties of southernwood, some safer than others. The scent on her fingers as she pinched the leaves reminded her how useful it was to repel flying insects and also how any student of herbs must take care to know both its harmful properties as well as its beneficial ones, and how to tell the varieties apart. Any careless mistake in identification could prove fatal.

But now her concern was being overshadowed by what had happened last night, by her personal admission of her feelings for Santo Datini and by his overwhelming expressions of desire for her. She had not evaded the truth by telling the priest that she did not know exactly what Santo felt for her, apart from desire, but nor would she risk hearing Santo's avoidance of the issue, for if she had learnt anything at all from her relationship with his brother, it was that a too-generous heart had its dangers. The main problem was, of course, that her body had its own treacherous agenda.

Twisting a head of the daisy-like feverfew between her fingers, she watched the leisurely approach of the one who filled her dreams, preparing herself for the explanation she knew he would request, for he had been in the courtyard with his men as Father Vickery had left. '*Madonna,*' he said, softly. 'The priest is concerned?'

'Yes, and so am I,' she said. 'And so should you be.'

'I am,' he said. 'May I ask what he said? He has advice to offer?'

'That we must put a stop to the gossip, before it's too late.'

'Too late for what?'

'For your honour to survive. For my reputation. I would like to be able to say I care nothing for that, but I do. I must continue to live here.'

'So he doesn't think the gossip will die away?'

'Not if Master Pearce has anything to do with it. Besides, Father Vickery was in the garden at dawn this morning when you escorted me back to my house. He saw. And me in my nightgown.' She glanced up at his shocked face and was quick to reassure him. 'No more than that. But I can imagine how it looked to him.'

'Did you explain?'

'No. There was little point, really.'

'What, little point in telling him I didn't seduce you? So you want him to...'

'It doesn't matter, does it? The damage is done, whatever he or anybody thinks. I can see no way round this. The village is talking.'

It was not true to say she could see no way round this. She could. But to drag a declaration of love out of a man in circumstances such as these would be a recipe for disaster and was certainly not a strategy she would consider. If there was any excuse to be made for her behaviour, it was that the situation had been initiated by Santo himself last night when he had taken her in his arms. She had not made it too hard for him, but nor had she thrown herself under his feet. She had revealed her desire, but no more than he, and for all he knew, her heart was still her own.

'And it matters to you, does it, that there is silly gossip? Do you not think they'll all get over it?'

'*Signor*, you must understand,' she said, heatedly. 'Of course it matters to me. I would have thought it would matter to you, too. But then, you can simply walk away and return to Italy, never to be heard of again. Unfortunately, I have to see and work with these people and earn their trust and friendship. I need their support if I'm to carry on my uncle's work here, supplying herbs. Which I'm not going to get if they disapprove of me. Am I?'

'Walk away? Return to Italy? Is that what you want me to do, Aphra?'

The argument was going nowhere and Aphra had no reply for him for he must have known, she thought, that her needs had suddenly become unreasonable. He waited only a moment before taking her arm, drawing her gently off the path to the outer wall of the whitewashed stillroom. It was now deserted, hidden by a wicker tunnel of roses sprouting from a bed of lavender. Against the wall, she was turned by the shoulders only a bare moment before his body pressed her against its warmth, his lips taking hers in the only reply either of them could think of, hungry for physical contact rather than words. Breathless, she slid her mouth to his lean cheek. 'This will not do,' she said, breathlessly.

'No, it won't do for me, either,' he said. 'I want you, Aphra. I cannot simply walk away from you.'

'That is what you *must* do, *signor*. But…oh… if only…'

'If only what? This?' Tenderly, knowingly, his hand slipped down the front of her bodice where her breasts were lifted by the boned corset, but not bound. She felt his warm fingers find the fullness, cupping it while his mouth took in her cry of ecstasy, playing over her lips as his hand kneaded and pressed, trapping the tender nipple to send waves of weakness deep into the caverns of her body. Dizzy with sensation, with the thudding rhythm of her heart, with the pressure of his legs against hers, holding her captive, her need of him was almost too great to bear. With a cry of pure desire, she held his head as it bent to kiss her breast, then her throat, tasting his thick hair as it passed close to her lips, delighting in his sensuous male warmth. Her body melted under his hands. Her eyes opened as he brought his caresses to an end and adjusted her bodice. Her arms dropped away, her trembling hands holding his wrists.

'I shall come back to you, Aphra,' he whispered. 'I cannot leave things like this, with so much unfinished business.'

Tears gathered in her eyes as the words found an echo in her memory, causing a surge of months-old cynicism to spill out before she could stop it. 'Yes,' she said. 'That's what your brother said, too.'

'Must you bring him into it?' he said, frowning. 'May we not have a moment to ourselves without Leon or Ben? Must they dictate to us, still?'

Turning her head away, something inside her urged on the perverse direction of her reasoning. 'But they do, don't they? Both of them are why we're here. You must return his notes and I must find out more about my uncle. I owe it to him. He left me *this* place, didn't he?' She waved a hand towards the garden. 'The least I can do is to put his soul to rest.'

'Your curiosity, you mean,' he replied, releasing her from the closeness of his body. 'It's more likely to be your prying into his affairs that's keeping his soul from resting, Aphra. Is it not time you let him go now? What's to be gained by all this?'

Like lightning, her hand flew up to strike at his face, but his reflexes were faster and her wrist was caught and held away, countering all her efforts to continue the assault. 'Prying?' she growled, struggling in his grasp. 'Let him go? What *are* you talking about? He *has* gone. Or hadn't you noticed?'

'No, I had not!' he said. 'Far from it! He inhabits every damn thing you do. And as long as you pursue these ridiculous theories of yours, woman, you'll never be free to give your heart, will you? At least half of it will be out there, in that grave.' He tipped his head in the direction of the graveyard, his pitiless words striking at her heart as no physical blow could have done, forcing her to see herself through his eyes, now coldly angry.

Hot scalding tears rolled down her cheeks as she watched him stride away along the path, his long legs covering the ground as if to put as much distance between them as possible, brushing against the bushy sage and creeping thyme. Now he would go, she said to herself, seeing a sea of swimming greens through her tears. That would be the last she would see of him. And was it indeed Ben who had come between them? No, she knew it was not, although that was how it looked to Santo.

Leaning against the wall, she allowed her hand to comfort the breast he had taunted so tenderly, where still the imprint of his caress lingered on her skin. 'Damn you! Damn you!' she growled. 'And damn your *feckless* brother, too!' Bending down to retrieve the feverfew she had dropped, she studied it before discarding it again, muttering its common name. 'Bachelor's buttons,' she said. 'How fitting!'

That particular Sunday morning continued to be no more like a day of rest than any weekday when her steward, Master Fletcher, interrupted her duties at midday to relate some serious news concerning the mill. 'Oh, not again!' she said. 'What is it this time?' She saw from his flushed face that he had been running. 'Will you be seated, Master Fletcher?'

'Thank you, mistress. I came to tell you that Master Pearce has been beaten up by his own men. He's in a bad way, they say.'

'Start at the beginning, if you will. What has that to do with the mill?'

'Earlier this morning,' he said, wondering how far back to go, 'he'd sent two of his men to wreck the mill while Miller was at church, mistress.'

'But Master Miller was not at church, was he?'

'No, as it happens, he didn't go because his two sons were visiting. So they were there when these two turned up and started to hack at the mill wheel. Miller and his lads ran out to stop them and there was a bust-up, mistress, and it turned out that Miller and his lads threw them into the millpond and nearly drowned 'em. They managed to climb out, then went off to Pearce's house.'

'Where they failed to find him.'

'Aye, he was at church, so they waited for him and when he came home and heard what had happened, he was roaring mad at them. He refused to pay them what he'd promised, so they beat *him* up instead of Miller, then they wrecked his house and took his gold, and went off.'

'But that's very serious. You say he's badly hurt?'

'Aye, he certainly is. He was not too fit to start with, was he, but now it looks as if he's got what he deserves, after all his bullying.'

Aphra had never wished any harm to befall Master Pearce. 'Does he have any help?' she said. 'I wonder if I should go to see what I can do.'

'Nay, mistress,' Fletcher said. 'Best to stay away. The quack is with him at the moment, but I heard from his housekeeper that there's little anyone can do. She's not too sorry, either. She tells me she's not been paid for months. She was there at the house to see it all happen.'

'Don't repeat that to anyone, if you please, Master Fletcher. Not to feel some sympathy for a badly injured man is unworthy of us.'

Fletcher looked suitably contrite and she thought he would have answered, but at that moment the barking of hounds and the clatter of hooves outside made them both peer through the window to see what was the cause of the commotion.

'Where is Signor Datini?' she said, unable to identify anyone through the wobbly green glass.

'Over in his lodging, mistress. Packing his bags, I believe. Again,' he added.

Aphra sent him a sharp glance, then was obliged to smile at the comment. 'Run over and ask him to come, Master Fletcher. We have guests. Again.'

The unexpected visit that day was one Aphra could not have wished for more, being exactly the kind of understanding and support for which she had been longing during the trials of the last week. The homes of Lord and Lady Somerville at Mortlake and London's Cheapside were not close enough to Sandrock Priory to make visits easy, so their last meeting had been at Ben's funeral earlier that year. Lady Henrietta Somerville had married only last year after a stormy courtship during which Aphra, her stepcousin, had stayed with her as chaperon. Aphra was two years her senior and had virtually grown up with Etta, who now came towards her with an enchanting smile and arms open wide to engulf her in brocade and velvet of violet blue, pale fur, cream silk, lace and a soft flowery perfume brought in, Aphra guessed, on one of Baron Somerville's merchant ships.

'Aphie!' said Etta, favouring her dear friend with a look of mock reproach. 'Did you really send them away... Uncle Paul and Aunt Venetia? You won't send Nic and me away, will you?'

Aphra hugged her, laughing and shamefaced. 'It wasn't like that,' she said. 'So they told you, then? Is that why you've come?'

'No, I persuaded Nic you needed us,' Etta said, linking her arm through Aphra's, 'so you must convince him you do. You do, don't you? Say you do.'

'As a matter of fact, I do,' Aphra said. 'Your timing is perfect.'

'Good. Excellent. So where is this great handsome Italian that Aunt Venetia fancies? Oh... Aphie! Is *that* him?' she whispered, looking across to where Santo and Lord Somerville were talking together like old friends. 'Well, look at that! Merchants can recognise each other from a mile away, can't they? You'd think they'd known each other for years. Now they'll be talking business all evening.'

'If Signor Datini stays as long as that,' Aphra said. 'I believe he's already packing his bags.'

'Why, Aphie? You've not quarrelled again, have you? Aunt Venetia said she thought...well... never mind that.'

'What did she think? That I was not keen on him being here?'

'No-oo!' Etta drawled, fumbling for an appropriate expression. 'Uncertain, more like. She seemed to think you'd make a fine pair, except for the fact that he's Leon's big brother.'

'That, and a few more facts that Aunt Venetia knows nothing of,' said Aphra, tartly. 'Look, I'll tell you more later, dearest. Let me go and welcome Nic. It was good of him to come all this way with you. Will you stay a while?'

When she had hugged her cousin's husband with a genuine warmth, she asked the same question of him, although it was a formality for already their trunks and bags were being unloaded from a train of packhorses by a retinue of liveried servants. Etta and her wealthy merchant husband always travelled in style. As an important member of the Mercers' Guild, he had an image to maintain, of which his lovely wife played her part to the full. 'Of course we'll stay,' the tall, good-looking mercer said. 'Signor Datini and I have some talking to do.' Being a very perceptive man, however, he noticed the look of doubt that passed between the Italian and their hostess. He was also an experienced diplomat. 'But we haven't come here to organise you, Aphie. Let's go inside and talk over a glass of Ben's finest claret.'

If Santo had expected to leave Sandrock Priory that day, he showed no sign of it as he was introduced to Queen Elizabeth's half-sister whose likeness to the young Queen was quite remarkable, though Etta was the lovelier of the two. Nor did Aphra indicate that she wanted Santo to go when the timely arrival of her cousin seemed to offer a chance to discuss matters and perhaps to resolve them. Not that she could disregard what was being said in the village, or what Santo had said to her in the garden, but somehow the presence of those whose opinions mattered to her was a consolation she badly needed. As they entered the house, she managed to ask him if he'd heard about Master Pearce's predicament.

'The news is all over the village,' he said. 'I hope the two men responsible have got well away by now. They'll be in deep trouble if Pearce doesn't recover.'

'I don't suppose that's what they intended.'

'We can all say that, *madonna*,' he whispered as they moved away.

Quite what he meant by that enigmatic remark Aphra was unable to decide, wondering if he referred to himself, or her. In the absence of even the smallest show of warmth, however, she could only contemplate the near future in which she might be expected to offer him some form of encouragement, some way out of the impasse in which they found themselves. Perhaps, she thought, Etta and her sensible husband might suggest something, for it was clear that Uncle Paul and Aunt Venetia had discussed the situation with them. They would also have discussed their brief visit to Aphra's parents in London, which put a certain pressure on her to do the right thing, whatever the right thing was.

While Lord and Lady Somerville were being shown to their room, last occupied by Uncle Paul and Aunt Venetia, Aphra took the chance to speak again to Santo, if only to offer him the chance to explain his intentions.

'*Signor,*' she said, stopping him before he could leave. 'Santo. A moment?' She quailed at the sadness in his dark eyes and how sad it was, she thought, that his warmth could cool so fast after his passion only a few hours earlier.

'*Madonna?*'

'You were preparing to leave?'

'That seemed the obvious thing to do. My mission has failed. You are not ready to move on. I expected too much. Why would I stay?'

She felt the ache of despair well up inside her at his reading of the situation, yet there was no dignified way to remove the barriers between them. In so many ways he was right, but how was she to move on inside a cloud of mystery?

'I just…just wondered,' she said, looking beyond him to the wilting bluebells on the windowsill, 'if you might stay just long enough to discuss things with my…with Etta and Nic. Perhaps overnight? I trust them. I helped them when they needed similar advice, so I would not mind if they offered me…us…some.'

'You mean you would take it? Even if it was not what you hoped for?'

'Yes. I would. Oh… Santo!' Her voice shook at the image of how the years ahead would feel without him. She thought how the loss of his brother had brought unbearable pain, but now saw that it was anger and humiliation at his rejection rather than the awful emptiness of unfulfilled desire she felt for his brother, his great, handsome sibling who had taken over every waking thought since his appearance, despite all her protests. But this time, it was she who moved forward into his arms, fearing that this might be the last time she would feel his warm strength and be pressed against his body. 'Hold me,' she whispered.

He needed no persuading. Carefully removing the black-velvet cap she wore over her hair, he nuzzled her cheek and sought her mouth for the mutual comfort they so desperately needed. Lifting his face from hers, he held her chin with his tender fingers, speaking softly. 'Yes, I will stay for one more night, Aphra, but you must be realistic about this. Your cousin and her husband will not persuade me to stay longer, for now you know the reason for my journey and I must return to Padua.'

'With or without the notes?' she said, taking his hand away to hold it.

'With or without them. But I am hoping that your advisors will persuade you that there is no point in you keeping them merely to revenge yourself on Leon. That would serve no good purpose. Besides that, my presence here is causing problems, as you said it might.'

'Then you'll be here this evening when we discuss what to do?'

'I already know what to do. But, yes, we'll talk about it, if that will make matters easier for you.'

'Nothing will make things easier for me. Not until I've found some answers. But at least we both know what must be done and that we appear to be moving in different directions.'

Unable to hear any compromise in her tone, Santo held her away with gentle hands on her shoulders. 'And now I think I should go and prepare for my journey tomorrow. You will have duties to perform. Their visit is timely, is it not?'

She nodded. 'I have you to thank for that. Had you not been here, they'd not have come.'

'And if I *do* come back to you, Aphra, will your uncle still come between us? Will he still claim half your heart? Because if that is to be the case, our farewells must be for ever. I am not a man to be satisfied with anything less than all of you. A smaller portion will not do for me. There. I've said it. Now you know how I feel.'

It was not the way she wanted to hear it without the one word that mattered most to her. 'No, I don't know how you feel, *signor*,' she said. 'I know no more about your heart than you know about mine. Lovemaking is not about a man's heart, is it? It's about desire. See, I've learnt that much from your brother. And not only that, *signor*. I've learnt not to commit myself too soon, for that way leads to trouble. It's been only a matter of days. Hardly time enough for me to know what I feel for you, whether half of my heart or indeed any of it at all.' Her voice wavered as she forced out the lies, the cold, uncaring, dignified deceptions. 'Perhaps I shall allow you to take your brother's research after all,' she continued, struggling for control. 'As a gesture. I cannot do more than that. See, here is the key.' She pulled up the thong that held her bunch of household keys, snapped one off the ring and handed it to him. 'There, take it. Take the notes. That's what you came for. Now your journey has not been wasted and your brother will be able to continue his fine career and earn a good living.' She would have turned away, but Santo placed an arm across her, turning her to him. She stiffened, refusing to soften into him.

'Still so bitter,' he whispered, tipping his head to see into her watery eyes. 'You think I cannot understand, but I do, Aphra. It's happened too fast for you. Too soon. I should not have let it happen, but it did.'

'Nothing happened,' she said. 'Nothing. Now, I must go and prepare and so must you. Leave the key on my work bench when you've removed the notes, if you please.'

'Aphra.'

'Supper in half an hour,' she said, pulling herself out of his grasp. 'We shall expect Enrico and Dante, too.' She had thought to evade him, to stop this distressing talk that so carefully avoided any mention of love, as if what had happened between them had not quite reached that lofty pinnacle of emotion. But she refused to be seen as the pleading one again, nor would she offer to forget about her concern for her deceased uncle who had no one but her willing to investigate his tragedy. Santo had agreed to help her in this, but now his presence was being seen as scandalous and he was being obliged to spare her good name, offering her nothing in place of his absence except the vague possibility that he might return, one day. She had already experienced the disappearance of hope. She would not cling to it a second time. 'Let me go, *signor*,' she said, trying to shake off the hand beneath her arm. 'Please…let me go!'

'No,' he said, harshly. 'Not without this.' His mouth covered hers to stifle her cry of anger, shocking her with the force and passion of his kiss.

Pulled once more against him, she felt his rock-hard arm across her back and his grasp under her head, extinguishing her anger in an instant and transforming it into the blinding passion of love. So close were the two emotions that, for a few moments, she fought him with flailing arms that soon tired and wrapped his head in an embrace, her hand burying into the thick dark waves, sending shivers of stark desire down to melt her knees. She knew it was meant to provoke some kind of commitment from her, to remind her, if she needed it, of what she would be missing. 'You are asking too much of me, *signor*,' she murmured against his lips as they lifted from hers. 'Neither of us can see where this will lead. Too many things are in the way. Don't ask me for more than I can give, other than what you came for. Make that do.'

'For now, Aphra. But if I return, I shall expect more from you than words.'

If he returned? The doubt seared her heart and provoked a whirlwind of questions without a hope of answers. When? Why? How long? More than words? What more? Was this simply a repetition of his brother's empty promises? And if it was, would she be able to bear it? Again?

Supper that evening was an ordeal alleviated mostly with Etta's help, the beloved cousin who had herself experienced an emotional tangle and who knew what Aphra was suffering. On the surface, the two protagonists gave every sign of having accepted the situation calmly, sensibly and without an excess of regret while, inside, both hearts bled with new wounds no apothecary had a cure for, though some claimed otherwise. During the meal, Aphra's discipline helped her to play the part of the smiling gracious hostess, betraying none of the awareness that this would be the last time she would entertain the three Italians at her table and the emptiness she would have to bear, after this. While Etta's husband enquired about Santo's merchanting ventures, they heard about his flourishing business in the spice and luxury goods trade and the mutual friends they had in the Mercers' Guild.

For once, Santo seemed not to mind talking about himself, as if it might give Aphra some comfort to know more of his earlier years in Venice about which she had purposely refrained from asking so as not to betray her growing interest. He told them how, at thirteen years old, being headstrong and at odds with his father's strictness, he had stowed away on a merchant galley, but had been returned to Venice by the unsympathetic captain. From then on, his father had employed a man to tutor him in the arts of navigation by land and sea. Asked about missing family life while travelling far and wide, it was Enrico and Dante whose gentle teasing implied that their employer, being a man of the world, had been looking to find a woman of intelligence as well as beauty. They had meant it, of course, as a compliment, not seeing the significance of the smiles exchanged between the English merchant and his wife. Santo could hardly avoid any mention of his brother Leon, though it became obvious to them all that the two were close, despite their different temperaments.

Aphra was studying the deep wrinkles of a walnut on her plate and would have asked questions of her own. But words seemed to fly past only half-heard, the food tasted of nothing on her palate and the colourful table was merely a blur of shapes. Time dragged on into space, into an echo chamber of sound, into the darkness and beckoning emptiness of years without him. Then she could no longer deny that love, real love, had rushed upon her in all its splendid fury to taunt and hurt her and to tell her that, if she had not already discovered it for herself, she was one of those women for whom love was never a simple act of falling, but more like an anguish and a suffering, and long cold spells of wintery yearning. Sadly, love only offered the balm of time to remedy the situation. Which nobody ever accepted.

When the talk eventually turned to the need for Santo to return to Padua, Enrico and Dante made their excuses to go and continue the packing, leaving the four of them to say yet again what had already been decided, as if to give it a last seal of approval. Aphra's reputation, they agreed, was of paramount importance in a village of this size and, since she was in effect 'Lord of the Manor', she could not afford to ignore damaging gossip, even if Nic and Etta were to remain there for a few weeks. Weeks, she had said? Yes, why not weeks, until the gossip died down? Their concern for her almost brought tears to her eyes.

They had entirely understood, in a way Aphra had refused to, how essential it was to claim his brother's valuable research and return it without delay. For Leon to justify his year of study with Dr Ben and to continue his future profession, he must have access to everything he had learned, of which the two books of notes represented his latest findings. With that argument weighted against her, Aphra was relieved to have already reached that decision, even if not for exactly the same reasons. To wish to hurt him, she told herself, was a perfectly natural reaction and it was not out of pity for Leon she had relented, but for love of his brother. That, too, was a perfectly natural reaction, even though he was not aware of it.

Fortunately for Santo's powers of imaginative truth-stretching, Nic withheld the one question on the tip of his tongue about why Santo had not said what he had come for at the beginning instead of putting it about that he was Aphra's lawyer employed to help. However, Nic suspected the answer to this when he heard how close Aphra had come to shooing him off the estate at their first emotional meeting, for although an air of fragility surrounded her, Nic

knew at first hand of her courage and the quality
of her affection. As for the Italian's offer of help
to unravel the strange and unsettling facts surrounding Ben's sudden demise and his mysterious studies, both Nic and Etta assured them that
they would do everything necessary to get to the
bottom of it. Knowing Dr Ben better than Santo
did, they would be well placed to see things he
might miss.

If more reasons had been needed why Santo
must leave without delay, it came in the form of
an exhausted messenger who clattered into the
courtyard on a sweat-lathered horse as darkness
fell. Suspecting something amiss, Nic offered to
go and find out, returning with one of Santo's
own sailors sent by the captain of the galley still
waiting at Southampton. Santo leapt to his feet.
'What is it, man?' he said. 'Bad news?'

The news poured out in a rush of Venetian dialect that only Santo and Nic could follow. 'Captain wants to know what your orders are, *signor*,'
he said, accepting a glass of brandy from Nic.
'It's the pilgrims. They've been waiting on the
dockside now for three days and nights, and it's
costing them money just to eat. They'll take another galley if we wait any longer, then we shall
be half-empty and…'

'Yes…yes. I can see the problem,' Santo said, imagining the loss of revenue.

'Pilgrims?' said Aphra. 'Is that what he said?'

'Yes, we usually fill up with them on the return journey at this time of year. We take them as far as Spain, then another batch from there to Venice. Some stop there and others go on to Jerusalem. They pay well for the passage.' He turned to her, seeking her acceptance as if it mattered to him. 'I cannot keep them waiting any longer without…'

'No, of course not. You must be away at first light. I'll have some food prepared for your man and a bed for the night.'

'Thank you. I'm afraid I must ask to borrow one of your men to bring back the horses from Southampton.'

'I'll see to it, Aphra,' said Nic. 'You stay here with Etta.'

So, she thought, this was how they must part, with only a kiss to her knuckles and a look from him that held so many unspoken thoughts and, from her, a movement of her lips that tried, and failed, to say goodbye. Had it really all been said? He had got what he'd come for and more besides, and yet again she was left to pine over what more she would like to have given, but could not. She had raised no objection when Nic assumed control, but had been drawn into Etta's embrace, struggling to manage yet another grief that had taken her emotions by storm and left her helpless in its wake.

Rocking her, Etta thought that talking might help. 'Did he make demands on you, dearest?' she whispered, pushing back wisps of hair from Aphra's cheek. 'Was it all a bit too soon...too much...too fast? Men are always in such a hurry for an answer. But he couldn't stay, love. You must see that.'

'I do see that.' Aphra said, trying to hold herself together. 'I do. I do. But I don't know if he'll ever return, Ettie.'

'Did he not say?' Etta said, holding her away with a frown.

'I would not offer him any hope. He thinks it's because of Ben.'

'Ben? How could he think that?'

'I suppose he could hardly think otherwise when I've talked of little else since he came. I think you're the only one who understands how it is with me, when my heart is telling me one thing and my conscience another. I feel I owe it to Ben's memory to find out the real cause of his death and I have no idea how long that might take, Ettie. So how can I invite Santo to return to me while he believes my heart belongs to a deceased uncle, of all things? No man would be encouraged by that, would he?'

'He doesn't think your heart still belongs to Leon, then?'

Shaking her head, Aphra looked down at their entwined hands. 'Whoever said that love remains constant no matter what, was wrong,' she said. 'It doesn't. Why should it? The grief I felt at Leon's behaviour was based on anger, Ettie. Santo has made me see that. I would not cross the oceans for a man such as that.'

'But you would for Santo?'

'Yes, when I've solved Ben's mystery, I would. But not before.'

'Then how will Santo ever know that, dearest?'

The clasp of hands parted for Aphra to cover her face, moaning with the conflict. 'I don't know. Unless I give him something to hope for, I shall lose him.'

'Aphie,' Etta whispered, taking her cousin's wrists, 'Ben would not have wanted this. We all know of his special affection for you, but he was the dearest and most understanding of men. I doubt if he would have regarded Leon's actions in the same light as you do. He liked and trusted him. He could not have been more pleased by what happened between you and Leon, and I'm sure he would be saying to you now, if he were still alive, that Leon must have had very good reasons for what he did. He must be very torn between his love for you and keeping his name as an honourable man. Who would trust him after going back on his word to marry the woman he was betrothed to? His future would be ruined, Aphie.'

'I know… I know…but—'

'But listen,' Etta said, cutting off the direction of Aphra's protest. 'Ben would want you to move on, love, not to waste precious time in delving into matters that will wait. Of all things, he would want your happiness. And if you've found a man who can give you that happiness, then hold on to him, whatever it takes.'

'Ettie, I don't know that Santo loves me. He's never spoken of love.'

Etta sighed, shaking her head. 'Have you not seen his eyes when he looks at you? Have you not seen them glowing with love for you?'

'I've seen them darken with desire,' Aphra said, smiling modestly.

'Tch! Innocent!' Etta said. 'He's an elder son, remember. He's not going to declare his love for you until he knows he's on sure ground, unlike his younger brother who did just the opposite. Neither of you is sure of the other, at the moment.

So if you want him to take some hope with him when he leaves, it's up to you to give him some. One or two words would be enough, dearest. Even if you were to see him off at dawn. Wish him Godspeed? A token, perhaps?'

Aphra nodded, bending her bright head to kiss Etta's knuckles. 'Yes,' she said. 'You're right. A token. I think I can manage that.'

The large complex of priory buildings was quiet and in total darkness except for the faint glow of a single candle in the visiting abbots' house where Santo was preparing for his last night at Sandrock. Aphra had seen it from her own windows and now, as she rounded the corner and entered the spacious fragrant area where the scent of freshly dug soil mingled with that of pungent rosemary, the flickering light lured her on. No plan had formed in her mind. No words, either of explanation or hope. No picture of what she might find. No expectation of welcome, surprise or rebuff. All she knew was that the choking farewell she had attempted after supper would not do. Even if it had been enough for him, it was not enough for her. She must see him, one more time.

Treading quietly so as not to creak the stairs, she was taken aback when, halfway up, the door at the top opened for her as if he had seen her coming. Santo's large figure, lit dimly from behind, moved aside for her to enter, his hand beneath her elbow to ease her over the lip of the door frame, no word passing between them, no smile of satisfaction from him. She was thankful for that.

His hand slid down her arm to lead her nearer to the candle before he leaned over to blow out the flame, plunging her immediately into the intimate warmth of the darkness and the close comforting safety of his arms, telling her that this was what he, too, had wanted. She knew that his smoothing hands over her back would be able to feel, through the soft silk velvet of her night robe, how her body trembled. Then, she felt him gather the long thick tresses of her hair into his hand and hold it up on top of her head, felt the kisses to her neck, then her throat, and it did not occur to her once, neither then nor later, that this was a risk they ought not to be taking.

Linking her arms around his neck, she hung on as her feet left the floor, her body swung up close to his and carried to his bed. Still mouth to mouth, they rolled on to sheets and furs, feather pillows and soft wool blankets, floating on bedding that offered no resistance or hindrance as they disrobed each other in an accommodating tangle of fabrics. Aphra was as eager and enquiring as he, only faintly registering in her mind exactly where their roaming hands might lead as the touch of his upon her skin claimed every fibre of her senses. But it was the warm exciting weight of his body over hers that made her moan with the rapture that anticipates possession. Those moments of thrilling helplessness, of being brought to that point of desire, were quite new to her, making her catch at his hand with a gasp that Santo apparently recognised as inexperience.

He slowed, waiting for her to catch up. 'Do you want me to stop?' he whispered. 'It's not too late, beloved. I shall not take more than you are willing to give.'

'I want to give you something to take with you. Something special.'

'As much as this? Are you sure?'

Moving her hips against him, she savoured the closeness and the tantalising warmth of his skin, his hardness pressing her for an answer, his hand capturing her breast. 'Yes, I am sure. I want to give you this, Santo, before you go. Show me what to do.'

His kisses were soft and gentle upon her face, giving her yet another chance to change her mind, to assess the risk, to see where this might lead. But his skilful lovemaking had already taken her beyond that point and when he whispered, 'Lift your legs...enclose me...yes...like that', she willingly drew him into her with little more than a gasp at the momentary pain before the sweetness of the sensation. Entering a new world of intimately shared delights more exquisite than anything she could have imagined, Aphra knew in her heart that there must be some mysterious reason why she had saved this gift for him alone and that she had been granted these last few hours in which to bestow it, whatever the consequences. Then all thoughts deserted her as the magnificent lover of one night took her through each exciting phase, teaching her to appreciate the experience with every one of her senses, rewarding her with the caresses of his body, making her realise, vaguely, that he was giving to her no less than she was giving to him.

Thrilled by her receptiveness and the subtle signs that her pleasure was soon to reach its climax, Santo's vigorous surge of energy raced through them both in a whirlwind of passion, bringing them quickly to an earth-shattering finale that held them, weightless, for those few last seconds of matchless bliss.

Calling his name while mewing with delighted surprise, Aphra was cradled in his arms, seeking no words to add to the experience. If she wondered, just once, what difference her gift would make to their unspecified relationship, no answer presented itself, not even when Santo murmured the most bewitching endearments, praising her surpassing beauty and her natural ability to give pleasure. He would treasure her gift, he said, for all time.

For all time? She fell asleep before the words could be examined for an exact meaning but, waking later to find herself in close contact with his body, she realised she must be the one to make a move. Stealthily, so as not to wake him, she extricated herself from the warm comfort, found her clothes and kid slippers and pulled them on without making a sound. As a last memento of their night together, she took Santo's brown-velvet cap that lay on the small table ready for his journey. He would surely have another, she told herself before tiptoeing to his side of the bed to place a light kiss upon his brow, insubstantial enough to be absorbed into his dreams.

Back in her own room, she found her maid Tilda in her bed. 'Keeping it warm for you,' the maid said, drowsily moving over. 'You all right?'

'Yes,' Aphra whispered. 'I think so. I don't really know.'

Tilda spooned herself into Aphra's back and

rested her arm in the dip of her waist. 'Try to sleep. You can think about it tomorrow,' she said.

But it was already tomorrow for Aphra and dawn came well before those too-recent memories had settled rationally into the corners of her mind. Nor did the sound of hooves from the courtyard and their gradual fading into the distance do anything to help Aphra's inevitable fears of abandonment.

Chapter Seven

Hoping to hide her secret behind a mask of non-chalance, Aphra had no reply to her cousin's one-word greeting of 'Well?' the next morning before breakfast. They tried to read each other's eyes, but Aphra's gaze fell before the laughter in Etta's. 'Oh, Ettie! Does it show?'

Etta would not tease her. It was much too serious for that. Instead, she drew Aphra into her embrace for the comfort of her understanding. 'Only to me, love. Because I know how you must be feeling. Are you all right?'

It was what Tilda had asked. The reply was the same. 'Yes, I think so. I don't know, really. How does anyone feel at gaining something and losing it at the same time? Bereft?' Then, because she had to speak his name, she whispered into Etta's neck, 'Santo's gone, Ettie. Shall I ever see him again?'

'Of course you will. Now,' Etta said, holding Aphra away, 'the best thing for you will be to tackle the problem of Ben. So let's get breakfast over and then make a start. Shall we? That must take priority. I'm sure we'll find an explanation.'

Lord Somerville was of the same mind, and while their kindly efforts to lift her spirits deserved some positive response, Aphra took them up to her workroom where her first investigations had caused her some concern, if not alarm. But the workroom held other memories for her of how, two nights ago, Santo had made her confront her desires and reveal something of the way her heart had changed course more quickly than she had ever thought possible. Never having thought of herself as impulsive, she now reeled from the suddenness and speed of events, alarmed by self-doubt, thoughts of wanton behaviour and that generosity she had disdained only hours before practising it, this time as great as she could make it. Is that what love did? Take her to the heights of joy before plunging her into emptiness? Would he return? Had she given too much? Again?

'Aphie!' Etta whispered, nudging her gently.

'The keys? We have to get into these cupboards, love.'

'Oh…yes! Sorry.' Sorting through the various keys, she snapped them off the chain and handed them over, pointing out the cupboards so far unlocked, still holding their secrets, however innocent. One of them held shelves of books, many of them in Latin or translated from French, two volumes of antidotes as a guide for students and a volume on aphrodisiacs next to *The Physicians of Myddfai*.

'Aphrodisiacs?' Lord Somerville murmured, glancing through the yellowed pages. 'Why would he…?'

Etta removed it from his hands and replaced it on the shelf. 'Keep your mind on the task, if you please, my lord. He was an apothecary. Remember?'

'Wait,' he said, taking it out again. 'What was that? Cockerels' testicles? Oysters, asparagus, truffles, candied eringo root? Good grief, the list is endless. But what's this?' Reaching into the space behind where the book had been, he drew out a small package wrapped with linen and handed it to Aphra. 'Do you want to see what it is?' he said, softly.

Curiosity overcame her scruples. This was for Ben's sake, not her own, she told herself.

Inside the linen wrapping lay a piece of dark dried wood as long as her thumb and, beneath it, a scrap of parchment with the words *Lignum Sanctae Crucis* written on it. Reading it out loud, she translated, 'Wood of the Holy Cross'.

'I suppose it must have belonged to the priory,' Etta said. 'Not so surprising, really.

'But beyond price,' Aphra said. 'To add to his collection of rare objects.'

By the time she had finished examining it, Nic had removed several more weighty volumes to see what might be hidden behind where only a tall man would have noticed how the cavity contained more parcels. Lifting them out, he placed them one by one on the bench. 'It looks,' he said, 'as if Ben didn't want anyone to see these, whatever they are. Touching the rounded top of the largest item, he offered an opinion. 'I wouldn't be surprised if this was a skull.'

'Oh, Nic!' said Etta. 'What would he want a skull for?'

'As an anatomist,' Aphra said, taking off the linen wrap, 'he might have needed it. But…oh, heavens! You're right, Nic. It is a skull. A woman's, by its size.'

'Or a child?' he said, looking at the white teeth. 'No, those are not a child's teeth. It's a female.'

Aphra and Etta were silent, not wishing to speculate on the reasons why such a thing should be hidden away in Ben's cupboard except for its rarity value. The next item was equally bizarre. 'A goat's horn,' Etta said, turning it over in her hands. 'Looks as if the wide end has been filed.' Touching the white smooth patch, a dusting of white powder was left on her finger. 'Powder of goat's horn?' she murmured.

'Sounds magical to me,' said Nic.

'You must not be frivolous,' Etta said, passing it to Aphra.

'I was not being frivolous, my dear,' he replied. 'The goat has…associations.'

'Associations with what?' Aphra said. 'With magic?'

'Yes. So does the powdered female skull, in some societies.'

Etta and Aphra both frowned at him. 'Are you serious, my lord?' Aphra said.

'My dear, I would not jest about any of this, knowing what it means to you. But from what you've told me so far about his collection of rare and precious things—the gemstones, the Murano glasses, the mistletoe objects, the rare essences, the words pinned to his gown and so on—I cannot help but think that Ben was striving for something beyond the reach of normal pharmacy. None of these things have anything to do with herbal medicine, no matter how much we may want the connection. We have to start thinking of what else this might mean, Aphie. Clearly, you've ruled out his studies of insomnia and pain relief, otherwise he'd not have needed Leon's research to see him through his lecture, would he?'

The two women were silent. Etta sighed, shifting uneasily with a discreet rustle of silk. Aphra touched the tallest item, still wrapped. 'So what will this reveal, I wonder?' she said. 'A rare plant, perhaps?'

As the wrapping fell away with the string that tied it, all they saw was a jar containing two small grey organs with a few fine blood vessels still attached, submerged in a clear fluid. Holding it up to the light made identification no easier until Etta picked up the label threaded on to the string. '"Castoreum",' she read.

'Castor is the beaver,' Aphra said. 'So which bit of beaver is this?'

'Another very expensive item,' Nic said. 'Or so I'm told. If one cannot get hold of what's known as Castor sacs, that is beaver glands, one uses the gall bladder of a dog instead. They look very similar and they're easier to acquire. I have no idea which one this might be, but it's not going to be a herbal cure, is it? What would Ben need it for and why would he hide it away at the back of a cupboard? Did he keep his notebooks somewhere, Aphie?'

'There's one more here,' she said, picking up a flat oblong wrapped in parchment. 'Could this be a book of notes?'

It was not a book, but a small framed portrait of a white-bearded saint whose eyes stared back at them with an expression of deep pity. Beneath, only just visible to Aphra's keen eyes, was the name Saint Valentin. It was obvious, from the discoloured wood at each side, that the saint had been consulted regularly. 'Not a saint I'm familiar with,' she said. 'I know of *Valentine*, but this is not him.' She turned the picture over to look at the back, peering closely at the faded ink in Dr Ben's handwriting. 'Ritual of Three,' she said, reading the words with difficulty. 'Recite three Paternosters and three Ave Marias.' Blankly, she looked at Etta, then Nic to see if it meant anything to them. 'Ritual of Three?'

'Things in threes,' Nic said. 'Those names...'

'The three magi. Three precious gifts. Three wings on the Murano glasses. Three objects made from mistletoe,' she said. 'In other words, the Trinity.'

Etta was examining the piece of wood from

the Holy Cross. 'This has a small hole at one end,' she said. 'Looks as if he may have worn it as a pendant.'

'For what purpose?' Nic said. 'I never got the impression that Ben was any more religious than the rest of us, even though he was brought up by the monks. He was certainly not pious, or he'd not have kept a book on aphrodisiacs, would he?'

'That doesn't follow,' his wife said. 'He would need to know such things. But all this makes me think of the Elixir of Life that so many men seek. Remember Dr Dee and how he was obsessed with the idea? Still is, I suppose. He and Ben would talk for hours, closeted together.'

'Interesting,' Aphra said, looking out of the window. 'That's the way my thoughts have been heading since I began to look into why Ben died so suddenly. I still cannot believe it was simply a problem with his heart. I think it's more likely to have been accidental. Except that Ben was always so careful.'

Succinct as ever, Nic could not contain his opinion any longer. 'Elixir of Life. Elixir of Death,' he said, under his breath. But the two women heard it.

'Oh, Nic!' said Etta. 'We don't know enough to be sure of that.'

'No,' he said. '*We* don't. But I know someone who might.'

'Who? Doctor Dee, you mean? Or Paul?' she said.

'No, Leon. Master Leon of Padua. Sorry, Aphie. But surely you agree?'

'Well,' she said in a small voice, 'knowing that is not going to help us much, is it? I shall not be sending a request for *his* help. Let's see if we can find those notebooks.'

The notebooks, although plentiful and full of information, meant very little to them, even to Aphra whose knowledge of herbs was better than theirs. There were notes in his diary to record two visits from Dr Dee, the Queen's astrologer, and another showing that Ben had been called to London to arbitrate over a dispute of medical negligence, all of which indicated that his reputation had never been better. They packed the notebooks away, still clinging to the only conclusion that seemed to make any sense to them, that Dr Ben's research, beneath a cloak of pain relief, was all about a desire to prolong life by some means more mystical than herbal. Knowing Ben as they did, however, they found it almost impossible to reconcile the dear sensible man they had loved with the strange discoveries made by Aphra and Santo, then by themselves.

And was it only coincidence that Ben's set of Murano glasses had come from a factory owned by Leon's father? Like other skilled men, apothecaries were sometimes paid in kind instead of money, so could they have been a payment from someone in Italy, during Ben's travels?

Later that day, after making an assessment of all the high-value items and substances in Dr Ben's store, stillroom and cupboards, Aphra and Etta went to sit at the table out in the garden. The sky was cloudless, skimming with swallows catching at invisible food. The women wore their hair loose, letting the thick tresses hang down their backs as they raised their faces to the sun. 'We shall be very unfashionably sunburnt,' said Etta. 'And I don't care.'

'Santo will be almost at Southampton by now,' Aphra said.

Etta reached out a hand to her. 'Yes, love. He will indeed.'

A servant brought a tray of glasses, jugs of ale and elderflower wine, warm biscuits and chunks of fruit cake, reaching them only moments before Lord Somerville. 'Just received some news,' he said, stepping over the long bench, 'about your good friend Master Pearce.'

'Oh? He's on the mend?' said Aphra.

'Afraid not. He died this morning. Just spoken to your steward. He seems to have his finger on the pulse of the village. No more trouble from that quarter then, Aphie?'

'May his soul rest in peace,' she whispered. 'That's very sad.'

'They've caught the two men,' he continued, passing a glass of the pale wine over to her. 'In fact, they were not far away, so that will save some time. Wine, or ale, Etta?'

'Does anything move you?' Etta scolded. 'Wine, please.'

Nic's mouth twitched, mischievously. 'Occasionally,' he said. 'Now, Aphra, my dear, tell me how committed you are to finding more out about Dr Ben. You may not wish to send to Leon for help, but there is another way of doing it, you know.' He poured the wine while waiting for Aphra's response, which appeared to be taking some time.

At last, she said, 'What other way? *You* write to him, you mean?'

'No, we don't write. We go. To Italy. To Padua.'

'Nic!' Etta said, sharply. 'Don't tease! You know very well—'

'Wife!' Nic barked at her. 'I am not aware that I have done anything to deserve a reputation for teasing a lady on such a sensitive issue. Well, not lately, anyway. So calm down and allow Aphra to speak, if you please.'

'It's all right,' Aphra said. 'I'm just not sure of what you're suggesting, Nic.'

'I'm suggesting that there's now no good reason why I should not take you to Padua to find out what you need to know. I have ships waiting at the port of London and I'm due for a visit to Venice.'

'Venice?' Etta said, unable to keep the excitement from her voice. '*Venice?* I've always wanted to go there…oh, Nic…do take me… *please*?'

The thudding inside Aphra's chest made her breathless at the thought of having to speak to Leon, to see his wife, his family and, most of all, his elder brother. Here was her chance to ask Leon what he knew and, at the same time, to see again the one from whom each day apart was going to be torture. How could she turn down such an offer? But how could she accept it while her duty as mistress of Sandrock demanded her presence here?

'Ettie,' said her husband, good naturedly, 'Aphra is trying to think. If I might remind you, Aphie,' he said, 'the problem of Master Pearce and his bullying has now disappeared. Your men are more than capable of running the place while you're away, just as they did for Ben. This is the perfect time of year to sail, and I have the means to get us there in reasonable comfort, if you don't mind a few weeks at sea. Of course it would be more than my life is worth to leave my beloved wife behind, so I'm afraid we'd have to take her along…but—'

His beloved wife chose to stop his explanation by launching herself at him in the most unladylike manner, almost strangling him with her arms while covering his face with a thick mantle of hair.

Aphra made a grab at Nic's ale before it was knocked flying. 'It's a very kind offer,' she said, 'but I don't know. I'd like to give it some thought.'

But Etta had already done that. Sitting down close to Nic, she set about planning the voyage and its passengers. 'And we'd have to take Aunt Venetia, Nic. She has family there…we could stay with them…and Uncle Paul could call it a business visit for fabrics…well, yes… Aphie's father, too, for the same reason, and little Flora… she's learning to speak Italian, and…' Suddenly she found that a large strong hand had clamped itself over her mouth, shocking her into silence. Prising it away, she rolled her eyes towards her husband in mock meekness. 'Sorry, Aphie,' she mouthed, her eyes dancing with laughter.

'As I was saying,' Nic said with a stern glance at Etta, 'we could get there and back well before the autumn storms. It seems to me that this is going to be the only way to find out what we need to know. Ben trusted Leon and no one would know more about his studies than him. Now, would you trust me to look after you? We can take your father along, too, if you wish. There's plenty of room on board.'

'Thank you,' Aphra said. 'Yes, Sandrock can do without me for a few weeks and I like the idea of taking my father. I think it might help. And I owe Uncle Paul and Aunt Venetia a favour after cutting short their visit. That would be a nice touch, wouldn't it?'

'So, a day for you to pack and organise things here. A day to reach London. Better send some messages straight away. We can set sail by the end of the week.'

Reaching for cake and biscuits, each of them thought from different angles of the same event. 'Velvets,' Etta whispered, 'and those Italian brocades and Venetian lace. Some of the women bleach their hair in the sun to make it even paler. Did you know that, Aphie?'

Aphra smiled and shook her head, already

imagining too far ahead how the Datini family might regard this invasion—with surprise, embarrassment, or annoyance at the intrusion, perhaps? How would she face the deceiving Leon while asking him for information? Was that really her prime reason for accepting Lord Somerville's offer, or did she dare to admit to herself that it was not so much to solve the mystery of Ben's death, but a chance to be reunited with the man she had come to adore? Yet the terrible doubt lurked in her mind that she was taking a huge risk in supposing that Santo would be pleased to see her. What if he already had a relationship with a woman? She knew so little about him. There had been so little time to find out.

She turned her head to look at Nic, to say to him that, no, this was a big mistake, she could not go ahead with this plan. But Nic's experiences of his wife's mercurial changes of mind had stood him in good stead and now he reached out to lay a hand on Aphra's arm, to let her know that her fears were acceptable, not foolish. 'It's all right,' he said, softly. 'You need not fear. Santo's a good man. So is his brother. You'll see.'

There had been a time, early in their marriage, when Aphra had given Nic some very similar advice, helping him to understand her wayward cousin. Now he appeared to be doing the same for her, letting her know that her private reasons for going on such a voyage were as sound, if not more so, than the reason they would give to the other passengers.

'Yes,' she said. 'Thank you. Whatever the outcome, it will not be wasted, will it?'

By sailing so soon, Nic told them, they would be only a few days behind Santo, although it was anybody's guess which of them might arrive first at Venice, for although Santo's galley was faster than Nic's carrack, it would have to make frequent stops to take on more water and food for the crew and pilgrims. The carrack was large enough to take on board all it needed without stopping once, so it would be sensible, he told them, to take something to do during those interminable weeks.

A day of non-stop preparations was followed by a day on the road, the Somerville cavalcade now augmented by Aphra, Tilda, two packhorses, and two grooms to bring the horses home again. On reaching Aphra's parents in London, it was not too difficult to persuade Sir George to join them, just as Lady Betterton needed none to stay behind. Weeks at sea, she said, were not her idea of adventure, even if Venice *was* at the end of it.

Their visit to Paul D'Arvall and Aunt Venetia was timed to perfection, for it was young Flora's birthday and such an invitation was beyond her dreams. Her twin brother Marius, however, must stay behind for his lessons. The other reason they gave was that such a journey would tax his strength, and though they were adamant, and Marius himself was philosophical, Aphra and Etta could not see why they were being so protective. If Aunt Venetia had had her way, her own packing might have taken an extra week, but the thought of seeing her own family after so many years acted as an incentive to keep to Nic's timetable, especially when Aphra was trying to make amends for their curtailed visit to Sandrock.

Even at thirteen years old, Flora understood what this visit meant to her father and how deeply he had been affected by the death of his brother at their home. She knew he felt he ought to have been present at that moment and that there was still something to be revealed about it, something he ought to have been able to prevent. Her mother, perhaps to comfort him, had disagreed, had said that, if the authorities were satisfied to attribute the death to Ben's heart problem, of which he was aware, then Paul should let the matter rest there. Flora had learnt a good deal by listening, asking questions and saying little, absorbing snippets of information dropped during adult conversation. Intrigued by her lovely cousin Aphra and the recent afflictions of her life, she welcomed the chance to be with her for longer than their last meeting, hoping that, in some small way, she might contribute to her happiness. She would also be meeting her grandparents for the first time. 'I shall practise my Italian on them,' she told her mother, 'if only they will speak to me more slowly than you do.'

In the busy port of London on the wide River Thames, ships of all shapes and sizes sailed on the tide or rocked alongside the many wharves and jetties. Water-washed stairs led directly into warehouses or to garden doors with glimpses of green lawn beyond. Nic's gigantic carrack was amongst the largest of the bulky merchant ships, its high sides towering above them, with even higher decks, fore and aft, like tiers of windowed buildings shining with gold paint on carved mouldings. The two cousins were familiar with such sights, but this was the first time Aphra had been on board one of them and, although Etta had told her of what she might expect, the panelled comfort and luxury of the cabins took her quite by surprise.

But as Tilda bustled about to arrange her mistress's belongings within the compact space, Aphra stood by the multi-paned window that seemed to hang over the murky brown water, letting her mind fly over the hundreds of miles she must sail to reach the man she wanted. Her lips moved in silent prayer as she asked, not so much for her own safety, but that Santo would still want her as much, if not more, as he had on that memorable night when she had given him her most valuable possession.

Like his wife, Nic was well aware of Aphra's true mission as opposed to the alternate one believed by their other relatives. Aphra's father, Sir George Betterton, saw every reason to pursue the mystery surrounding Ben's death and had thanked Nic heartily for making the expedition possible.

For Aphra, there was still time for her to envisage every kind of greeting, welcome, and situation they might find at their journey's end although, as both Aunt Venetia and Etta had said, together they would overcome any obstacles they might encounter, of which Venetia's family would not be one. They would be ecstatic, she assured them. So with such positive speculations to help them, they endured and came to enjoy those weeks at sea during which there was no need for them to call at any port but only to catch sight, very occasionally, of land in the far distance.

There was little to mark their progress except the passing days and nights, each one shortening the time before Aphra would meet Santo. She thought how strange it was that she should now be so desperate to see him again after her earlier insistence that he must leave her and never return. What would the stern father, Signor Datini, think about her sudden appearance after forbidding his younger son to return to her? Would Santo have told him about his feelings for her, whatever they were? Would he accept that a woman's heart could find another love so soon after losing one? Or would he understand that, as a novice, she had at last found the difference between a sweet first love and the earth-shattering emotions of the real kind, capable of turning a cautious careful woman into a determined risk-taker? Obviously, the father was capable of exerting considerable influence over his sons. But would there be a reason, she wondered, for him to forbid Santo from encouraging her? Or would Santo find his own reasons?

Plagued by doubts, fears and flimsy hopes, Aphra's usual patience was tested to the full as each plunge and dip of the carrack took them, mile by slow mile, towards her uncertain future, relieved only by the expectation of learning why her beloved uncle had departed this life so abruptly. That, at least, would be no wild goose chase.

Aboard Santo's galley, the beat of the drum thudded rhythmically above the heads of the crowded pilgrims, many of whom were already collecting their belongings and preparing to climb the ladder to the upper deck, now occupied by row upon row of sweating oarsmen. They felt each pull and surge as the galley moved gracefully past the ancient lighthouse and into the Spanish port of A Coruña. The fresh air and exercise would be a welcome relief after their confinement, although the long trek ahead of them to Santiago de Compostela would tax many to their limits, especially the physically frail, the very young and aged. The voyage from England, by Santo's standards, had been relatively easy but, to these poor souls whose stomachs were not as robust as his, it had been a penance to add to their woes. There had been two deaths already, with the comfort of others always to hand, even in those cramped conditions.

Things would be quite different, however, for the lovely young woman who sat sideways on her grey silky-maned gelding surrounded by her attendants and her luggage. She had waited on the quayside all morning and for the last three days for the sleek galley that sped towards its moorings. She had not given up hope, for Santo had promised that he would, eventually, come to collect her, and Santo always kept his word. Shading her eyes against the glare from the water, she saw the name painted on the bows, *La Speranza*, and knew that, from the other almost identical galleys, this was the one. 'Come,' she said to her attendants, 'the *signor* is here at last.'

Scanning the quay crowded with more pilgrims waiting to embark, Santo saw the one he was looking for, her trim figure perched high above the proud arch of her horse's neck. Well dressed as always, even after a journey of fifty miles, she dismounted ready to greet him, her slender form encased in deep wine-coloured silk that shone gold in the bright light. Her hair was immaculate, too, drawn back from her face and gathered at the back of her head with a jewelled band from which a profuse bunch of red-gold hair sprung in tiny coils, covering her back and shoulders. No one watching this lovely creature assumed for one moment that she would be joining the jostling crowd of eager pilgrims in the smelly hold of any ship.

'I'm late, *madonna*,' Santo called, holding out his hands to her. 'Forgive me.'

Affectionately, they kissed both cheeks and stood back to smile. 'No matter,' she said. 'You're here and safe.'

'Your mission?' he said, still smiling. 'Successful, was it?'

'Interesting. Very moving. We shall not know how successful until we get home. And did you get what you went for?'

'I did,' he said. The smile faded amongst the memories, but thankfully the lady was too preoccupied to notice as she watched her luggage being moved into position.

'Do we sail today, or shall we rest at the inn overnight? I can vouch for the comfort, although...'

'No, you're right,' he said. 'We must not delay. We'll take on water, clean out, reload and get away on the next tide. Your quarters have been made ready.'

Expressing no surprise at Santo's success, the lady prepared to occupy the area in the bows of the galley safely covered over with a stout awning of canvas, as private as one could be on such a ship. Santo's success had not surprised her because, in her experience, this remarkable man was as unfamiliar with any kind of failure as she was to being ignored. So the stares she received as she and her retinue went aboard were, although gratifying, nothing very unusual.

Relieved not to have been delayed a moment longer than was necessary, Santo moved out of A Coruña's harbour on the next high tide, even though his galley relied less on deep water than the larger ships. His oarsmen were not convicts, as many others were, but paid, well-fed and well-treated men who enjoyed the life and the reputation of being the fastest and strongest in Venice. Trained in seamanship, they worked the sails once the ship had left harbour and soon they were skimming through the sea with their new cargo of pilgrims, baskets of fresh food, water, fish newly caught, eels still wriggling, crabs still clambering. And a fair young woman returning home with the hope that her prayers at the shrine of St James might be answered.

With long days and nights at sea behind him, Santo's thoughts returned again and again to that last night spent in Aphra's arms and to the days before that in which her emotions, understandably confused, had veered like the wind in his sails. Pushed to the last few hours of his stay at Sandrock, she had come to him as a homing pigeon finds its roost, revealing to him her needs, giving him what his body craved without bargaining or explaining. No words of love had been spoken, for no doubt she had learned that to do so was almost as dangerous a commitment as the gift of her body and he had not been able to discover whether she would ever give her heart, too, as long as her other love, a certain Dr Ben Spenney, claimed it. So he had not spoken of it, not wishing to force a decision or to ask for more than she was offering. The tragedy was that, with no chance for him to stay there longer and with so many miles now between them, the situation, delicate, fragile and inconclusive, was hardly likely to improve or be resolved. Not for some time, anyway.

One thing he took from it, however, was the certain knowledge that he had been the first to receive her gift. He had not asked his brother about that part of their relationship and Leon had not ventured the information. Nor would he ever have asked Aphra. But now he knew that she, too, would be remembering that night, wondering the same things, reconstructing those ecstatic moments of bliss. By comparison, his own gift to her had been bestowed before in other places, given without any devotion. But Aphra was not one of those casual acquaintances and, although he had willingly pushed that aspect of their loving to the back of his mind at the time, it had come back to haunt him every day since. What if he had made her pregnant? What would his father say to *that*? he wondered. Had he been any less of a fool than Leon?

To the Italians, the begetting of illegitimate children was not frowned upon in the same way as it was in England. At home, even popes fathered them, including illegitimate boys in their wills like those born within the family. But for a woman like Mistress Betterton, such a scandal would send shockwaves through her family, for Santo doubted that any relative of hers would condone such intimacy with the brother of the man who had deceived her, and to become pregnant after such a short acquaintance would never be understood, however much they tried. That he had taken advantage, not only of the situation, but of her parents' absence, too, was bad enough, but to leave her at such a time was worse. Yet he had had little choice, as Signora Margaretta, now comfortably installed on *La Speranza*, would certainly agree.

Those weeks spent at sea in Lord Somerville's sturdy carrack had not been as difficult for his passengers as any of them had first supposed when they were given the chance to get to know each other better than at any other time in their lives. Bearing no grudge against Aphra for cutting short their visit to Sandrock, her uncle Paul and aunt Venetia were happy to discuss Ben and the priory with her while telling her more about their three children, proud but never boastful.

Privately, Venetia believed that Aphra's mission was not quite what she would have them believe and that her relationship with the handsome and charismatic Santo Datini was what occupied her thoughts rather more than Ben's tragedy. Eventually, she said as much to Etta, who would surely know the truth of the matter. She did and, while wording her opinions with the utmost discretion, confirmed that Venetia had got it right, both of them agreeing that neither Venetia's husband nor Aphra's father ought to be party to this information. One never quite knew what men were going to do with women's secrets, did one? So, to establish firmly in her husband's mind that the mission was about his brother and nothing else, Venetia made sure to remind him of this, casually and privately in their cabin, while Flora was 'asleep'.

For herself, Venetia could not understand why any woman would not fall desperately in love with Santo at first sight, as she might have done had not her own Paul kept a close guard on her heart.

As the distant coastline of Italy slipped past them on the port side, Venetia's thoughts turned to their personal appearance, by which she meant Aphra and Etta, her own not having been allowed to suffer from a lack of audience. Or anything else, for that matter. Venetian women, she told them, would never be seen anywhere looking less than their best. Having a husband who worked at the Royal Wardrobe was a good way to stay ahead of fashion, both in England and abroad, though she did not forget that Etta's husband, Lord Somerville, was the one who supplied the Royal Wardrobe with exotic fabrics from Venice.

So now, she told them, they could leave off their starched ruffs for the more comfortable stand-up half-collars of lace, leave off their heavily jewelled hoods in favour of a single jewel or a tiny cap, leave off their farthingales to hold out their skirts and dispense with the layers of flashy jewellery, choosing only one or two of the best pieces for more impact. She knew what she was talking about. The effect of the radiant silks, figured brocades, velvets and gauzy veils, the sleek hairstyles and pearl-covered nets of gold mesh made the three men gasp at the transformation and, as they appeared on deck, the stares of the crew made their efforts more than worthwhile.

Emerging from her cabin into the bright honey-gold sparkle of Venice, Aphra could hardly believe what she was seeing, even though Venetia had tried to prepare her. The buildings, a mass of intricate lace-like patterns, seemed to float on their shimmering reflections under a sky of brilliant blue pierced with towers, pinnacles and domes. Ahead of them at anchor, long wicked-looking galleys with spiky furled sails unloaded their precious cargoes into small boats. In the square of San Marco, swarms of people moved like worker ants stranded on a maze of waterways. She had slept little on the previous night, wondering what she might see, hear and say, knowing the futility of such anticipation, but unable to prevent it. But no overworked imagination could have prepared her for the sparkling brightness, the colours, the elegance and the glassy images reflected on the dancing green waters of the lagoon.

'Magic!' she breathed. 'This is so…beautiful! How could you leave such a place to live in London, Aunt?'

Uncle Paul answered for her. 'Blame me.' He grinned. 'I insisted.'

With no warning of their arrival, Aphra had

assumed that Venetia's family might not appreciate such a large invasion of their hospitality,
though Venetia had brushed off her concerns
with a wave of her hand. 'Nonsense!' she had
said. 'Ca' Cappello is an enormous place. More
rooms than I can count. And they *love* having
guests to stay, especially family. They've never
seen Flora. They'll be *delighted*.'

After more than five weeks at sea, the firm
paving beneath their feet seemed to rock until
their balance was restored. Groups of pilgrims
stood patiently beneath the banners of agents
selling passages to the Holy Land, as gondoliers
took others out to the ships. Shading his eyes,
Lord Somerville scrutinised the names on some
of these, at last striding off towards a group of
merchants to whom he introduced himself, pointing to the nearest vessel. *'La Speranza?'* he said.
'Is that the Datini galley, *signor*?' Without him
noticing, young Flora, eager to hear her cousin's
lordly husband exercise his Venetian dialect, had
followed him and now slipped her hand into his,
standing quietly beside him.

'Indeed it is, my lord,' said one merchant, so-
berly dressed in a calf-length gown with a bulging leather pouch hanging from his belt. 'Lovely
thing, isn't she?'

'Yes. Do you know when she docked?'

'Three days ago. The Datini son was on board. Had a young woman with him. She was a lovely thing, too.' Smiling at the memory, he blew a kiss from his fingertips.

'Really?' Nic said, smiling in reply. 'His wife, was she?'

'Oh, no, my lord. That one will not be marrying for a while yet. Too busy. No, I don't know the lady, but noble, from the look of her. They went off straight to Padua, I believe. That's where the Datini live in summer. Where do you and your daughter stay?'

Conspiratorially, Nic squeezed Flora's hand. 'With the Cappellos,' he said.

As he slid his smile towards Flora, the merchant's assumptions took flight. 'Ah,' he said, 'of course. This young lady has the looks of a Cappello, *sì*?'

'*Grazie, signor,*' Flora said, dimpling at him. 'My mama's looks.'

The smile was indulgent now. 'Fortunate papa,' the merchant said, winking.

Nodding to the men, Nic led Flora away, almost bumping into Aphra in the crowded square. 'Three days ago,' he said, 'so he didn't linger. Good timing.'

'He's here, then?' she said, looking about her

as if he might be somewhere in the crowd. 'Here in Venice?'

Like a brother, he linked her arm through his as they watched Flora skip back to her mother. 'In Padua,' he said. 'I shall send a message to them to tell them we're here and wait to hear when they wish to receive us.'

'And if they don't want to?' she whispered.

Trapping her arm tightly against him, he soothed her like a child. 'Of course they'll want to, Aphie. Why would they not? We shall be with you. Our business with them is perfectly legitimate. Remember?'

Our business. 'Yes,' she said, smiling as they reached Flora, who was excitedly telling her mother, as far as she was able, what the merchant had said. Venetia's expression was hard to read as it changed from a frown to a darting glance of concern at Nic, then to a rather forced smile at Flora's probably mistaken Italian.

'Quale?' Venetia said.

'What?' Aphra said.

'Nothing,' Nic said. 'Come on, let's get a move on. I'm starving. Paul, get one of the men to hail a gondola for us, will you? And find out from Venetia where Ca' Cappello is. Flora, my dear, I think you'll have to carry little Grace now. She's getting thoroughly confused.'

Venetia glanced down at the shivering little Italian greyhound. 'She's not the only one,' she murmured.

Signora Angela and Signor Pietro Cappello were on the first floor of their beautiful old house overlooking the Grand Canal and so were afforded a good view of their unexpected guests' arrival before the servants. Well, Angela was. 'Do you know, Pietro,' she said, 'that looks remarkably like our Venetia down there.'

'Oh, more than likely,' said her elderly but remarkably sharp husband. 'After all, she lives only a few hundred miles away.' He continued to read his book through a very large magnifying glass made on a nearby island. He was used to his wife's pronouncements by now. He owned a pair of leather-bound spectacles, too, made on the same island, but they had recently made a sore place on his nose.

But when his wife crossed the room to the reception hall, he recognised something in her purposeful step, lowered his book, then stood up to follow her, hearing the sound of voices from below. A female called, then an answering shriek from Angela, and before Pietro could register through bleary eyes who was who, figures surged up the grand staircase from the offices below into the clear glossy hall, its shining floor reflecting a sea of colour from their skirts.

Neither of the elderly couple, however, would admit to complete surprise. 'We knew you'd come, one day,' they said, hugging their daughter and her husband. Their joy at seeing Flora for the first time was very moving for all of them. 'Such a beautiful child,' they said, forgetting how a girl of thirteen was fast leaving childhood behind. 'How old, now?'

'Where are the boys?'

'And Lady Somerville...how like Elizabeth!'

'And Mistress Aphra...we've heard...'

'My lord...welcome...and Sir George...'

The excited chatter flowed fast enough to sweep away, for a time, Aphra's concerns about whether their visit to Padua would be as successful, or as appreciated, as this one.

Later on, after they had been shown to magnificent bedrooms, she had intended to ask Flora what the Italian merchant had said, but found that her father had already mentioned the Datini family to Pietro Cappello as they sat round the table. 'Oh, yes,' the old gentleman told them, putting down his glass of wine. 'I was over at San Marco when the Datini galley came in. I didn't realise the eldest son had been away until I saw him come ashore. I don't have much to do with them, you see. They're not in my line of business. Luxury goods, you know. I deal in silks.'

Having been taught to add something to the conversation, within the family, Flora put her social skills to the test. 'We're told that Signor Datini had a beautiful young lady with him, Grandfather. Did you see her? They said she was *una bellezza*,' she said, using the exotic words with gusto. 'Was she?'

Her mother sent an apologetic glance in Etta's direction.

The hairs on Aphra's head prickled as her heart thudded uncomfortably within her bodice. Her knife clattered on to her plate before she could lay a hand over it.

'Now that,' Pietro said, 'is not something I am able to confirm or deny, Flora, my dear. My eyes do not see what they used to when I was younger. But if I were you, I would beware of accepting all that Italian merchants say. Anyway, you're off to visit them at Padua, so you'll be able to see for yourself, won't you?'

The room was suddenly very quiet and it was Angela who sensed that there was something here not to be developed further. 'Sir George,' she said, 'I understand you supply your young

Queen with Venetian fabrics. What does she prefer, these days?'

But although the conversation resumed easily enough, Aphra felt physically sick at the thought of Santo and his beautiful companion within the intimate confines of a galley, day after day, week after week.

Chapter Eight

At any other time, the well-appointed bedroom lined with tapestries would have received all Aphra's attention, but now she stood by the arched window where light reflected on her face from the water below. 'I knew it, Ettie,' she whispered through her fingers. 'I knew there must be somebody. Why could he not have said?'

Placing herself on the cushioned window seat in front of her cousin, Etta tried her best to produce the alternative view. 'Dearest, there could be any number of reasons why she was there. She may be his sister…'

'He *has* no sister.'

'…or a cousin, or just a friend.'

'Hah! A young and beautiful friend.'

'You cannot jump to conclusions like this,

Aphie. He has shown his feelings for you. You should not doubt him, but give him a chance, love. I'm sure it's all perfectly innocent.'

'Has Nic sent a message?'

'To Padua? Yes, but it's quite a way, so the messenger won't be back until dark. We may as well let Venetia show us round and let Tilda get on with your unpacking.'

'Ettie, I think this has been a dreadful mistake.'

Etta stood to place her arms around Aphra, willing the situation to be better than it appeared. 'Hush now,' she said. 'This is not like you. Try to concentrate on the other matter. That's why your father and Uncle Paul have come, isn't it? We don't want them to get diverted with anything else at present. We have to find out what we can about Ben.'

'Yes, you're right, love. One thing at a time. I'm strong, Ettie, and we've come through heartaches before, haven't we?'

Etta held her by the shoulders to look into the grey eyes rimmed with black that gave so much away about her feelings that it was almost impossible for her to hide behind them, as others often could. 'Aphie, this is not going to be a heartache. There's a simple explanation. Santo is trustworthy. You *must* believe it.' A gentle shake made

Aphra look at her and smile, at last. 'There, see? That's better. Come on, let's start enjoying ourselves. Where does this door lead, I wonder?'

It was not until bedtime that Aphra was given the chance to dwell on what she might encounter on the morrow. Although she had not expected to sleep well, the feather bed that neither rocked nor lurched, the complete silence beyond the window and the good food and wine of the meal brought sleep almost immediately.

Downstairs in the comfortable salon where only the last shouts of the gondoliers broke the silence, Venetia and Paul sat with their hosts, laughingly apologising for the invasion, but happy to be here, at last. As Pietro and Angela Cappello had suspected, however, the surprise visit had a hidden agenda which, out of politeness, they deserved to know.

'We didn't want to discuss it over our meal,' Venetia said. 'We've had over five weeks to talk about the whys and wherefores, and although Aphra is keen to know what Dr Ben was up to, it's Paul who really *needs* to know more about his brother. This business has really begun to concern him, since they told us what they'd found.'

'Your brother,' said Angela, taking her husband's knobbly hand in hers, 'came to stay with us some years ago, didn't he? He's the one who dashed in and out as if we were an inn for travellers. We saw very little of him, really.'

'Very clever man,' said Pietro, nodding sagely. 'What's the problem?'

So in the soft evening light that washed pink ripples over the wooden shutters, they sat together to hear the story that neither of Venetia's parents had known, about Aphra's connection with the younger Datini, Dr Ben's death, Santo Datini's visit, their own visit to Sandrock, the lecture notes and what they had discovered that was puzzling them.

The death of Dr Ben saddened them, prompting Pietro to recall how, on one rare evening of conversation just before Ben's departure, they had shown him a set of Murano drinking glasses because he had been telling them how he was making a collection of rare objects. 'He told us it was a pastime of his,' said Angela, 'and how he regretted he'd not had time to visit Murano. His ship was to depart the next day.'

'Yes, we thought that was a sad omission,' said Pietro, 'so on the spur of the moment, we gave our set to him. He protested, of course, but he accepted them.'

'He was overjoyed,' said Angela. 'Shed tears

of gratitude, I remember, as if his life depended on owning them. We were glad to have parted with them to such a brilliant man. I'm so sorry he's gone.'

'So he didn't pay you for them?' said Venetia.

'Oh, no, dear. Certainly not. They'd been given to us as a wedding present by Pietro's old aunt, so we hadn't paid for them either. We rarely used them. Didn't care for them much. Too ostentatious. Nor did we bother to replace them. Not at our time of life. We had them packed up in wool and they went off with his luggage.'

'Well,' said Paul, 'only a few weeks ago, Venetia and I drank from them at Sandrock Priory.'

'The same set? Are you sure?' said Pietro.

'Positive. Santo Datini was there, too. He said they'd come from his father's glass factory on Murano. Told us how they were made, but no one knew how they'd got to Sandrock.'

'The world is getting smaller these days,' Pietro said, wistfully. 'We knew he was your brother-in-law, Venetia dear, which is why we were happy to receive him, but not for a moment did we think the glasses would be so significant to his collection. What did you call this obsession with the number three, Paul?'

'The Ritual of Three, Aphra called it,' Paul replied. 'Don't ask me what it's all about. We shall be hoping for some answers tomorrow, if the Datini family will co-operate with us.'

'I shall see you travel safely, then,' said Pietro, smiling, 'and in some style.'

Word had come, said Pietro Cappello on the next morning, that Signor Datini would be happy to see them. Happy, that is, in the polite sense, for the wording of the letter had a slightly defensive ring to it. Signor Datini could not guess the reason for their visit unless, perhaps, it was to clarify the situation after his younger son's previous unfortunate relationship with Sir George's daughter. If this was so, he would be happy to explain the matter further.

'I would have thought,' said Sir George as they sat at breakfast, 'that Santo had already made our feelings known about that. It is not something we need to discuss further. Now, my child,' he said to Aphra in his fatherly tone, 'will you have a little of this, whatever it is?'

'It's butter, Father,' she said, rolling her eyes.

The restful night had helped to calm her nerves, as had her first warm bath for weeks. Tilda had made ready one of her most attractive dresses, pale gold brocade with long slashed sleeves that showed the white linen undergown at elbow, arm and frilled wrist. Over this she wore a long sleeveless gown of pink velvet that hung straight to the floor, a more comfortable style, she thought, than the profusion of bones and wires she was used to. Her hair had been parted in the centre, then coiled up to fit snugly to her head at the sides and back, Tilda having been instructed by Angela's maid. Her only adornment was a pair of long gold and topaz earrings that set off the honeyed tones of her skin. Subconsciously, she hoped to make a good impression on the Datini parents by her sophisticated appearance whilst at the same time showing Santo something other than the working dress he had seen so often.

Etta had chosen a similar style in blue, while Aunt Venetia's blonde maturity was enhanced by a silken grey-violet, but now all three had left off those stiff black-velvet hoods that hid their hair. Showing off their enviable fairness, they attracted more than the usual attention as they were taken along the Grand Canal and across to the mainland in Signor Cappello's impressively fine gondola worked by two uniformed gondoliers. From this point, the River Brenta had been converted into a canal that continued all the way to Padua, a distance of some twenty-two miles through summer landscapes, under bridges and past the fine villas of wealthy Venetians. Heads turned this way and that as Aunt Venetia pointed out the sights, the gardens, the towns and palaces with their elegant boats.

Sir George kindly took Aphra's hand upon his lap, sensing her anxiety. 'If Master Leon is at home,' he said for her ears only, 'don't let it concern you, love. And don't let your hurt show. What's done is done. We'll not find out what we need to know about Ben and his necromancy unless we can talk as friends.'

'Is that what you believe, Father? That Ben was practising magic?'

'This Elixir of Life theory,' he said, 'sounds likely, but how well your findings tie in with magic, only Leon will be able to pass an opinion. After his experience with Ben, he'll soon be in line for some teaching post at the university, I don't doubt.'

'You may well be right, Father,' she said. She had purposely not told him that Santo had been sent to collect his brother's research notes, but Nic had unwittingly parted with the information while they were at sea, causing Sir George to show a certain indignation that he and Lady Betterton had been misled about the reason for Santo's visit, which they had thought was merely to enquire about Aphra's welfare. Fortunately, Nic had been able to see both sides, pointing out to Sir George that neither Santo nor Leon had known about Dr Ben's death when he set out for England, so had not expected his niece to be at Sandrock, making the success of his visit so much more complicated. He could quite see, of course, why Leon would need his notes rather urgently, for such a bright scholar would have great ambitions. He could also see how the Datini family might, even now, be assuming that this visit was more to do with Aphra and Leon than with Dr Ben. Sir George and Lady Betterton's occasional attendances at court had, however, kept their diplomatic skills well exercised, though Sir George knew that his daughter would need all her courage, too.

At this time of the morning, the perfect geometry of the gardens at the Villa Datini was empty of all except the two brothers who strolled along the gravel pathways, stopping and starting, deep in discussion. Or was it an argument? 'I've told you,' the elder brother was saying, 'I know no more than you do, Leo. This is a complete surprise to me, too.'

Leon pulled his long dark gown away from the low-growing edge of the plot. His dress marked him as a student, as did the high collar and small round beret capping his dark hair, though none of the usual epithets flung at 'scruffy students' ever applied to him. 'Did Mistress Betterton give you no indication that she might come? None at all?' he said.

'No. None at all. But it looks to me as if the cousin and her husband who arrived just before I left may have persuaded her to follow it up.' It was a slip of the tongue that he instantly regretted.

'Follow *what* up?'

Santo's dark eyes narrowed, searching the extensive garden for a reason. Leon had stopped, challenging him to explain what he would rather not. 'Your decision,' Santo said, lamely, knowing Leon's keen mind was unlikely to be fooled by that.

'Wait a moment,' Leon said, laying his long fingers over Santo's sleeve. 'There's something here you're not telling me, isn't there? You've been home three days, Sant, and in that time all you've said about her is that she's now living at the priory, hoping to continue growing the herbs. Not once have you mentioned her state of mind, her beauty, her gentle character...nothing! Were you so unimpressed by such a lovely creature, or is it that you're hiding something from me? From us all?'

'No, of course not. I *was* impressed. Of course I was. Who wouldn't be?'

'So what happened?'

'Look… Leo… I've done what you wanted. I've got your notes back. Now leave it!'

'No, I won't leave it! You got the notes, but you didn't say *how*. Well, now we're alone you can tell me. *Tell* me, Sant. Did you threaten her? Seduce her?' He stopped and gasped, open-mouthed. 'My God! You *did*! You *did*, didn't you, you bastard! Did you think that was the only way to get what you wanted?' He let out a roar, almost incoherent with rage. *'She was mine!'* Grabbing at the two edges of his brother's jerkin, he pulled at him, then with a mighty shove pushed him away, ready to swing a clumsy fist.

But Santo was faster and more powerful. To stop his brother's rage, he swung first, landing a hard thud on Leon's cheek that knocked him backwards over the low hedge and into a bed of spiky lavender. The sight of his younger brother lying in a bed of flattened lavender with a hand over his face, too distressed to retaliate, almost broke his heart.

How could he ever tell him how it had been at Sandrock, that he'd had no need to seduce this beautiful, tender, passionately angry woman, that she had offered herself without reservation, and that he had taken her gift as her farewell, neither of them able to predict their future, either together or apart. To give Leon the facts without any of the details would do neither of them any favours for, to his ears, it would sound quite out of character and loveless. And that word, love, was the one neither could be sure of in the other and Leon had lost out for good.

Stepping into the lavender behind Leon, Santo heaved him to his feet, almost lifting him on to the path. 'Come on, Brother. This won't do. Let me look.' Tenderly, he pressed his handkerchief, meant only for show, on to Leon's damaged face and held it there with his other hand behind his head.

'My beret,' Leon mumbled.

'I'll get it. Hold that. There, you'll be all right.'

'I shall *not* be all right. You bastard, Sant. You had no need to take her—'

'Shut up! It wasn't like that. It had nothing to do with the notes.'

'But she let you have them. You didn't tell her about Bianca and me?'

'No. She didn't want to discuss you. Wouldn't hear your name.'

'Thank you for that,' Leon mumbled into the kerchief. 'So why is she coming all this way, then? To see…oh…no! She cannot be! No…no!'

His eyes were darkly furious and wild. With one of them rapidly closing up, he glared at Santo.

'No, it can't be that,' said Santo. 'There's not enough time elapsed since…'

'Since what? Since you bedded her? How many times? Did you—'

'*Shut up*, Leo! I've told you, it was *not* like that.'

'So what *was* it like? I never took her that far. I had too much respect for her. You've always had it too easy, Sant. Did you promise her marriage, too?'

'No. I didn't promise her anything.'

'Oh, well done!'

'It was not well done, Leo. And please don't tell Father about this.'

Leon examined the kerchief, then touched his eyelid gingerly. 'I can't go to class looking like this,' he said. 'As for not telling Father, it sounds as if neither of us will need to, if that's the reason she's coming.'

'I don't believe it *is* the reason. I don't believe she's coming to see either of us, actually.'

'What? Why not? Why else would she come with all the rest of them to back her up?'

'It's more likely to do with Dr Ben. I think he's the only reason she'd come all this way. Not for you. Not for me. But for Dr Ben Spenney, who left her the priory in his will.'

Leon stared at him through one eye, his other now completely closed and puffy. His red nose, his finely chiselled features and tanned skin turning blotchy after their ill usage added more disturbance to the dark shadows beneath his eyes. Santo had been shocked to see how the laughter had disappeared from them since his return to Italy. This impending visit would do nothing to ease the burden weighing on Leon's heart and now he himself wished that Aphra had not taken this decision at this particular time to compound Leon's troubles. It could not possibly help matters. What was more, he did not agree with Leon's fears that he might have made her pregnant. It was much too soon to know that.

Placing an arm around Leon's shoulders, he drew him along the path towards the vine-covered *allée* where a wooden bench ran through the centre to the far end. 'Come and sit a while,' he said, 'and I'll tell you why I think so.' But whatever it was that Santo wished to reveal, if only to clarify his own thoughts, was not said after all, for as soon as Leon sat, his body and his head fell forward into his hands. 'Don't,' Santo whispered. 'Oh…don't…please!' His hand stroked tenderly over his brother's back, feeling

the shaking sobs while the deep muffled roars
of despair mingled with the mocking laughter of
tinkling water in a nearby fountain.

None of the occupants of the large gondola
had quite appreciated how long the journey to
Padua might take, nor had the elder Cappello
remembered to warn them. The gondoliers expected to rest. Stops were required for refreshment. There were delays through the waterside
towns of Oriago and Dolo, as well as sightseers
at the huge villas that lined the canal. And so, by
the time they had reached the outskirts of the university town and the last of the grand mansions,
Villa Datini, it was well into the afternoon with
some voiced concerns about a return in daylight.

Sir George was not one of them. 'There will
be plenty of places to stay in Padua,' he said,
'if the Datini family don't offer us hospitality.'

The villa could be seen from the stone steps
leading up to an imposing arch from which steps
led to a veranda overlooking a perfect pattern of
plots. Vases, statues, fountains and seats punc-
tuated the design beyond which the main building was set against a background of colonnades,
bushes, trees and hills that brought the countryside right to the edge of the garden. A wide
stream of water rushed along one side to fall like

a fold of satin into the canal, while on the other side stood a raised summerhouse with open sides from which a couple descended to greet them, unsmiling, but eager.

To Flora's disappointment, they spoke in perfect English, introducing themselves as Lorenzo and Juna Datini, parents of Santo and Leon whose good looks could now be understood more easily in the light of this handsome pair. Stately, broad-shouldered and square-jawed with a head of thick white hair, Lorenzo Datini would be the exact model, Aphra thought, for his eldest son, whereas Leon favoured his mother's light frame and gentle features. Like Aunt Venetia, Juna Datini wore her years graciously, her silvered dark hair drawn back into a net of gold, her brocade gown the colour of new grass. Looking into her eyes was like looking into Leon's before he and Aphra had parted, though now they held a reserve and some caution.

As the senior member of the party, Sir George performed the introductions, beginning with Baron and Lady Somerville, whose titles usually lent some gravitas to any performance. Aunt Venetia saw no harm in pointing out the Cappello connection, a family of whom they were aware, and her husband, Paul D'Arvall, who was the elder brother of the late Dr Ben Spenney, their younger son's tutor and mentor in England. This caused a long studied perusal as if to find something in Paul of the brother they'd heard so much about.

Finally, it was Aphra's turn to be scrutinised, an ordeal for which she had been preparing all the weeks of her voyage, for now the Datini parents would be able to see, at last, the woman they had forbidden their son to return to. And although she had now accepted the reasons for this, there was still a tender wound on the surface of her heart that resented the enforcement that had affected her so deeply at the time. So it disturbed her very little if they still believed she had not recovered from it, though it would have helped her to know if Santo had told them anything about the relationship he and she had formed. On the other hand, she had told herself repeatedly, if he had said nothing about this, that would surely indicate that the woman who had travelled with him was already one of the family and not to be informed of Santo's romantic capers while on his brother's business.

As if she had needed the advice, Sir George had suggested to her that it would be best to allow the Datini elders to bring up the subject of Dr Ben in their own time, which would be the perfect opening, he said, for her to say why they had requested a meeting. Since this would have to include Leon, Aphra hoped that, by the time he appeared, his parents might have warmed to her by a few degrees, or at least lowered the guarded looks they gave her as she rose from her curtsy.

Their heads bowed in response. 'Mistress Betterton,' they said.

'*Signor. Signora.* Thank you for receiving us.' She felt their eyes picking over every detail of her dress and silently thanked Aunt Venetia and Etta for their guidance.

Indicating the elevated summerhouse, Signora Datini led them up the stone staircase into the open room where, above them, a richly painted ceiling showed a hunting scene. In the centre of the room was a table covered with white linen and an array of cold foods, the covers of which were being whisked off by servants as they entered. Seated in strict order of precedence, Aphra found herself placed between her father and Etta, midway between her hosts at each end, and for some time as the sumptuous meal got under way, the conversation concerned their voyage, their well-being and the Cappello connection. All very neutral in content.

Flora yawned and was nudged by her mother until Signora Juna noticed Grace, and was instantly taken by her. From then on, Flora was given the chance to try out more Italian words and it was she who unwittingly became the catalyst that kept the innocuous conversation flowing, feeding their hosts with information, including the fact that her Cousin Aphra was now the new mistress of Sandrock Priory, once owned by their dear departed Dr Ben. At which Venetia laid a hand on Flora's arm with, 'That's enough now, Flora. Eat your peach.'

Signor Lorenzo was the first to recover from the surprise. 'We were not aware that you are now the new *owner* of the priory, Mistress Betterton,' he said. 'We assumed you simply lived there. Of course, we heard of the sad death of your uncle… your *brother*,' he said, turning to Paul. 'Please accept our condolences. He was much revered here by the university scholars and tutors. A great loss.'

'Indeed, *signor*. He is a great loss to us, too,' Paul replied.

'May I ask the circumstances, sir? Or is it too painful still?'

Paul dabbed at the corners of his mouth with his napkin. 'My brother was staying with our family in London at the time,' he said. 'It came as a shock to us.'

Glancing round the table, Signora Juna took advantage of the lull. 'Shall we adjourn into the house?' she said to her husband. 'We can sit there in comfort without being plagued by midges all evening. That's one of the pests we have to endure when we live so close to the water.' She smiled at her guests and led the way, taking Flora by the hand and speaking to her in Italian, slowly, to her delight.

A double outside stairway reached over the ground-floor offices up to the grand salon, shining and glittering with glass, cool marble floors, brass chandeliers and painted wood, tapestries and swags of velvet, tiles and marble busts of ancient Greeks and Romans, small tables and cushioned cross-legged chairs and stout chests. Aphra compared this elegant luxury with her own medieval priory, its small rooms and little windows of green glass, and wondered if Santo and Leon had been amused by the difference. Even their gardens were spotlessly clean and clipped.

Signor Datini was intent on resuming the earlier topic of conversation while Aphra wondered at what stage the brothers might appear and why they had not done so already. 'You say your brother's death came as a shock, Master Paul. By which you mean it was unexpected?'

'Totally unexpected,' Paul said, taking an upright wooden chair next to Venetia.

'Perhaps,' said Nic, 'this might be a good time

to explain to Signor and Signora Datini that Dr Ben is the purpose of our visit.' He spoke with quiet authority.

Lowering his head a little, rather like a doubting magistrate, Lorenzo Datini peered at his lordship, then at Paul, then at Sir George, all of whom stared respectfully back at him while taking note of his frown. 'The purpose?' he said. 'I had assumed that Mistress Betterton had come to take issue with our youngest son, or perhaps to seek some recompense for...well...' Whether he meant it or not, his eyes flickered over her torso, as if he had missed something.

'Signor Datini,' said Aphra, interrupting him, 'I can see that your eldest son has not yet talked with you about his visit to Sandrock. If he had, I am sure you would have known by now that there is nothing further from my mind at the moment than taking issue with anyone in your family, not for any reason at all, nor would I have wished to trouble you with a request for some help in the matter of my beloved uncle's untimely death if there had been any other way for us to discover what went wrong during his stay in London.' It was a very long sentence after her previous silence, so she made it last, speaking slowly and clearly.

Then she took advantage of their rapt attention to continue. 'Unfortunately, there is only one person who may be able to help us, who may possibly know more than we do about the research Dr Ben was working on when he met his death. It was generally believed that he was investigating the problems of insomnia and pain relief. Indeed, this is what he was going to lecture on at the Apothecaries' Hall the next day, but I have found cause to believe that his research was veering in very strange directions which none of us can find an explanation for. The notes he was apparently going to use were those your son left behind for that very purpose. Yes, they were good enough for Dr Ben to use for his lecture. Master Leon's own notes. Naturally, he wished to have them back to continue his studies and obtain his final degree, and this I agreed to. What we now need to know is whether your son can tell us anything about Dr Ben's research that might put our concerns to rest, one way or the other. We are not convinced, you see, that Dr Ben's so-called heart problem was the cause of his death.'

'So called?' said Signor Datini. 'Whose diagnosis was this?'

'It was his own,' said Paul. 'As a medical man, he recognised the symptoms. The officials decided there was no need for an inquest, since my brother had informed me of his suspicions. He even discussed his will with me. It was only later when my niece began to examine his belongings at Sandrock that she began to suspect that the talk of a heart problem might be a cover for something more sinister. Especially as my brother had never spoken about his heart to anyone but me. We wondered if he might have mentioned it to your son when he was in England, since they had become close friends and colleagues, but we have no way of knowing this unless we are allowed to ask him, here, in Padua.'

If there was a note of censure in Paul's last remark, the Datini parents did not take the bait. But now another Datini had joined the group, appearing silently from the shadows to lean on a marble pillar, his arms folded across his wide chest, his eyes gliding over the company, recognising them, stooping down to fondle Grace's silky ears. She sniffed at his feet and trotted back to sleepy Flora.

His father glanced at him. 'Join us,' he said. 'You know our guests, do you?'

Santo stepped forward into the room, his grey-velvet tunic catching the last pink rays of light from the sky. 'Signor Padre. Signora Madre,' he said, bowing respectfully to his parents. 'Honoured guests. Welcome to Padua.'

'Your mother and I have already done that, Santo. Where were you?'

Santo chose to ignore the reprimand. 'My brother sends his regrets,' he said. 'He is not well, but will join you tomorrow. Do you stay in Padua overnight, Sir George?'

'We shall find somewhere to stay nearby,' Sir George said. 'Our business is with Master Leon, so with your permission, *signor*, we shall hope to see him tomorrow.'

'Then you must stay here with us,' Santo's mother said to Venetia. 'Mistress Flora is almost asleep. It would be such a pity to disturb her. Follow me, *signora*. I have rooms always ready for guests.'

If Santo had been away from home when they arrived, Aphra thought, there would presumably have been an explanation for not coming immediately to greet her, to smile an assurance that all was well, that she had done the right thing in coming. But he *had* been here and decided not to join them, which was as clear an indication as she could ever need that he was not as eager to see her as she had been to see him.

A cold numbing fear swept across her heart, making her arms prickle, making the soft subdued colours of evening swirl madly before her, shapeless, like a grey fog. She felt sick. She wanted to run to him and beat at his chest, to make him take her in his arms and to soothe away those terrible memories of rejection she knew so well. Now they were with her again and, this time, she did not think she would recover, for this man had become part of her, once, and she was his for all time.

The arrangements to accommodate them, so kindly meant, passed over her head as she heard Santo's father ask him where Leon was in a simple Italian she could understand. 'I put him to bed,' Santo replied.

'Has he eaten?'

'Just a little.'

'And Bianca?'

'Margaretta is with her. She'll stay.'

Aphra pretended not to hear, but looked away, refusing to catch Santo's eyes. So, this Margaretta. Was she the woman he'd brought back home on his galley? Would she be obliged to meet her? Had he made love to her, too? Had he held her under him and shown her those same visions of ecstasy he'd shown her, just once? Had those hands caressed and explored this woman, since that night at Sandrock? Did it mean so little to him, then? Had those endearments been learned by rote, used for years in other brief encounters? How she wished she had not come here, forcing herself into this ridiculous situation where she had to pretend that Ben's tragedy was more important to her than seeing Santo again, hearing his voice, tasting his kisses.

It was obvious to her now that he had said nothing to his parents about their relationship, yet another indication that she was not, after all, to be a part of his life. But then, she had given him little hope, had she? Only that one precious gift which apparently had not been enough to convince him of her commitment. For some time now she had thought that Santo and his brother would never display the same duplicity. She had given him the benefit of the doubt. Now she saw how mistaken she had been. How naïve and trusting. And what a fool, too.

The guest room she had been given overlooked the garden at the front of the house where the set of four windows opened on to a stone balcony above the outside stairway. The problem of luggage, or lack of it, concerned Signora Juna not at all, for she had everything they could possibly need for an overnight stay. She was, she told them, quite used to unexpected guests staying longer than intended, though she said it so graciously that they felt no awkwardness. Etta had come for a chat before saying goodnight, telling

her that of course Santo could not have spoken
to her this evening with a father like *that* watching them. Santo was obviously choosing his moment, Etta suggested, and as Leon was unwell,
would surely wish to be with him. Aphra was
unconvinced.

The room was beautiful and fragrant with
scents from the garden. The distant tinkle of
water drew her to the window where the plots,
bathed in moonlight, were laid out like tiles on
a palace floor. Such a lot to be explored, she
thought, wondering if Leon grew herbs here. A
shadow moved into the central pathway, a man
of Santo's stature, standing quite still to face her
window. She knew he had seen her. He turned
and walked towards the summerhouse where
they had dined earlier. He meant her to follow,
to go down and meet him there. But by now the
wall of rejection and hurt was growing steadily
around her heart, building on previous founda-
tions, stout and protective.

Let him sit there alone. Go to bed. Taste the
cup of bitterness once more. Let him think you
came for Ben's sake, not his. Love is for fools.

She had slept badly and fitfully, and at dawn
she dressed in the nightrobe left for her use and,
without waking Tilda, crept downstairs and

across empty salons and out into the pale slumbering garden. Walking quietly round the edge, she reached the stone summerhouse and climbed the stairs from where she could see more than she had yesterday. She saw, however, more than she had expected when Santo greeted her from a corner bench, wearing the same suit of grey velvet, his shirt open at the neck to contrast sharply with his tanned skin and unshaven chin. 'You're late,' he said, almost whispering.

'You've been here all night?'

'All night. You came to me once before at night. Remember?'

'No. Why should I? Perhaps I should not have come here at all.'

He uncoiled himself from the corner. 'Where, here? Or Italy?'

'Both. I was foolish enough to think you might have said something about me to your parents. Not knowing how much they know makes things difficult for me.'

'I've been back home only four days, Aphra. I don't part with all my news to my father so quickly. You've seen him. A cynic. Plays by the rulebook. No imagination. Everything is black or white to him. He would not understand.'

Aphra was still standing and uncomfortable at being here with him after expecting at least another day of non-communication. She had not prepared herself for this. She looked round for a place to sit. Her legs were suddenly weak and she knew now how it felt to be at a disadvantage as a guest, as he had probably been at Sandrock. Here she felt no longer in control, as she had been there. Well, for most of the time. 'Four days?' she said. 'And that is not long enough?'

She saw that she had angered him. 'For what?' he said. 'What did you want me to tell him? That I seduced you before I left? Or that you came to me that last night, in spite of you forgetting? Or that…'

'Or that, despite you denying you had a lover or a wife, you had a beautiful young woman with you in your galley for several weeks, however long it was? Did you tell him *that*, or are you still waiting for something?'

He had not expected that. She could tell. His eyes narrowed like two daggers and she wanted him to be as hurt as she was while at the same time wanting to throw herself into his arms and be told that she was mistaken. Except that she was not.

'How do you know that?' he said. 'Who told you?'

'We all know it. All of us. So now you can stop pretending you are free, can't you?'

He paused for her words to take effect, denying nothing. 'But you are not free, either, Aphra. Are you?' he said. 'And you never will be as long as your interfering in Dr Ben's affairs continues. Then you'll be old and bitter, like my father. And cynical. And lonely.'

'But I shall not be a deceiver, like you and your brother,' she retorted, wishing the words back as soon as they had gone.

In the early light, with more shadows than substance, she was not quick enough to move away as he took two fast strides towards her, grabbing her shoulder and the thick mass of her long hair, forcing her face up to his where she could see deep into his angry eyes. Her lips parted to begin a protest, but they were taken by his in a hard kiss that was clearly intended to stop any more of her hurtful contempt. As if to revenge himself for his wait throughout the night, he took his fill of her mouth until her knees began to give way. Then, hooking his hands under her armpits, he held her to him for a final kiss, softening, making the most of her weakness, roaming over her eyelids, earlobes and throat, sending shivers into her thighs as she recalled that night together when all had been equal and well. That, she was sure, would have to be her last memory of him.

'There,' he said at last. 'Take that with you into your poor cold memory. You might have done better to ask me about her instead of telling me what you expect to hear. One bad experience has made a cynic of you, Aphra Betterton. Get over it, woman, or you'll be a bitter old crone before you know it. And stop leaping to your stupid conclusions. For a beautiful and passionate woman, you can be unbelievably opinionated.'

Breathless, and furiously angered by his lecture as well as the rough treatment, she snarled as she wriggled free, 'And as a woman, I'm not supposed to think for myself. Is that it?'

'Think for yourself by all means, but not for others. Especially not for me. I can do my own thinking, thank you. And if I want to bring an extra pilgrim back here to Padua, I shall not ask your permission, mistress. Is that clear?'

Although she had moved away, he moved with her, not menacing, but with authority. 'Bring whoever you like whenever you like,' she said, holding the back of her hand to her bruised lips. 'I'm sure I have no interest in your extra pilgrims. I bid you good morning, *signor*.' She turned to go down the steps, but he held her arm.

'Just one more thing,' he said, holding her back.

'More? Your lectures grow tedious.'

'Too bad. Leon will be with us today. He's not quite himself. Be careful with him. Try to remember that he obeyed our father. That's all there is to it.'

'Finished?'

'For the moment.'

Tugging her arms out of his grasp, she stalked towards the house that was flushed with pale pink light, its windows staring at her indignantly, accusingly. Had she become cynical? Would she be a bitter old crone? Had she misjudged him?

The answers brought a threat of tears to her eyes and a terrible misgiving that she had handled things very clumsily, so far, and that if indeed he was being driven away by her mishandling of things, then she had only herself to blame.

The day had begun disastrously and now Aphra knew she would need to draw on all her reserves of strength during the rest of it when she must go through with the ordeal of discussing Dr Ben's business. She would rather have met Leon alone, or perhaps with Uncle Paul, but the rest of them had already gathered after breaking their fast, except for Leon who, for some reason, ate with his wife in their apartment. She had not asked, but Signora Juna had explained that Leon and Bianca lived on an upper floor in their own rooms with their own servants, since he was still attending the University of Padua and was expecting to qualify this year. His final exams were only weeks away.

Hence the urgency to acquire his notes, Aphra thought, appreciating at the same time that neither he nor his wife would be in any particular hurry to meet her and her family after all that had happened. Santo had asked her to be careful with him and she would. What would it serve to be otherwise? Not simply because she needed his help, but also because she sensed that all was not well since their parting, less than a year ago. He had been obliged to obey his father, Santo had said, and now she could see, having met the patriarch, that Leon would have lost more than he could afford, had he disobeyed. As the new mistress of Sandrock, that would not have mattered to her so much, but there had been the added element of honour to consider, which would certainly matter to the Datini family.

After the hostile interlude with Santo, which had made Aphra consider anew her assumptions, the first change she decided to adopt would be her public attitude towards him which, if she continued with her cold-shoulder treatment, would cause some comment of an adverse kind. This would not serve any purpose, either. It was a personal indulgence she could not afford. Obviously, her visit had come at an inconvenient time for him, but now they were here, he would have to make the best of it, as she would. So it was her cousin Etta who pointed out to her, when she commented on Aphra's swollen lips, that Santo must have cared enough about her to stay up all night to wait, in the hope of mending the rift that appeared to have opened up between them. What was more, she said, if the unknown lady on his galley had been his lover, he would surely have thought it best to tell her so, rather than have her believe that she stood a chance with him after coming all this way. It was time, Etta said, that she started to think more rationally. Aphra had not argued with that.

To look at Santo, however, no one would have thought he'd spent a sleepless night out in the garden. Years on the open sea had toughened him. By breakfast, he had changed into his long merchant's gown of chestnut-brown brocade with long hanging fur-edged sleeves and an open front that showed a tunic of pale grey silk. His chin had been shaved and he was still as healthily handsome, still able to stop Aphra's breath with the effortless virility of a man in his prime.

With a slight lift of his square chin, he held her eye with a steady gaze as if to judge how much, if at all, she had been affected by their hostile confrontation and by his harsh criticism of her. She met his eyes, but not for long could she manage the defiance she had intended and it was her own lids that dropped first in a blink of sudden embarrassment, amounting almost to shame at her shrewishness. She knew his eyes remained on her as a blush rose from neck to cheeks, but she took some comfort from her attire, which he could see now in daylight, and the careful braiding of her hair.

The preparation of her mind was not so easy, for no anticipation had quite matched her picture of Master Leon Datini that had stayed with her over the bitter months of their parting. Once gay and full of zest for life, he now appeared rather shorter than she remembered and certainly not as smiling as the man she had once felt a deep affection for. Besides which, someone or something had given him a black eye. The lack of smile she could understand, but the apologetic and uncertain attitude almost broke her composure.

Before both families, she held out her hands to

him, keeping them there until he stepped forward and hesitantly lifted them into his own, raising first one and then the other to place a courteous kiss on her fingers. She felt the warmth of his lips and knew for a certainty that his love was still in place, recalling how those kisses had once been in other more sensitive places. And as if rehearsing a stately dance without music, their hands parted, feet took a step backwards, and heads bowed before Aphra broke the silence with, 'Master Leon.' She withheld her smile, thinking it would be too much to expect one from him, in the circumstances.

'*Madonna,*' he said. 'You are well?'

'I am well, I thank you. But you…?'

'You have come a long way. I was sorry to hear about Dr Spenney. A great loss.' The loss appeared to show in his eyes, one of which was almost closed, swollen and bruised with a crimson ring around the tender skin. His other eye showed signs of weeping, with a dark shadow beneath, and Aphra's heart ached with pity for his obvious unhappiness, all the nurtured stores of heartache at her own plight now transferred to him in a single instant.

'It is indeed,' she said, gently. 'And I must beg your forgiveness for troubling you at this time. If I had known…' She had to stop, unable to find the words that would express a sympathy the details of which she could not begin to guess.

'No,' he said, putting out a hand to stop her, 'it is no matter, *madonna*. I will do whatever I can to help your enquiries. My brother and my father have told me of your concerns.'

'Yes. Thank you. We are all concerned…but of course…you have met us all, haven't you? Father…?' Re-introducing them, she managed a glance at Santo who stood beside his brother and was heartened to see the slight nod of his head and a slow blink to accompany it. *Approval. Well done.* And even though she still had reason to believe she might have lost him, his silent praise mattered to her.

To her great relief, the two Datini parents, having realised that they had no role to play in what was a very private concern, announced that they would leave the business to their sons and guests to deal with, suggesting that they should occupy the stone summerhouse at the end of the garden. Here they would be secluded from the rest of the household and servants had been instructed to attend them with refreshments. Flora was more than happy for herself and Grace to stay with Signora Juna in the garden and more particularly to impress the lady with her knowledge of plants, their names and uses.

Visiting the summerhouse again so soon, Aphra found that her recent memories were making her ache with longing, Santo's voice still ringing in her ears, his kisses still hard on her lips. Now able to compare the brothers, she saw their differences in detail, Leon's eyes that had once been soft and appealing, Santo's more usually squeezed hard against the sun and wind, alert and penetrating. His shoulders were wider than Leon's, his frame altogether stronger and more robust. She had felt the hardness of him, the power and energy, and the lash of his tongue. All the affection she had once felt for Leon, thought of as love, was now a deep sadness for all the misery he had suffered and was still suffering, apparently. Would she have time, she wondered, to help him through it, or would her presence here only make things worse for him?

Just as importantly, she saw as if for the first time that her feelings for Leon had come nowhere near the passion she now felt for Santo and that the pain of betrayal and fury at the mention of a rival was something she had heard of but never experienced for herself. Jealousy. Etta had told her it could do terrible things and now, experiencing its insidious coils squeezing the joy from her heart, she knew Etta to be right. Etta had once felt it, too, and had suffered badly.

Aphra remembered her cousin's despair. Whatever the truth of the matter she herself must not fall prey to that hideously ugly emotion.

Chapter Nine

Ever since Santo had informed Aphra that he had helped his brother to write the letter telling her he wouldn't be returning, she had wondered about the nature of the relationship between them. Was it really as close as he had made it sound? Now she saw that it was when Santo took the chair next to Leon, gently touching his shoulder as they sat. She sat opposite them with Uncle Paul, though it was her father who addressed Leon first.

'Master Leon,' he said. 'Thank you for taking the time to help us with our concerns. We appreciate that you are anxious to resume your studies, so we shall not overstay our welcome, I assure you. But your presence means a lot to us all.'

Leon's expression was far from his usual geniality and they could see he was making an effort to concentrate. 'Thank you for sending my notes back, *madonna*,' he said to Aphra. 'I believe Dr Ben would have approved of that.'

She longed to put him at his ease, glancing at Santo for a spark of kindness. She found it and was able to put her question before her father, who had already cleared his throat in anticipation. 'Yes, I believe he would,' she said, 'but I wonder if you could tell us why Dr Ben needed to use your notes for his lecture instead of his own?'

'I think we already know that, don't we?' said Sir George, pursing his lips.

'No,' Paul replied, glancing at his brother-in-law. 'We *suspect*. We'd like to hear what Master Leon has to say about it.'

Leon was already agreeing. 'I think you should know,' he said in a quiet voice, 'that neither Dr Ben nor myself ever thought anyone would discover that the lecture notes were not his own, but mine. He asked a great favour of me, but he'd once lent me *his* notes, so it was my way of repaying him and he said he would mention my name. That would have been a great honour. There appeared to be no problem, except that I was obliged to return to Italy without them. Then, when it was clear that…that I would…not be…returning…' His voice wavered and slowed, only gaining strength from Santo's quiet presence beside him. 'Returning… I asked my brother to call on Dr Ben to collect them, not knowing until later that…well, you know—' his hand flapped idly on the table '—Dr Ben had gone.'

'Yes,' Aphra said, gently. 'That came as a shock to all of us. But Dr Ben was regarded as an expert on sleeplessness and the relief of pain, wasn't he? So why did he need…?'

'We were both working on the same subject,' he said, anticipating her question, 'but he had not kept up to date with his studies and I had. You will ask why. Because he'd been concentrating more on other areas of research. He'd had meetings with Dr Dee and he'd been following other lines, rather than his own. It's easily done.' He looked directly at Paul in whose house Dr Ben had died. 'Can you tell me how the accident happened, sir?'

Paul told him, leaving out no detail, not even the half-consumed potion that smelled strange.

'That would have been a tincture of arnica and calendula…marigold,' Leon said. 'He took it… well…for various reasons, usually to help him sleep better.' Reaching across the table, he drew towards him the piece of parchment found on the lining of Ben's gown, the pouch found hanging round his neck containing the three exotic gifts and the mistletoe items from his satchel. Reverently, he touched them as if they were familiar to him, nodding his head wisely.

He soon got into his stride as, one after another, mention was made of all the other anomalies found at Sandrock, items that did not surprise Leon as much as the rest of them: the rare metals and gemstones, the vessels in the dining cupboard, the spices and expensive ingredients in the stillroom, the curiosities in his book cupboard. Leon agreed that these had all been part of Dr Ben's research so, when Paul asked him, quite bluntly, if this had anything to do with the Elixir of Life, Leon's reaction was to sink his head slowly into his hands, elbows on the table.

'Are you all right?' Santo said. 'Need a rest?'

Leon shook his head, recovering himself. 'No,' he whispered. 'It's all right. I owe it to these good people to tell them everything. It's obvious that all these things have nothing to do with pain relief and I cannot blame anyone for thinking it has more to do with magic than with medicine.'

He took a deep breath and sat up straight and, in that moment, Aphra saw again the Leon she had known, bright, intelligent and in control of the situation. She caught Santo's eyes, but could not read their message. She wondered if he was remembering, as she was, that night in the workroom at Sandrock when he had exposed her feelings for him after she had worn his cap. Surely, she thought, that had not been an act, put on in order to get what he'd come for. Had it? A tremor shivered its way down through her body as she recalled his masculine closeness, his arms, the warm scent of him, making it an effort of will to drag her mind back to the business in hand. As she must.

Leon was speaking while all of them watched and listened. 'The Elixir of Life would appear to explain this,' he said, 'and indeed that's what it *was* all about. In a way.'

To those of them who had known Ben best, however, this did not ring true and the first to say so was Nic. 'Master Leon. We have known each other well and, although I am not doubting your interpretation of this mystery, you have not yet suggested how this Elixir of Life theory could have led to his death. How could a man like Dr Ben, an authority on pain relief, have abandoned such an important subject to chase after something as foolish as the hope of living for ever? It is totally out of character, isn't it? And if I may say so, I believe there may be something you're not telling us. In a way, you said. In *what* way?'

Leon heaved a sigh, then took a sip of water from his glass. 'My dilemma, my lord,' he said, looking at Nic, 'is that I was sworn to secrecy on a certain matter that I have always been careful to honour. But now he is no longer with us, I believe his grieving relatives should also share his secret.' He took another sip as everyone at the table leaned forward, as if to anticipate the revelation of some unethical dealings of which Ben may have been ashamed. 'I first encountered the problem one evening when we were studying alone in his workroom. He had been reading aloud when his voice tailed off and stopped, and he simply fell off his stool.' Leon slapped the table. 'Just like that! I went to pick him up, but he was shaking and trembling uncontrollably, his legs…his whole body convulsed…his eyes rolling…foaming at the mouth. I'd never seen anything like it, but I recognised it to be…'

'The falling sickness!' Paul whispered. 'Lord have mercy upon us!' The colour had drained from his face as Venetia gave a cry. Her hand stole across to his, grasping it tightly.

'Yes indeed, sir,' said Leon. 'He was having an epileptic fit. He was quite unconscious. I knew what to do. I put my gown under his head, laid him on his side, shoved something between his teeth and sat by him. In a few minutes, he stopped thrashing about and then he slept for a while, holding my hand. That, my friends, is what he feared more than anything in the world. If it had got out that Dr Ben Spenney was a victim of epilepsy, his career would have been ruined.'

If the effect of Leon's story was like an earthquake to the others, to Aphra it was more like a painful ache deep within her heart for the terrible secret Dr Ben had carried alone for so many years. Why could he not have shared it with her? Had he not trusted her quite enough? Or had he hoped to cure it before it was discovered? Had he been afraid of her reaction, and could she have contained it without revealing the slightest sign of her deep concern? Questions too new to answer. Too soon. Too painful. Too heart-achingly tragic. Dear Ben. Poor dear forlorn Ben, dying alone. Tears poured silently down her face. Shattered was their memory of the man who had appeared to have the most brilliant future with every material advantage to take him as far as any professional man could go. But fate had taken a hand in it. By now, Paul and Venetia were quietly sobbing and shaking in each other's arms, the rest of them either holding their faces or staring down at their clenched fists, feeling the horror of such a serious affliction. Believed to be caused by malevolent diabolical sources within the body, sufferers were never accepted by hospitals because of the disruption they were likely to cause. Mostly, they were shunned as being possessed by demons. And now, all those unexplained possessions found in Dr Ben's workroom were, apparently, supposed cures for this condition or preventatives against it. All of them there that morning could easily imagine what might have happened if Ben had had an attack while he was lecturing.

'Yes,' Leon said into the silence of the room, 'the portrait of St Valentin, patron saint of epileptics, the Ritual of Three, the desperate search to find antidotes however strange or expensive, the time taken away from his other research, all this was to ward off another attack which he dreaded might happen in public. There was no theory he neglected to investigate, however bizarre.'

'Why didn't we know sooner?' said Sir George. 'My wife and Paul and Ben didn't grow up together because Ben was kept at Sandrock for his first twenty years or so. But his uncle the prior said nothing of it. Why?'

'I believe the answer, sir, was that it only

started later in Dr Ben's life. It can do that, I've heard. When he was preparing for the lecture, he may well have taken too strong a draught of his tincture that brought on a fit while he was alone and made him fall...'

'No...*no*!' Paul shouted. 'That's not the whole story.' Tears flooded into his eyes as he clung to Venetia's hand. 'There's another explanation. You tell them, my love.'

Venetia knuckled away a tear. 'Paul is referring,' she said in a trembling voice, 'to that evening, the day before Ben's lecture. In hindsight, if we'd known what we know now, we would not have told him...but...'

'Told him what, dear?' said Etta.

'That our son Marius, Flora's twin, also suffers from epilepsy. This is why we have the boys educated at home. He could never go to school. Oh, if only we'd known. We would not have told him at that time. He was very upset. Oh, Paul, what have we done?'

'Uncle and nephew,' Sir George said. 'The sins of the fathers.'

'Then why not *me*?' Paul said, his voice breaking with grief. 'Why Marius?'

'Because the affliction can skip a generation,' Leon said. 'Or sometimes it fades out altogether.

It can appear for no apparent reason. But whose sinful father do you refer to, Sir George?'

'My wife's,' he said. 'Paul and Ben's. Sir Walter D'Arvall. The boys' mother was not Lady Agnes D'Arvall, but a local abbess. Sir Walter was unfaithful. *"The sins of the fathers are visited upon the children,"'* he quoted, rather pompously.

'As an apothecary, Sir George,' Leon replied, 'I would prefer to believe that epilepsy, or any other ailment, for that matter, can afflict anyone whether they have sinful parents or not. I find *that* theory more comforting. It's a medical condition we don't yet understand, so we can hardly blame Dr Ben for being so determined to hold it off, can we? He even wore a cramp ring on his finger to ward off convulsions, but no one would have recognised it as such.'

'It went with him,' Venetia said, quietly.

'Then may he rest in peace,' said Leon.

Aphra had watched Leon closely as these disturbing facts were uncovered, peeling back each layer of their understanding, putting each item in its proper context, stemming the awful doubts that each of them had carried. As the distressing enquiry progressed, she had seen the change in Leon's posture and the light in his one good eye shine more brightly as he answered the queries and then, at the end, voice an opinion to her father that in any other setting might have sounded remarkably like a contradiction. Unforgivable in a young man to his elder, but Sir George had accepted it like a lamb because, Aphra believed, Leon had said it with an authority they all admired. Herself included. She had thought, perhaps they all had, that he would flounder under the pressure of so many sensitive questions but, as she watched, his discomforts fell away and his stature grew, making it easy for her to see how he would shine as a teacher, sure of his subject. She had not seen him in this mode for some time, capable, assured and articulate.

How much of this was down to his brother's presence at his side Aphra could only guess. She was the first to move as the rest of the party sat in silence, too stunned to speak. She held out her hands to Leon again, holding them firmly, like a friend. 'Thank you,' she said. 'That was not easy, but you handled it well. I cannot explain what a difference this makes to our family to know what was concerning Ben so much that he could abandon his studies. We can all understand it now. But would his so-called remedies have worked, do you think? Did he discuss them with you?'

For the first time that morning, he smiled. 'Thank you, *madonna*,' he said. 'It was a disappointment to him that I would not enter into any discussion about his remedies and he was bound to realise that I had no belief in them. For a man like him, a down-to-earth realist, it is quite ridiculous to put one's faith in charms and chants and such.'

Santo, who was listening, tempered his brother's opinion. 'Ah, but if one is as desperate as Dr Ben was to keep his position, it's any port in a storm, as they say. Who knows, we might all at some time have to believe in the intangibles, if we cannot find anything else.'

To Aphra, this had a ring of something personal to them alone, but she did not want to explore his meaning at that moment. 'Then will you try, before they leave, to explain to my uncle and aunt what you know of this falling sickness? I wouldn't like them to think that all the things Ben collected were in any way beneficial, if they're not. And what danger is there of Flora being affected, too? Could you put their minds at rest on that? They believed he had a problem with his heart, too. Perhaps you know something of that?'

'I will talk to them, I promise. I feel so sorry for them, but I still think there are worse illnesses than epilepsy.'

'I cannot imagine any,' Aphra said, sadly shaking her head.

'I can,' he said. 'Believe me, I can.'

He was an apothecary. He should know. Aphra let the matter rest.

As refreshments arrived, Leon was now in demand to add details to some of the matters already touched upon and, as the comforting process continued, Santo took Aphra's elbow to lead her away into the garden.

'Where are *they* going?' said Sir George, suddenly protective.

'They're going for a walk, George,' Nic said, pressing him back down into his seat. 'They're adults. Leave them be.'

Under the table, Etta nudged her husband's foot.

For the first time in many weeks, Aphra's personal concerns were slowly being replaced by those of others who, that morning, had shown her the darker side of fate's dealings. Her aunt and uncle were distraught and shocked to discover what they would prefer to have known years ago. Then perhaps they might have been of some comfort to the brother they had loved. And so might Ben to them. Santo was clearly concerned about his brother and had now convinced Aphra about Leon's continuing love for her. Apart from the injury to his eye, his sadness was plain to see. The Datini parents, for all their courteous hospitality, were concerned about the reason for their visit and Aphra could tell, even after a brief acquaintance, how the father's authority was a powerful force to be reckoned with.

The huge garden, ordered and peaceful, had a calming effect on Aphra's earlier confusion. More than once, during that discussion, she had told herself how unlikely it would be that both her objectives in coming to Padua would be resolved in her favour. That would be too much to expect. 'Santo,' she said, once they had moved well away, 'I've come to realise that…well… some of what you said is quite true. I have, in the past, been remarkably critical…'

'You certainly have, mistress.'

'Yes…well…thank you, but now I see…' She floundered. She ought to have rehearsed it. 'Oh, dear, I don't know how to say this.'

'That's new. You usually manage to say what you feel without too much trouble.'

'And that's not helpful, is it? You could help me to…'

'What? Help you to apologise? Not I. I did that once before.'

Aphra came to a stop on the gravel and the

sigh she gave was meant to be heard. 'I was not going to apologise. I was going to explain why I came here and what I hoped to achieve, and why I now realise…'

Santo had continued walking slowly ahead of her. 'I know why you came,' he said without turning round. 'You came to find out about your beloved uncle. I was under no illusions about that. Did you think I might be?'

Desperately, she searched her mind for a suitable, sensible reply while her heart dropped like a weight inside her, slowing her reasoning to a standstill. 'Santo,' she whispered. 'Santo, I knew you might think so, but that was not the only reason I came. And now I wish I had not expected so much. I have embarrassed you and made you angry. But I had to see you again. That's all. Just to see you. Even though you have someone else, I had to take that risk. Perhaps I should…should not have done, because now…my heart is…'

Santo had turned ahead of her and now he approached, treading like a cat, stealthily so as not to startle her. 'What did you say? What is your heart doing?'

'Hurting me,' she whispered, pressing the back of her hand under her nose to stop the gathering sobs. 'I love you, Santo…oh…don't listen…you have your lady here…'

Reaching her, he took her wrist away from her face in a grasp so fierce that her feet trotted forward of their own accord to follow his growled instruction. 'Come with me,' he said, pulling her along the path to where a white marble wall sheltered them from all prying eyes. The wall pressed hard against her back as he held her with both hands, his face lowering to hers, his eyes searching her soul. 'Say it again!' he commanded. 'Say it!'

'I must not,' she said, watching his beautiful mouth. 'You have another...'

'Never mind that. Say it, Aphra.'

'I love you, Santo. I love you.'

His kiss was soft, tender, warm and very prolonged, his arms supportive, his thighs hard against her softness, melting her, making her cry his name as her arms wrapped around his head. 'I am not angry,' he said between kisses, 'or embarrassed. But we have both been dogged by misunderstandings and now it's hard for us to see things as they are, sweetheart. I have been just as guilty as you in that. Forgive me if I've shown my jealousy. I loved you from the very beginning, you see. You must have guessed that, *madonna*.'

Guessed? Wondered. Hoped. Doubted. Dreamed. Yearned.

'I found it hard to trust,' she said against his lips, 'after what happened. I wanted you to love me, but I didn't make it easy for you, did I? I couldn't trust my emotions, either. You say you've been jealous, Santo, but I'm still suffering. It's tying me in knots. Is she your mistress, the woman you say was a pilgrim?'

To her relief, he did not laugh. Instead, he took her face between his hands, kissing it from forehead to chin, lingering over her mouth. 'No, she isn't,' he said.

'But they said she was…wait…*una bellezza…* is that right?'

'Very beautiful, yes, but nowhere near as beautiful as you, my love.'

'But you and she were together on your galley.'

'And you think…? Oh, my beloved Aphra, do you really believe…? No, I'm not even going to tell you how wrong you are except to say she's a relative. I'll explain the rest all in good time. And believe it or not, my love, I am free and so are you, now you've discovered about your uncle.'

'I was free before, Santo. My heart, I mean. But if I had not come here to follow up Ben's problems, Uncle Paul would not have been any wiser about the epilepsy, would he? And that would have been serious. You can see why it mattered, can't you? But I never wanted to cause problems for Leon and I think I might have, even so. What caused his black eye, Santo?'

'I did. He was about to thump me, but I got there first. Nothing new in that.'

With all the hidden undercurrents swirling around their relationships, past and present, Aphra chose not to dig too deeply into the precise reasons for the brotherly quarrel, for she could hazard a guess about what might have caused Leon to react so violently. 'I'm sorry,' she said, nestling into his arms, her cheek against his chest. 'Truly, I am so sorry. I wish there was something I could do, or say, to make things better for him. I hate to see him like this. I had no idea how badly he's been affected. Do you suppose that, if I were to meet his wife and show her I'm no threat, would that help, d'ye think?'

'When do you return to England?' he said.

'I have no idea. It will depend on the others.' She noticed that he had not answered her question, most likely, she thought, because he would not know what might help Leon. But after another stroll along the pathways, followed by a short interlude hidden behind a well-covered trellis, they went to rejoin the rest of the party on their way to the house, while Aphra's heart sang so loudly of Santo's love that she felt sure

they would all hear it and smile. Except her father, who she did not think would be quite so
approving.

As the simple midday meal drew to an end
Santo took his brother aside where the rattle of
water in the stream covered the sound of their
voices. Together, they sat on a low stone wall in
the shade of a lemon tree.

'She was kind,' Leon said, studying a cushion
of green moss by his side. 'After all that, she was
kind to me. I don't know why I should be surprised. She's a remarkable woman. I suppose I
ought to have expected you to fall for her, Santo.'

'She wishes to meet Bianca,' Santo said with
a glance at his brother.

Leon sat up straight, frowning his disapproval. 'No,' he said. 'Simply no.'

The silence between them seemed to indicate
that there was more to be said on the subject.
Gently, Santo persisted. 'Think about it,' he said.
'Who can it hurt? Bianca wants to see her.'

'Has she said so?'

'Not in so many words, but she knows she's
here and she'd like to know more about her. And
there may be a time, in the future, when they will
have to meet. In public.'

'When you make Aphra yours…yes… I can see that, but…'

'Don't be bitter, Leo. It doesn't help matters to be bitter. Aphra is not likely to make things more difficult than they are, is she? You've seen how kind she is and, if the two of them wish it, who are we to prevent it? Shall we give it a try? There'll never be a better time. Privately. Just us.'

'Margaretta will be there with her, I expect.'

'Good. Then we can kill two birds with one stone, as the English say.'

'Meaning?'

'Aphra thought she was my mistress.'

Leon smiled at that, wincing at the discomfort. 'So you've been in the doghouse. Good. Serves you damn well right.'

'So what was I to do, then?' Santo said, standing up. 'Suggest that she swim back home? Too many people in Venice with not enough to do but gossip, that's the problem.'

'Yes, and too many of them know Father. I'll go up and speak to the women.'

Lorenzo Datini was holding forth, as he liked to do, just as Santo entered the cool salon. He was telling his guests about his younger son's expectation of being offered a position at Padua University as a teacher of botany. According to him it was a foregone conclusion, subject to Leon's good grades in the examination. To which Aphra would like to have reminded him of her part in sending back Leon's notes. She caught Santo's smile, their thoughts running along the same lines, their lips still alive with the memory of those recent stolen kisses.

'As for Santo,' Lorenzo continued along his favourite route of outlining his plans for his sons, 'Santo will become the manager of my glass factory. Our workshops are on Murano,' he said, waving an arm, 'so we shall be seeing more of him than we do at present, when he's abroad most of the time. Another year or so, when plans are in place. Our present manager is getting old. We need fresh ideas. Yes, Santo?' He looked towards his son, smiling broadly while hoping to manoeuvre him into an agreement under the public eyes of his guests.

His son was wise to his father's methods. 'It's something we have to discuss, Signor Padre,' he said. 'Another time, perhaps.'

The smile fell. 'Oh, I know you fancy yourself as a merchant now, but you'll get tired of all that. I know it. A change is as good as a cure, eh?'

'A cure from what, Father? Doing well?'

Aphra could see now why Santo would not have discussed her with his parents. He would have to choose the right moment for that, too, especially since his father clearly wanted him to stay near the family. What chance would she have against the authority of such a man, having already experienced his firm hand over Leon's future?

For all his domineering, Lorenzo was astute enough to see that Santo's agreement could not be forced in this manner, out of politeness to their guests. Sir George, Nic and Paul also recognised that it was time for them to take their leave, having achieved the purpose of their visit.

But Signora Juna, Santo's mother, was reluctant to lose the company of the English guests who had brought a touch of warmth to her villa and shown such an interest in it. 'Stay a little longer,' she pleaded. 'I have not yet shown you my Giotto. This you must see. Just a small panel, but one of his finest, I'm told. Do come.'

Santo signalled to Aphra. 'You still wish to meet Bianca?' he whispered.

'Indeed I do. Now? Leon doesn't mind?'

Beyond them, Venetia cleverly slipped her arm through that of Signor Lorenzo, looking up admiringly into his face and following his wife's lead while chattering excitedly to him.

'Leon understands,' Santo said.

'And Bianca will not be jealous, I hope?'

'I cannot say, sweetheart. You must judge for yourself.' Aphra might have asked why the Lady Bianca had not come down to meet them, since she lived here, but perhaps that would have placed both of them under some considerable strain. So it was with the expectation of having to suffer the curiosity and some questioning from Leon's wife, the woman he had been obliged to marry, that Aphra put on her bravest face and told herself that this was to help Leon through his wretchedness. To have Santo beside her gave her the courage she needed.

Leon's apartments were as luxurious as the rest of the villa's interior, causing Aphra once again to compare the rambling ancient priory where she was now mistress and where Leon might have become master, had things been different. The lady's room was vast and dimmed by a screen of linen pulled down over the large windows and, over by a high tapestry-covered wall, a very large canopied bed with half-closed blue-velvet curtains appeared to occupy centre stage. Carved and painted marriage chests stood solidly against the walls where several small gold-glittering portraits of saints and virgins waited to receive prayers. The room smelled of medication and a want of fresh air.

As they entered, Leon came towards them. A

lady rose from a stool near the bed, a lithe and lovely creature with a mass of tight curls tumbling round her face. Her smile was for Aphra alone as they were introduced. Margaretta Rossi, sister of Signora Bianca, Leon's wife. Gracefully, she dipped a curtsy and so mischievous was her glance at Santo that Aphra was immediately aware that her mistake had been discussed. *Santo's sister-in-law.*

Stop leaping to your stupid conclusions, he had said, in exasperation.

The young lady was proudly wearing a pewter shell pinned to her shoulder, like those pilgrims who had visited Santiago de Compostela. 'Welcome,' she said, sweetly. 'We hoped you'd come up to see us, since we cannot come down, you see.' She looked towards the great bed where, under the stark white line of a linen sheet across the bedspread, a hardly discernible bump showed that someone was there, her white gown and close-fitting cap merging with the pillow, her white face turned towards the sound of voices.

Oh, Leon! Why did you not tell...? She stopped herself. Questions would wait until later. Regrets were useless. It was help they needed, not pity. She must hide her shock, summon every ounce of fortitude and do something to help. Anything. Smile, at least.

'Madonna...' Leon began, hoping to explain.

Aphra laid a hand on his arm. *Not now.* A familiar gesture from one who was not related, but allowable, she thought. Smiling was not as difficult as she'd feared, nor was it hard for her to walk towards the shadowy patient or to take up the soft hand being offered to her and to hold it gently in her own, to curtsy, then to sit on the stool vacated by Margaretta. She was close enough to hear the whispered words of welcome. Instinctively, Aphra knew that there was love in the weary heavy-lidded eyes that glanced quickly over at Leon as he stood apart, just as she knew how much she and this woman had shared hopes, fears, disappointments and betrayals. All was written in this poor woman's lovely face, ravaged by pain. And she, Aphra, had foolishly thought that she alone had been the one to suffer. 'Bianca,' she whispered as tears burned behind her eyes, 'forgive me. I didn't know.'

'How could you?' Bianca replied, wearily. 'I was only given half the story, so I expected you would be, too. Men. They believe it's kindness, but it isn't, is it?'

To be given only half the story and to expect that to suffice? To expect any woman to rebuild her life on half-truths? No, it was a strange kindness not to have told her of this when she might have understood sooner the reasons for Leon's change of heart, wanting her, Aphra, rather than an invalid. But wait! Was she leaping to conclusions again? 'Will you tell me about it?' she said, keeping hold of Bianca's hand.

But the frail young woman was drowsy, and obviously not up to the sustained effort of conversation. 'Stay with me,' she said, closing her eyes.

'Your sister...?' Aphra ventured, hoping to regain her interest.

Margaretta came to sit on the bed, taking over her sister's voice. 'I live with my husband and children in Venice,' she said. Touching the shell on her shoulder, she explained, 'Santo picked me up from A Coruña to bring me back to Venice. I went to ask for a miracle for my sister, you see.' Her eyes softened as they rested on Bianca's face, apparently sleeping. 'It may already be happening.'

'Yes,' Aphra said, shamefaced. 'My thoughts... sometimes...run on ahead of me. I am not proud of them.'

Margaretta nodded, touching Aphra's arm with her fingertips in a gesture of complete understanding. 'It happens. But you would not have expected...?'

'To see your sister like this? No, indeed. If only I'd been told. How long?'

'It started after Leon went to England. They were betrothed, you know. She was well until then. Signor Lorenzo wrote to him telling him how Bianca had become weak, her legs painful, not working properly. She was not sleeping.'

'Has the illness been diagnosed?'

'The doctors cannot identify it. She's in constant pain. Fortunately, Leon has been able to prescribe a new medication for her, now he has his notes returned. Santo says you were willing for Leon to have them back. That was kind of you.'

Aphra's look across to where Santo and Leon stood talking was intercepted, as if they both knew which bit of information was being exchanged. 'New medication,' she said, sliding her eyes to the table on which stood a flask of whitish liquid amongst a collection of beakers and bottles. 'Straight from your English notebooks? Your research notes? Pain relief? Insomnia? The latest treatments?'

Bianca's eyes opened wide enough for Aphra to see the adoring expression sent to Leon's bewildered face, hoping for the smile that refused to respond. Aphra waited, scarcely breathing, for him to make some kindly remark to his wife while, for her, the dense cloud of misunderstanding began slowly to dissolve in her mind. Of course. This was behind the urgency to have the notebooks returned. Not for his studies or exams. Not for his ambition to secure a good position or to earn a good salary, but for his wife's sake, an invalid in perpetual pain.

Slowly, the two men approached the bed, suspecting that, between them, they had handled this whole affair rather badly. Before Aphra could say 'why didn't you tell me', Santo began his own justification. 'Yes, that is why he needed them, Aphra, but please try to understand how difficult it was for me, at the time, when you were…'

'Yes, I know all that, Santo. But this is not about my feelings, it's about Bianca's needs. There must be something…'

Bianca waved a feeble hand from the bed, reminding them that she was still in the room, although appearing to sleep. 'I need Aphra to stay,' she said, plaintively. 'We have things to say to each other. Margaretta must return home tomorrow to Alberto and the children, and then I shall be alone again.'

'Your ladies come in and out,' Leon said, as if that should have been enough.

'I know,' she said, 'but that's not the same, is it?'

'No,' Aphra said, before Leon could develop

his argument. 'Bianca needs to talk and so do I. Santo, do you think your mother would allow me to stay a while longer to be with Bianca? I could do such a lot to help.' It took her some effort not to launch immediately into the details of how she'd move that damn blind aside, for one thing, throw the windows open, move the bed for a better view, move Bianca out of this dark, dreary place into the garden. She needed someone to read to her, play music, make her smile, take her mind off the pain. And Leon needed showing how she could become a blessing to him instead of a burden. Surely, she thought, this tragic situation could be made more bearable.

'I know my mother would be happy for you to stay here as long as you wish,' Santo said. 'She'd probably invite you all to stay, but I know your aunt and uncle wish to see more of the Cappellos while they're in Venice. But why not ask Lady Somerville to remain with you, Aphra? If Lord Somerville would not object?'

'As I did for her in London. To be my chaperon. That's inspired,' Aphra said, wondering if she was being fair in denying Etta the amazing experience of seeing Venice's many attractions. And would it be fair on Nic, who had already done so much to help?

Leon, Bianca and Margaretta were all in favour of Aphra's offer, at least two of them well aware of Santo's other reasons for wanting her to stay. Leon, however, remained behind as Santo and Aphra took their leave of the two sisters, knowing how this latest revelation, whilst solving another part of the puzzle for Aphra, would also leave behind a trail of questions to which only time would provide the answers.

Escorted along the cool tiled corridors of the villa, she was still mentally reeling from a discovery that was as pitiful as it was unexpected. Uppermost in her mind was the grievance both she and Bianca shared concerning the lack of openness about what men preferred to see as a kindness, as if women were incapable of accepting the full story. Bianca's illness. Leon's urgent need of the notebooks. His deep unhappiness, only partly explained. Ben's predicament, which surely would have been better shared, in the circumstances. Then the silly mystery about Margaretta and her voyage back to Venice which, after all Aphra's fury, was actually no mystery at all. Yes, of course, Aphra admitted, she ought not to have formed her own conclusions about that, but what else was she to think, given that she and Santo had exchanged no definite assurances about their future, either together or apart? They had admitted their love for each other, but where did that leave them, he a successful merchant in Venice and she the owner of a large estate in England?

Santo knew exactly where her room was. Once inside, and with the heavy iron key turned in the lock, they clung tightly to each other, pressed against the door, kissing with a passionate relief, though in Aphra's case, this was combined with some anger, too. Santo was quick to recognise it. Bending swiftly, he picked her up in his arms and carried her over to the bed, holding her down with ease on the green-figured satin as her questions spilled out, between puffs of exertion. 'Explanations will wait,' he said in answer to her protests.

'They won't wait!' she said. 'Why could you not have told me? Why...?'

But Santo had seen the compassion in this astonishing woman about which Leon and others had told him and now the ache of love had grown almost beyond control. He knew also that some physical consolation was required to calm her fears about their future, for this was something that had been on his mind, too, though he could not have foreseen how she would be so generous with her time.

'Hush, beautiful creature,' he whispered, lifting the strands of silky blonde hair away from

her face. 'You were magnificent. Kind. For-
giving. Understanding. Unselfish.' With each
compliment, he planted a soft kiss upon her features, moving his mouth downwards to throat
and neck, and lower to the smooth mounds of her
breasts. The questions stopped, replaced by deep
sighs, by hands that caressed his head, sinking
into the deep dark waves as she had wanted to
so many times that day.

Although her mind was still in some turmoil,
the needs of her body demanded the kind of attention only Santo knew how to give, for that
one experience of his loving had been, so far,
the only memory of heaven she had been able to
cling to. That occasion had been dark and only
for feeling, not for seeing. This time, there was
to be no undressing, either, for the rest of the
family would be waiting downstairs, and Aphra
was every bit as eager to take whatever small
moments they could steal before time ran out
on them.

So rather than make a protest about the urgency, she found the lack of preparation exciting,
hardly mattering at all when the thrill of expectation was already rippling through her thighs
and into her secret parts to the tune of his hands
which, like a skilled lutenist, knew exactly which
chords to play upon. Her skin responded to his

knowing touch like a lock opening on the instant, placing herself shamelessly ready for him, lifting her hips to meet him, gasping with the sweetness of being possessed by such a man as this. Again. 'Santo,' she said. That was all. Just his name. It felt like honey on her lips.

They both wanted it to last, but knew it was not going to be possible, this time, so Aphra savoured every second of those precious attentions as the one who must forfeit the blinding climax she had known before. It did not matter, for when he came to the end even before he expected to, the beat of his powerful body against hers was a reward in itself, and she found herself laughing silently with joy, content to have given him, and herself, those few blissful fleeting moments of undiluted happiness.

Chapter Ten

Aphra's concerns that, in keeping Etta with her in Padua, she might be denying her the companionship of her husband were soon relieved when Santo's prediction was seen to be an accurate reading of his mother's generosity. So it was Signora Juna herself who insisted that, since Etta was to stay with Aphra here at Padua, then Nic and Sir George, Aphra's father, ought to be with them, too, since she did not share her husband's and son's view that Bianca's days should be dark, quiet and isolated from any kind of stimulation.

'I have always said,' she told them while Signor Lorenzo was in conversation with Leon, 'that what the poor girl needs is company and something to do to keep her mind off the pain. Her mother tells me she reads and paints well,

but of course she hasn't done any of that since…
well.' Her face tightened as if the thought pained
her.

'Since she became ill?' Etta said.

'Since they were married.' The flicker of her
eyes towards Leon revealed less of the sympathy Etta and Aphra had expected and more the
irritation of a mother disappointed in her son's
performance. 'I cannot interfere,' she whispered,
almost to herself. 'It's not my place to interfere.
But drugs and potions will only do so much,
won't they? And all they seem to be doing at the
moment is sending the poor girl to sleep. Maybe
that's how he prefers it. What do *I* know?'

There were questions Aphra would like to
have asked about Bianca's illness, but Margaretta had told her it had begun while Leon was
in England and there was a limit to the questions she might comfortably ask of Signora Juna,
who could so easily have become Aphra's own
mother-in-law. It would be best, she thought, to
exercise some discretion, the situation being still
so new to those concerned.

Paul and Venetia, suffering the shock of Ben's
problem, had preferred to return to Venice with
Flora. Leon had assured them that, as Marius's
twin, she need not be affected any more than
their elder brother Walter, but it was clear to ev-

eryone that their decision to leave the boys was worrying them. Nevertheless, they were glad to have spoken to Leon and their waves as the boat was rowed down the canal lasted until they were lost in a mass of colourful awnings swaying on the water.

Dazzled by the bright reflections, Aphra turned away, looking down at her pink and gold ensemble. 'This is all very well,' she whispered to Etta, 'but I had not thought to be wearing it for more than a day or so. It looks as if we shall have to play maid to each other, too.'

'I've thought of that,' Etta said. 'They're going to send our luggage tomorrow. Do you think we might get Bianca into something pretty?'

Aphra pretended to scribble on the palm of her hand as if it were a notebook. 'Improvement number three,' she mumbled. 'First some light and air in that room.'

'I think,' Etta said, 'that Master Leon should be first on the list, while we have him here. Do you think he'd talk about Bianca?'

Only a year ago, Master Leon had lived and studied for a time in the London home of Nic and Etta, then newly wedded, with Aphra as her cousin's companion. They had known each other well enough to talk of sentiments as well as practicalities and, although so much had changed between them in that year, it concerned the cousins to see Leon's misery. With some artful manoeuvring, they managed to steer the four men into a semi-circular alcove in a corner of the vast garden where embroidered cushions had been left on the marble benches, inviting them to rest. On purpose, Aphra sat next to her father rather than Santo, for until she knew more about her future, she saw no point in displaying her love, when her father would ask questions she could not answer.

But it was to Leon that Sir George directed a question, not his daughter. 'Your father believes you may be offered a post here at the university, Master Leon,' he said. 'Would you take it?'

Leon's gaze was far away as he replied, with little enthusiasm. 'Yes, I suppose so,' he said. 'Father has always wanted his sons to live near him.'

'But you,' said Sir George, 'is that what *you* want?'

It was well meant, but thoughtless. Santo came to the rescue. 'My father believes that the connection between our family and Bianca's was more important than Leon wanting to live in England. That's the way one's standing in society improves in Venice, these days. It's probably the same in England, Sir George.'

'Indeed. But there are occasions when one goes against those conventions, Santo.'

'Leon had no choice. There was a betrothal. By our laws, that may not be broken except in very particular circumstances.'

'I *had* a choice,' Leon whispered. The group were startled. His intervention was unexpected. They had thought that Santo would speak for him, protecting him.

'Can you talk about it, Leon?' Nic said. 'We're all on your side.'

'I think so. I don't want you to take sides, though,' Leon said. 'My father is an honourable man, but think how it would have looked if I'd insisted on renouncing the woman I was betrothed to, who had become seriously ill while waiting for my return. My father wrote to tell me of Bianca's illness, but I chose to ignore it, thinking that perhaps her family would withdraw from negotiations on the grounds of a serious impediment. It was foolish of me and selfish. My choice was whether to return to England... to Aphra...or to honour my promise to Bianca, who would have stood little chance of recovery otherwise. Which of them would be hurt most?'

'You believe your wife will recover, then?' Nic said.

'I *have* to believe it,' Leon said, quietly, 'but...'

Here, the thought of the alternative was too bitter to be spoken, although the rest of the group could have finished it for him.

But she will never be the one I dream of and love. She might never bear me a son.

'When I was in England, at the priory with Dr Ben, I realised then it was not the university life I wanted, but to do what he'd been doing, growing plants from the New World, discovering their properties, working on a system of naming them so that every botanist in the world could understand. That's gone, now,' he said, parting his hands to let it fly. 'All gone.'

Listening intently, they had all identified in some degree with the life-changing decisions Leon had been obliged to make, if only to lessen the hurt to the most vulnerable of the two women. They could all have contributed comfort, advice, or empathy, but it was Aphra who could not contain her response. 'Leon,' she said, leaning forward to make him look up. 'Listen to me. It isn't all gone. Nor has fate dealt you the blow you seem to think. Bianca *loves* you.' It was a risk, saying such a thing before others, not knowing how the private information might be received.

'What?' he said, only half-believing.

Santo added his opinion. 'She does, Leo. I know she does. I've seen it, too.'

Leon sat up straight, looking from one to the other, saying nothing. His lack of response confirmed what they already suspected. Nothing unusual for an arranged marriage. One partner loved, the other did not.

Aphra kept up the attack. 'She's a lovely woman,' she said. 'You must have seen that, when you agreed to marry her. And I know your medications will help her with the pain, but she needs more than that, Leon. Surely there's no reason for you to shut her up in a darkened room as if that's all she...' *she was good for* '...she could manage.'

Leon's hand went to his forehead as he saw the picture in his mind. 'I know, I know,' he said, 'but it's all *I* can manage. What else can I do?'

'Saints preserve us, Master Leon!' Sir George said, bringing some robust old-fashioned common sense into the conversation. 'Is that where your wife is? In a dark room? Then get her out of there. Bring her out here into the garden.'

'The sunlight hurts her eyes, sir.'

'Well, put her in the shade, then. Carry her out on a litter. Sit her out here in the flowerbeds. Sit her by the fountain and let her hear the birds.

Talk to her. Have a musician play for her. Bring her books. Does she read?'

'I believe so.' Leon had the grace to look guilty at not quite knowing.

'Bianca paints, too,' Aphra said. 'Did you know that?'

'No...no, I didn't know that. Perhaps I should...'

'There's no "perhaps" about it,' Santo said. 'You have a wife up there we're all eager to help. So now it's time you stopped feeling sorry for yourself and realised how blessed you are. She could be a boon to you, if you'd only give her the chance. Mother would do everything she could to make your marriage work. You know that.'

'We all would, Leon,' said Aphra, softly.

His look was gentle and kindly as he replied. 'Even you?' he said.

'Me more than anyone.'

If anyone had wondered how these plans would go down with Signor Lorenzo, they were not to be enlightened that evening as they sat around the long table for supper in the Datinis' dining room where the display of sparkling glass was far superior to anything Aphra had been able to produce at Sandrock. Gilt-edged, enam- elled and tinted, twisted, fluted and engraved, the bowls, drinking glasses, candelabra and plates seemed to be indicating to Santo what he could be director of, if he chose. On that occasion, however, nothing more was spoken about Santo's or Leon's futures if only because, this time, the host's attempts to direct the conversation were diverted by three articulate men and three women. Even he could not speak over the top of them.

For Aphra and Santo, the effort of hiding their love from their parents was a strain that found a release later, after dark, when Santo slid quietly through Aphra's bedroom door and into her waiting arms. When they found breath to speak, at last, they were both of the same mind. 'We shall have to tell them soon, beloved,' said Aphra, laying her cheek against the bare patch of chest showing inside his gown.

Santo agreed. 'I have to choose the right moment to break that kind of news to my father. I cannot see that he'll be so surprised, but it will certainly interfere with his plans for me. Meanwhile, sweetheart, I have my own plans for you.'

She knew what he meant. He had come to her in his long loose gown of forest-green velvet edged with satin, and she knew he wore nothing more beneath this than the exciting male scent of his warm skin. Unlike those early days when their talk was of anything but love, their moments together in Padua could not be squandered on discussion, even though she longed for some clarification of her part in Santo's future.

Yet each time she allowed her need of his wonderful loving to override her uncertainties, she was placing herself in a very dangerous position, one that could change the direction of her life for ever, if she failed to exercise some caution. Unlike her cousin Etta, whose heart had been known to rule her head, Aphra was by nature more cautious. Her unfortunate dealings with Leon had shown how right she had been not to allow the same intimacies she had initiated with Santo. Twice, she had risked pregnancy when her love for him had cried out for expression and, even now, her body yearned to be possessed, fired by passion, consumed and sated. Here, in her room, they would have a whole night in which the risk could easily become a certainty, if she allowed it.

She didn't want to put herself in that position when fate had given her a second chance at happiness, nor would she force Santo's hand by loading him with an extra responsibility. His father was a difficult man to persuade, once he had formed his own plans, and who could tell whether Santo would be obliged to comply, as Leon had been, or go his own way?

As his powerful body lay half over her on the bed, it was some moments before she could make him realise that she was trying to hold him off, not the opposite. His kisses were already luring her towards a blissful forgetting and the effort of discontinuing what had begun so naturally and easily was more difficult than she had thought.

'What is it, sweetheart?' he whispered, kissing her temple. 'Am I being too rough with you?'

'No. But I have something to tell you, Santo.'

His body was easy to read. The pause. The hand stealing over her abdomen, waiting for a sign. The deep look into her eyes, waiting for confirmation. 'Tell me?' he said.

'It's not what you think,' she said, unable to keep the smile from her voice, 'but it has to do with that.'

He lay beside her, drawing her close to nestle in his arms, his mouth breathing warmth on top of her head. 'That?' he said.

'We're taking an enormous risk, Santo. It's not one I can afford. Nor you.'

For some moments he made no response as his hand stroked the soft skin of her shoulder to show that words would come, eventually. 'I've been selfish,' he said. 'I know the risks. It's easy to pretend them away when I want you so much. I want you every time I look at you. Since that first time we met in the orchard, when you were so angry and upset. Then at last you came to me and the sky fell in.'

'Perhaps I should not have done. I don't regret it, beloved, and nothing came of it. That's not why I'm saying this, but neither of us is in a position to tempt fate and, who knows, we may already have gone too far. Can we make love without it, or is that too much to ask?'

At the sound of a compromise, he reared up on one elbow to look down into her face which, in the summer night light, was as pale as the moon. 'For your sake, my lovely, concerned, practical, sensible and utterly adorable woman, we will make love only so far and save those endings for when we are married. Then...*wow!*' He growled, earthily.

'Married, Santo? Is that what you said? You want to marry me?'

'Of course I do. Did you doubt it, my love? Marry you and make you mine for ever, make a family with you when you're ready, not before. A woman should always be allowed to choose her own time. I know you need to know what the future holds for us, but while I don't wish to alienate my father, I shall not allow him to direct my life, or yours. We belong together and you belong at Sandrock. I have not lost sight of that, my sweet Aphra. Leave me to sort out the details.'

'I knew there'd be complications, Santo. My being here, I mean.'

'Nonsense, darling woman. Nothing a Venetian merchant cannot sort out.' He kissed her lips, then thought of something. 'But you've not said yes, have you?'

'Haven't I? How remiss of me.' She laughed, drawing his face down to meet hers. Whatever words and half-words were attempted after that came to nothing in the heat of their delayed passion in which, at last, they could experience the delights of nakedness as if to make up for what they had just agreed to relinquish. Taking full advantage of the new diversion, they explored every surface using fingertips, palms and lips to fill their senses and to stir up reserves of excitement, new or long forgotten.

Finding a new reason for their lovemaking and with no particular aim in mind except that of giving and receiving pleasure, they rested at intervals to slumber before the next gentle awakening of hands, like an afterthought, to the accompaniment of more kisses and assertions of love. Until this, neither of them had known that two people could find such exquisite pleasure in the tender explorations of undulating surfaces, of crevice and muscle, bone, hair and those parts where hair begins, where ears fold, where a man is hard and a woman soft and yielding. Aphra had thought that Santo might find the situation too frustrating, but when dawn came and it was time for him to leave, she watched him, his muscles rippling, don his deep green robe and come to sit on the edge of the bed, bridging her with his arms. His tousled hair and devastating smile, catching the early light, melted her heart again.

She thought he would kiss her and be gone, but after gazing at her tumbled hair and sleepy eyes, he drew down the sheet covering her nakedness, sliding a hand over her beautiful body, fondling her breasts and watching the rosy peaks become firm and inviting. 'So,' he whispered, '*that's* what they are!' His head bent to her, kissing the delicate nubs, teasing them with his tongue before raising his head, softly laughing.

'*Idiota!*' she said, smiling and pulling up the sheet. 'You must go now.'

'I seem to remember you saying the same thing at regular intervals in England. Did you mean it?'

'No,' she said, shyly. 'Not often, anyway.'

'No, I didn't think you did.' He stood tall and slender in the new light of day. Like a god, she thought, following him to the door with her eyes and thinking also about how far they had come since his first visit to Sandrock.

Having made a start on Leon's sorry expectations of what his life with Bianca had to offer, Aphra found no resistance from him over her plans to make the invalid's days more comfortable, being convinced that living as she did would do her no good. For one thing, she did not think Leon would ever have agreed to marry a woman of little intelligence or character and, for another, she had seen in the somnolent bedridden wife a spark of life and coherent thought that, if gently fanned, could easily burn brightly enough to reveal her potential. Leon, she thought, had allowed his disappointment to cloud his compassion, for as his mother had remarked, drugs and potions were not the only cure.

So she and Etta lost no time in searching through Bianca's chests of beautiful clothes, many of them still unused, to find something colourful, comfortable and flattering for her to wear. Administering only a fraction of Leon's drugs, they discovered that Bianca could string many more sentences together, in English, without falling asleep and that the pain in her legs became less important to her than having her fine,

long, fair hair dressed and braided with blue rib-
bons to match her gown. All this was achieved
by the full light of day, the blinds having been
removed so that, for the first time in months,
Bianca could see the garden, the trees and sky,
hear the birds and the water fountains.

As an important part of Bianca's rehabilita-
tion, the two cousins managed to persuade Leon
that his presence was essential, for all their sakes.
On the third day, it was Etta who remarked to
him, when he came up to the room, that Bianca
had identified all the flowers and plants seen
from that window.

'All of them?' he said, hardly hiding his scepticism. 'You sure?'

'See over there,' she said, pointing to one
of the large bowls of blooms set by the flutter-
ing curtain. 'Bianca named all those, and when
Aphra asked her if she knew the Latin names,
she gave them all. We're going to take her down
into the garden tomorrow. In the shade.'

Leon shook his head, dazed and somewhat
shamefaced. 'Why didn't she tell me?' he said,
looking anew at Bianca's transformation. Reclin-
ing on a day-bed on the balcony, draped in colourful coverlets and wearing a dress of spring
green, Bianca's long wavy hair hung down over
her shoulders like a silken veil. Aphra was read-

ing to her in a hesitant Italian which Bianca corrected, amidst peals of laughter.

'Did you ever ask her?' Etta said.

'No, I'm afraid I didn't. I should have.'

'Well, there's time this evening. And tomorrow, perhaps you can help us to carry her outside. Your mother has found a litter.' She half-expected him to excuse himself, his exams being not far off, but he did not. 'If you're thinking about your revisions,' she said, 'you might find that she could help you.'

'What about the pain?'

'She's hardly mentioned it, Leon. But if you were to spend some time with her, just you two, that would help her to recover faster than anything else. What's more, if you'll forgive an old friend for saying so, you would recover faster, too. You have a treasure there, you know, if only you'll take time to discover it.'

As if Bianca knew she was being spoken of, she turned to look over her shoulder at Leon with a demure smile, her sparkling blue eyes filled with open adoration. But it would have been difficult to tell which of them benefitted most from that exchange, for Etta and Aphra had both caught the answering smile from Bianca's husband. He went over to the day-bed while

Aphra left them alone, touching Bianca's shoulder as she passed.

Etta winked at her with a hint of conspiracy. 'Come on,' she said.

'What did you say to him?'

'Say? I'd like to have taken him by the ears and shaken him.'

Aphra smiled at the forthright language, remembering how she herself had given Nic some advice concerning Etta's intransigence in the earliest days of their marriage. Though she had not wanted to shake him.

In the days that followed, Bianca's recovery was nothing short of remarkable. In the sunny garden the men erected an awning to shade her from the sun's glare while she reclined on a cushioned day-bed, taking in dainty morsels of tasty food as the others ate al fresco around her, involving her in the kind of conversation of which she had been starved for months. Unsurprisingly, they found that she was convent-educated, artistic, and scholarly. She was also highly sensitive, an intriguing discovery to which Aphra and Etta attributed her physical pain and the weakness in her legs, though they had the good sense not to discuss this with anyone else, since the only evidence they had was their own, albeit less dramatic testimony when the pain of jealousy and rejection had been almost tangible. And since Leon's growing interest in her, his attentions, appreciations and increasing admiration of her newly blossoming loveliness, she had been sleeping without the aid of his newest concoctions.

There was an occasion when Etta and Aphra were able to coax her to talk about those fast-disappearing symptoms of intolerable pain. It was towards the end of a day when the low sun cast an orange glow across the sky, catching the edges of tiny clouds with a silvery-pink and reflecting on the gathering tears in Bianca's eyes as she tried to explain how Leon's betrayal had affected her. She apologised as she said it to the one who was so closely involved. 'I wanted to die,' she whispered, hoarsely. 'I thought it would be best if I did. I knew he had found someone in England, his tutor's niece.' She put out a hand to hold Aphra's, begging her pardon for this recital of her personal woes.

'You knew?' said Aphra. 'He told you?'

'No. Signor Lorenzo discussed it with my parents. They told me. Both our parents were against any breaking of promises, even though I said I was willing to release him. I didn't want to go ahead with it, but they insisted. I made Leon so unhappy and neither of us was able to comfort the other. He said he'd discovered properties in some new plants that would help my pain, but he needed to get hold of his notes and recipes. He sent Santo to find them, but...'

'Yes...yes, I know. Please don't be distressed. It's over now, Bianca. Put it behind you and try to find ways of helping each other. That's what he needs, too. He's already finding out what you can do and tomorrow you can impress him even more. We'll bring your paintbox out here and together we'll do some botanical drawings. Etta, too.'

Etta protested. 'Me? You know I'm useless at...'

The crunch of gravel sounded from behind the awning. Leon appeared in his long student's gown. 'They told me you were still outside,' he said, sounding concerned. 'Isn't it time...? Sweetheart, what is it? You're weeping. Is it the pain?'

Like shadows, Aphra and Etta slowly rose and backed away as Leon, ignoring them, sat down on Bianca's day-bed to face her and take her in his arms.

'No...no,' she said. 'Not pain. That's going now, Leon.'

'What, then? What is it, little one? Tell me?' Rocking her, he stroked the wisps from her face and touched her nose with the tip of his own while, unnoticed, the cousins tiptoed away towards the house where lamps were being lit.

Unable to stem their curiosity, they went upstairs to see what they could of the day-bed, but it was too dark. Later, it was a very bemused Santo who told Aphra that he had seen Leon carrying Bianca in his arms to her room. 'What is the world coming to,' he said, slipping her silky gown off her shoulders and picking her up in a similar fashion, 'when a man has to carry a woman to her own bed?'

'I'd rather stay up and talk,' Aphra replied, saucily.

'Talk tomorrow,' he said, gruffly.

Looking back, it seemed to Aphra that they had reached a turning point in relationships, hers with Santo and Bianca's with Leon. She did not want to press the point too hard when Santo had assured her that he would himself attend to the details when he thought the time was right, but it was these same 'details' which concerned her most. Although Santo had agreed that she belonged at Sandrock Priory, it was a source of unease to her that a successful merchant like him could possibly wish to live in a place like that, in the wilds of the Hampshire countryside when

he had been used to living in the pristine splen-
dour of a huge villa like this, which he could expect to inherit one day. Was it any wonder, she
mused, that his father wanted his sons closer at
hand than England? Leon's needs were different. He had immersed himself in Dr Ben's life-
style, gardens, studies and all. Nothing would
have suited him more. But Santo? How could
she expect him to uproot himself from his thriv-
ing business in Venice? Had he thought of that?
What would his father have to say about having
his ambitions thwarted, all in the name of love?
Quite a lot, she imagined.

Their nights together had been blissful, chaste
and rewarding, both of them finding satisfaction in avoiding the risk of a pregnancy while
going as far as possible without making the effort unbearable. On the contrary, it was a tremen-
dous journey of wonder for them, more leisurely
without the usual goal, sweetened by stops and
starts that interrupted nothing but sleep. And if
Aphra had feared that Santo would try to persuade her to go further, out of sheer desire, she
found that he was fully able to control his needs,
understanding all the reasons for caution at this
particular time. She had to admit that he was
an amazing and unselfish lover, doing everything he could, within those limits, to give her
pleasure.

By day, because of their fathers' ignorance of the situation, Santo kept company with Etta's husband whose knowledge of overseas trade was extensive and interesting. Sir George appeared to enjoy the company of Signor Lorenzo who, although enjoying a reputation for domestic high-handedness, was not as unreasonable as he appeared when Sir George challenged his opinions, a process he was not used to. Their voices, raised in discussion, carried across the enclosed space of the Orto Botanico di Padua where, the day before, Leon had said he wished to take his wife and her 'carers'. Meaning everyone.

Torn between attending the university lectures in Padua and spending time with his wife, he combined the two by taking them all to the newly built botanical garden situated not far from the centre of the town. Enclosed by a stout wall, the circular space was arranged on the four points of the compass, since it mattered, he told them, where plants should grow in order to thrive. The square plots in each of the quadrants were subdivided into patterns of smaller plots, each containing plants with certain properties, all clearly labelled so that students of botany could identify them easily. He wished to encourage Bianca in her cushioned litter, with Aphra and Etta, to draw and paint from life, which would make them look more closely.

It soon became obvious that Leon and Bianca shared an interest in botany much more than any of his family had supposed. Including himself. With heads together, they discussed the fascinating garden, its layout and contents and, before anyone had noticed what was happening, Bianca had slid out of her litter to stand by him, leaning partly on him and partly on the fence to touch the leaves. Reluctant to stare at the couple, the two cousins bent their heads to their tasks, but the next time they looked, the litter was still empty with no sign of husband and wife.

Seated on a stone water trough by the western gateway, Signor Lorenzo Datini and Sir George Betterton were deep in conversation. Signora Juna was talking to a gardener about the shrubs along the edges. Sir George pulled his fur-edged coat clear of the water. 'Surely you must have noticed,' he said. 'An astute man like you?'

'Noticed what, George? I knew they were friendly. Well…naturally. But…'

'Friendly, my foot! Have you not seen the way they look at each other and carefully avoid any contact when we're with them? Clear as daylight.'

'What, my son and your daughter? Again?'

'Different son. That's not exactly "again", is it?'

'I thought she was still…'

'Getting over Leon? No such thing. She got over Leon months ago.'

'So how long have you known about it? Santo didn't say…'

'Of course he didn't. Nor has she. But I knew it before they knew it themselves. You can hardly expect a handsome brute like him not to be attracted to my Aphra. Besides, he made it plain after their first meeting that he liked the look of her. I knew something would come of it.'

'Well, nothing *is* going to come of it, George. I have nothing against your family, but your daughter owns a large property in England and I cannot see her wanting to live over here, which is where Santo needs to be.'

'Didn't you ought to let him make his own mind up?' Sir George said, eyeing a fat honey bee near his shoulder. 'You can't make their minds up for them on every matter, Lorenzo. They're men, not boys. It only makes for unhappiness, in the long run.'

'It's working in Leon's case, I think,' Lorenzo said, rather smugly.

'Well, that's not something you can claim the credit for, is it?'

'Eh? Why not?'

'Because it was due to Aphra's efforts. She

and Lady Somerville. Between them, they smoothed that path, I'd say.'

Lorenzo gave it some thought, while sounds of snatched conversation reached them from a group of black-capped students. 'Come to think of it, you're probably right, George. She's a remarkable woman to come over here and do that. I can't claim the credit for that transformation. You have a very special daughter. Quite different from the woman I expected.'

'Exceptional enough for your eldest son, then?'

Lorenzo's reply was prevented by the appearance of Santo and Aphra holding hands as they approached, putting on a brave show of confidence that was not backed up, in Aphra's case, by any hope of certain approval. 'We have something to tell you,' Santo said, as if a parental meeting needed to be explained.

Lorenzo, who liked to control such situations, would have preferred the lovers to run through the whole story from start to finish and to end with some special pleading, to which he could pretend to give in. It satisfied his ego to act as benefactor. But Sir George had no time for such nonsense. 'Yes, we know,' he said, rising from the trough and rubbing his behind where the stone had made a ridge. He held out a hand to the astonished Santo. 'You'll do no better than my Aphra,' he said, 'and you have my blessing, both of you. You'll be all right,' he said to Aphra, hugging her, 'with Santo. He's a sound man. He'll look after you.'

'Yes, Father.'

'Just a minute,' Lorenzo said, beckoning to his wife. 'Have we agreed on this?' Signora Juna came to his side, standing close to him for support.

'Lorenzo, you said just now that Mistress Aphra is a remarkable woman, so what more do you want for your son? And if I had not thought that he was a good, reliable and decent man, I would not have suggested he should stay with her at Sandrock Priory, would I? It's not any man you authorise to protect your daughter, you know, while her mother and I go off to London.'

Lorenzo Datini glanced fondly at his wife, who appeared to know what this was all about without being told. 'So we've agreed then, have we?' he said, rather dazed by the lightning-quick decision. 'Well then, I suppose we'd better wish you both well, although we haven't mentioned settlements yet, have we?' With a bemused chuckle, he clasped Aphra in his arms, then kissed both her hands. 'And as for you, you rogue,' he said to his son, 'you don't waste any time, do you? Just like me when I was a young man, eh, Juna?' He took her hand, like a young lad, smiling. 'Congratulations. Where are you going to live? Have you thought of that?'

At this point, Aphra thought it best to voice her concerns, if only to hear some discussion about the possibilities. But Santo did not hesitate. 'Yes, Father, I have. We shall be living at Sandrock Priory.'

'Santo! How can we do that when you need...?'

'Lord Somerville has invited me to go into business with him. I trade mainly from Southampton and he trades from London at the moment. Together, we can corner the market in fabrics and luxury goods, and take cargoes of whatever is available instead of waiting. We can steal a march on the Genoese that way. Lord Somerville uses carracks. I have galleys. And Southampton is in the same county as Sandrock. Living there will be no hardship, especially when we shall have agents at both ports. There now, how does that sound, Mistress Betterton?'

Resting her head on his arm, she held his hand tightly. 'It sounds very well, Signor Datini, thank you,' she murmured.

'Well!' said Lorenzo Datini, pulling at his chin repeatedly, 'I had hoped you'd take over the Murano factory. I don't know what we're going to do now for a new manager.'

'Father,' Santo said, gentling the old manipulator, 'you know perfectly well that Margaretta's husband Alberto is waiting to step into the manager's shoes. He knows more about the business than I do.'

'Aye, I suppose you're right. I'm beginning to think I can't have everything my own way any more, can I? All the same, it would have been… ah, well!'

'Etta! Nic! Over here!' Santo called across the plot.

They came while Aphra and Signora Juna were almost weeping in each other's arms, all smiles, holding out hands, anticipating the good news. 'Yes,' Nic called, beaming his handsome smile, 'it's going to work well, I'm sure. It's financially sound and very good for trade.'

'Financially sound?' Aphra said. 'Good for trade? What is?'

'Er… Santo and me…in business together. Isn't it?'

Etta rolled her eyes. 'They're going to *marry*, darling. Santo and Aphra. Remember? My cousin?'

Sir George was intrigued. 'So you knew about these two, as well, did you? And kept it to yourselves? So who else knows?'

Heads turned to look for signs of Leon and Bianca, but although the litter was still on the path, the couple were nowhere to be seen. Until, that is, they came strolling down the pathway with arms around each other, Leon supporting a slow-walking Bianca who, with hair waving down her back, wore a garland of honeysuckle on her head.

Supper at the villa that evening lasted well into the night, with so much to talk about and be thankful for. This time, Leon and Bianca were present, both looking happier than anyone remembered, even smiling at Signor Lorenzo's less than tactful remark that Bianca's silken gown of magenta shot with violet must surely have been chosen to match her husband's discoloured eye. Etta and Aphra had braided her hair with pearls and gold net, piling it up to form an intricate nest of plaits in the latest fashion, showing off every lovely feature and transforming the former white-clad invalid into a woman of style of whom Leon was clearly proud and delighted.

There were no speeches, only remarks about the success of the guests' visit, about the good fortune of the two brothers and the parents' contentment, Nic and Etta's assistance, and the more moving episode concerning Paul D'Arvall, his brother and his family. Touching on the subject of weddings, it was decided that, since they were already in Padua, Santo and Aphra should be married in a small family ceremony before leaving for England. To wait another day for the arrival of the Cappello family and Bianca's parents from Venice would give them time to arrange matters with the local priest. And for the English relatives, they would have a second ceremony at Sandrock Priory.

Although it might have appeared quite astonishing, after all that had happened, for Leon and Aphra to be so comfortable with each other, more like siblings than one-time lovers, the rest of the family were relieved to see the understanding and kindliness between them. Once he had passed his exams and Bianca was fully recovered, Santo said, they must visit Sandrock to see what he and Aphra were doing there. 'You could even bring a few students with you,' he said, 'to work in Dr Ben's gardens.'

To Leon, this was good news. 'You mean to keep them as they are?'

'More than that,' Aphra said. 'We shall extend them and provide apothecaries in the towns with plants they can't grow. And I shall paint better illustrations of them than those clumsy woodcuts that Fuchs did. Bianca might like to help me.'

To her delight, Bianca enclosed her gently in her arms and whispered words to her that filled Aphra's eyes with a sudden rush of tears. 'You have been so kind. Thank you for coming here. You and Etta. My sisters. Leon and I will come to see your *orto botanico* at Sandrock, I promise.'

When Aphra told Santo of the promise in the longed-for privacy of the night, Santo ventured an addition of his own. 'They might see more than that, if they wait long enough. Is the embargo to be lifted now, cruel mistress?'

Entwining her smooth naked limbs with his rough hairy ones, she gave a huff of laughter at his poorly concealed impatience. 'Embargo? That sounds like merchant talk,' she whispered, nuzzling the side of his warm throat. 'But we are not yet married, *signor*.' She was not quite prepared for his reaction, too fast for her to counter but, finding herself suddenly underneath him, had to concede that she was in no position to argue that a few hours were going to make much difference. Were they?

'No, *signor*,' she said, between kisses.

'No to what?'

'No, I can't wait, either.'

Their loving that night exceeded all their dreams, for now it was not only a longed-for release after their abstinence, but enriched by all they had practised, as if to prepare for the full performance. All that had gone before, all the denials, arguments, admissions and separations were fed into that experience, none of it wasted, but used to show who they were as individuals and what they needed from each other. Giving freely and taking with rapturous abandon, their lovemaking flowed and ebbed on tides of desire, flooding them with unbounded sensations. And for the first time, Aphra experienced a climax greater than that stolen virgin night at Sandrock, when doubts and fears had cast shadows over her gift. This time, she learnt to express herself in ways that gave pleasure to both of them without the anxiety of the consequences, and although she could not say why she was so certain, it was that relief from concern that made her sure she had conceived. In fact, it was Santo himself who suggested it might be so. 'Lie still, wonderful woman,' he said. 'That was incredible. That's how little Datinis are made, I believe.'

'Made with love, in Italy,' she murmured, sleepily.

Epilogue

The wedding at Padua, though smaller than Signora Juna would have liked, was the happiest and merriest occasion any of them could remember, all the more so for being unexpected. The guests were dressed magnificently, brightly coloured in the Venetian fashion, though few of them could understand why the lovely bride in a golden gown wore a man's brown-velvet cap until the moment when she exchanged vows with her husband, to whom it belonged.

Some private jest, the parents said, smiling indulgently.

Only a few weeks after the departure from Venice of Lord Somerville's carrack, Leon Datini heard that the marks for his exams at the university were the highest ever recorded, as a result of which he was offered a post as tutor there, with a healthy salary to match.

Later that year he and Bianca went to live in a house very near the Orto Botanico, with a court-yard where she could continue painting botanical specimens as part of her husband's studies. By then they were devoted to each other and went on to produce two beautiful girls. They all made annual voyages to Sandrock Priory to discuss the latest horticultural developments for which the priory became famous and from where Santo continued to trade via Southampton.

Uncle Paul and Aunt Venetia were happily re-united with their boys, to whom nothing sinister had happened in their absence—though Flora's newest Italian expressions and the sights of Ven-ice with which she regaled them were far worse, they said teasingly, than being without her.

The D'Arvalls visited Santo and Aphra for their second ceremony, which happened soon after their arrival in England. Aphra's mother wept with joy and other unnamed emotions, as mothers always did, and soon found another role for her motherliness in helping with the celebra-tions, a larger event than the first.

She was also called on to help when Aphra's twin boys, Paolo and Antonio, were born the following spring, at about the same time of year as Santo had first met the love of his life.

The Somerville Trading Company went from strength to strength and Etta's first child was born at Sandrock, quite unexpectedly, while Nic was being delayed by storms on the high seas. They called their son Robin, after their good friend and the child's godfather Robert 'Robin' Dudley, who became Earl of Leicester in 1564.

Edwin Betterton, Aphra's younger brother, found a young lady to love—which put a new perspective on his views about the whole process of loving. He and Santo became good friends after the wedding.

Master Fletcher, Aphra's steward, married his widowed housekeeper and became father to three healthy sons, one of whom succeeded him at Sandrock Priory.

* * * * *

If you enjoyed this story you won't want to miss these other novels by Juliet Landon

*CAPTIVE OF THE VIKING
TAMING THE TEMPESTUOUS TUDOR
BETRAYED, BETROTHED AND BEDDED
MISTRESS MASQUERADE*

Author Note

The *Mistress and the Merchant* is the third in a trilogy, the first of which was *Betrayed, Betrothed and Bedded*, the story of Etta's parentage and the lust of Henry VIII.

The second, called *Taming the Tempestuous Tudor*, is about how Etta came to love and marry Lord Somerville—Nic—in the first year of the reign of Elizabeth I.

Aphra appears in both these stories, first as a young child, then as a young gentlewoman who accompanies Etta to the royal court.

MILLS & BOON®

&HISTORICAL

AWAKEN THE ROMANCE OF THE PAST

MILLS & BOON®

Coming next month

THE MARQUESS TAMES HIS BRIDE
Annie Burrows

'Don't be ridiculous. I am not your fiancée. And I don't need your permission to do anything or go anywhere!' Clare said.

'That's better,' Rawcliffe said, leaning back in his chair, an infuriatingly satisfied smile playing about the lips that had so recently kissed her. 'You were beginning to droop. Now you are on fighting form again, we can have a proper discussion.'

'I don't want to have a discussion with you,' Clare said, barely managing to prevent herself from stamping her foot. 'Besides, oh, listen, can't you hear it?' It was the sound of a guard blowing on his horn to announce the arrival of the stage. The stage she needed to get on. 'I have a seat booked on that coach.'

'Nevertheless,' he said, striding over to the door and blocking her exit once again, 'you will not be getting on it.'

'Don't be absurd. Of course I am going to get on it.'

'You are mistaken. And if you don't acquiesce to your fate, quietly, then I am going to have to take desperate measures.'

'Oh, yes? And just what sort of measures,' she said, marching up to him and planting her hands on her hips, 'do you intend to take?'

He smiled. That wicked, knowing smile of his. Took her face in both hands. And kissed her.

And just as she was starting to forget exactly why she ought to be fighting him at all, he gentled the kiss. Gentled his hold. Changed the nature of his kiss from hard and masterful, to coaxing and...oh, his clever mouth. It knew just how to translate her fury into a sort of wild, pulsing ache. She ached all over. She began to tremble with what he was making her feel. Grew weaker by the second.

As if he knew her legs were on the verge of giving way, he scooped her up into his arms and carried her over to one of the upholstered chairs by the fire. Sat down without breaking his hold, so that she landed on his lap.

Continue reading
The Marquess Tames His Bride
Annie Burrows

Available next month
www.millsandboon.co.uk

LET'S TALK
Romance

For exclusive extracts, competitions
and special offers, find us online:

f facebook.com/millsandboon

🄾 @millsandboonuk

🐦 @millsandboon

Or get in touch on 0844 844 1351*

For all the latest titles coming soon, visit
millsandboon.co.uk/nextmonth